MW00984344

PROTECTOR OF MIDNIGHT

Midnight Chronicles Book1
DEBBIE CASSIDY

Cover by Covers by Julie

I adjusted my grip on the taser and looked the ripper straight in the eyes. "Drop the cat, Romeo. Just fucking drop it. I don't want to hurt you, but I will if you don't comply."

His eyes clouded in confusion.

Crap. Small words, Serenity. Rippers of Romeo's level in the hierarchy weren't too bright. "If you don't do as I say, I will have to hurt you," I enunciated.

Romeo opened his massive jaws and the cat tumbled to the ground. It lay still for a moment, then picked itself up and dashed off, a streak of black against the sunset. Romeo whimpered, and shook his head from side to side, a sure sign he was going to go off on one any second.

I pulled back the taser and held up my hands. A contrite Romeo was one thing, an agitated upset one was something even the taser wouldn't be able to calm down. My earpiece crackled.

"Serenity. You okay?" Nolan said.

"I'm fine. Don't break cover. I got this."

They knew I had this. I was the only damn member of the Sunset Police Department that Romeo ever listened to. In his human life, he'd been a jolly enough bloke, with mid spectrum autism, and then the magick of Arcadia had gotten under his skin, into his blood and twisted his genes, turning him into one of the scourge. Everyone had loved Romeo, and even though he was one of them now, we couldn't bear to hurt him.

Seeing me and hearing my voice usually calmed him down, but not today. Today, Romeo ducked his head, his bloodshot eyes hardening. Any traces of the guy I'd known melted away, leaving just a beast—a crush-you-in-my-jaws and pick-your-flesh-from-my-between-my-teeth-with-a-shard-of-your-bone monster. He'd gone under. The Romeo I'd known was gone. I'd seen it happen before, but this was the first time it'd been for someone I'd known and cared about. My throat tightened.

Romeo I could have reasoned with. But this wasn't him any longer.

I took a slow step back, hands still in the air. He'd been feeding off the local cat population, and yeah, that was better than going for the humans. I knew that, the SPD knew that, but the residences of Sunset district weren't having it. Scourge didn't usually venture into Sunset. This was unacceptable the district representative had said, his jowls wobbling with indignation. Fucking twat. And now I had an autistic, very aggressive, ripper looking to me to be his upgraded meal.

Romeo pressed his knuckles to the ground, his haunches bunching,

Shit, shit, shit. The van was a block away, too far to make a run for it, but damn if I wasn't going to try.

Romeo leapt, his body arcing toward me. I turned and ran. Boots pounding pavement, breath trapped in my throat, I sprinted down the street, away from Sunset and toward the inky black expanse that was Midnight.

Raspy breathes, way too loud, way too close, cut the air behind me.

I tapped my comm. "Pick up. Pick up now!"

But I was headed away from the van and farther into the dangerous territory. Midnight wasn't our jurisdiction. It belonged to the Protectorate and the Midnight Enforcement Department, and they didn't take kindly to Sunset's police department encroaching on their territory. Another mile and we'd cross the border into Midnight, and Romeo would be the Protectorates problem. My heart sank, because that only meant one thing for Romeo. Death.

But it was him or me, and there was no contest.

Sorry, Romeo. So sorry.

The screech of tires in the distance gave me a second wind. Back-up was here, not far behind.

"Serenity, what the fuck are you doing?" Nolan demanded.

"Getting Romeo out of Sunset."

"Dammit, woman!" Nolan's voice was a coil about to whiplash me into next week.

Man, he was pissed, and yeah, I'd get my ass chewed for this, but Romeo had gone under. He was a danger to the humans in Sunset, but damn if I had the breath to tell Nolan that while running for my life.

This far on the edge of Sunset, there was only the main road out of the district, creepy forest land to my left and barren wasteland to my right. It was the road less traveled, used only by humans being banished to Midnight, or the Midnight Protectorate here on invitation. Towers rose up high, housing border patrol—humans with guns. Because although the SPD wasn't permitted to carry lethal weapons inside of Sunset, the border patrol had authority to shoot to kill anything or anyone unauthorized trying to get over the border from Midnight. The crackle of the electric fence that stretched far to the left and right fizzed and popped in the air. It cut through the forest and across the wasteland, but it was old and filled with breaches we just couldn't afford to fix.

Thank goodness the scourge we dealt with in Sunset were nothing compared to the crap that lived under the inky sky up ahead. My legs screaming in protest, thighs burning and ready to cramp, I pushed the final few kilometers and crossed the unofficial border out of our territory and into theirs.

But there was no stopping, because Romeo was still on my tail.

Behind me the van screeched to a halt and Romeo's breath brushed the back of my neck.

Come on, where the fuck was the cavalry? Damn it. I was on my own, under a huge full moon, down empty slick streets, the sensation of eyes on my back. I needed to double back, but Midnight was not my terrain and the shortcuts were a mystery to me.

A howl ripped through the air to my left. Oh bloody heck. More of the beasts. The howls echoed, making it impossible to pinpoint which direction they were coming from. I took a left down a side street, cutting through onto a main road lined with stores. Humans turned to look at me and then scattered. Doors slammed and shutters came down.

Thanks a bunch. My heart was going to burst, like seriously just pop in my chest at any moment. Shadows zoomed in from either side—shadows with claws and fangs, joining in the hunt. And then two huge rippers landed in my path.

I slammed on the brakes, fell into a crouch and reached for my taser. Thanks to the district council and the no lethal weapon rule, I was surrounded by rippers with a bloody taser as my only defense.

The rippers circled me, sniffing the air and trading yips and grunts. Romeo growled. Yeah, he wasn't into the whole sharing thing, but the ripper in front of me was bigger, probably the alpha and these were his pack. Romeo was an outsider, and if he didn't back down, they'd tear him to shreds.

If I could just get close enough to touch one of them, just a brush, just a second of contact, enough to juice up and I could make a break for it. Leap over the smaller ripper to my left and into the alley, over the wall and double back to the border.

I just needed a moment of contact. The ripper in front of me snarled at Romeo.

Romeo finally buckled, ears going flat, head down. His wide mouthed face, so beastly yet still weirdly human, swung my way and then back to the alpha. He whined and took a step back.

Oh shit.

They were done talking.

It was time for the kill.

A low warning howl strummed the air. The rippers stopped and the hairs on the back of my neck quivered. Shit. Oh fucking shit. Something was coming, something that scared even the rippers.

Two, huge, barrel-chested guys, with arms slightly longer than the average human, strode into the road behind the scourge. Their eyes glinted like silver pennies in the moonlight.

The skin shifters backed up, bodies low to the ground in subservience. What the heck?

"House?" one of the dudes asked.

I swallowed hard. "What?"

"What is your house?"

My house, like where I lived?

"She has no brand," the other guy said. He lifted his chin and inhaled deeply. "No scent."

His companion's lips curled in a hungry smile. "Then she is fair game."

The tips of their fingers elongated, faces

melting and morphing until I was staring down two hairy snouts.

"Wait." I held up my hands. "I'm with the SPD. I'm here on official business. I — "

They attacked. Leaping at me in unison, a scream lodged in my throat and then something was hurtling toward me from a nearby building, bands of steel grabbed me around the waist and the ground rushed away.

What the heck?

"Don't struggle or I *will* drop you." The voice was deep, masculine and authoritative.

He was obviously used to being obeyed and, this high up, with the rippers looking like play figures below me, it was kinda difficult not to. But whatever had me wasn't human and that meant it was fair game. It was touching me, its bare arms wrapped around my torso.

A flat roof rushed toward me. We were about to land. I touched its skin, smooth and velvet and hard as marble, and cracked open my shields just a bit. The rush was immediate, heady and fast and whoa, what the fuck?

And then I was falling, hands out, ready to roll. The impact was jarring, rattling my teeth and skinning my palms. They never told you it would hurt this much in training, but then they had the cushy mats back at base.

Urgh, I came up in a crouch and scanned the night.

Where was it? Whatever had plucked me from the jaws of death? A shadow fell across the moon and a figure landed in front of me. Flashing blue eyes and short cropped dark hair, but it wasn't the chiseled face that arrested me. Nope. That gorgeous face was firmly on the backburner of my thoughts as the huge dark wings flexed at his back before folding closed.

I scrambled to my feet and took a step back. "You're a Black Wing."

He arched a brow and ran a hand over his arm...the arm I'd touched and fed off. The energy thrummed in my veins, like a warm cup of cocoa or a huge chocolate brownie.

His eyes narrowed and he cocked his head. "What did you do? What are you?"

He was one of *them*, one of the winged, and he'd caught me feeding but aside from that he'd just know. He'd smell, sense or see the taint inside me.

I swallowed hard and raised my chin. My shields were back in place. "I'm human."

He raised an index finger and wagged it from side to side. "*Tut tut*, lying is a sin. Now I might need to punish you." He took a step toward me and a scream, shrill and piercing, cut through the air.

His head whipped round toward the

sound.

I licked my lips, my muscles jittery with the need to move, to run away from this creature as fast as they could. "It looks like those things have found a substitute meal."

He locked gazes with me for a long beat, his jaw ticking, clearly torn between investigating me further and helping the innocent under attack. Black Wings didn't, as a general rule, give a shit about humans, but he'd helped me, so maybe he was the exception to the rule.

Another scream rose up toward us.

He took a step back. "Dammit, the scourge isn't meant to be running for weeks." He muttered to himself. His gaze narrowed. "Stay here. I'm not done with you." His wings shot out, and he launched himself up into the air.

Gone.

My shoulders sagged in relief, but there was no way I was sticking around until he came back. No one I knew had ever seen a Black Wing. They usually steered clear of humans and their issues, as if humans were beneath them somehow. The fact that this one was flying around helping people was just plain weird. And if I didn't have a secret to protect, I'd pump him for as much information on his kind as I could, but he knew what I was. If he reported me, then everything I'd worked so hard to build would be taken from me.

The ground was a no go right now with the rippers on the loose, but with the Black Wing's power still skimming through my veins, a little roof hopping would be a breeze. A spike of euphoria stabbed at my chest and I dropped my shields a fraction. This was something barred to me in Sunset, something my human guise didn't allow for, but for the next few minutes I could just be.

I ran full pelt toward the edge of the roof and jumped.

The van came into view, idling at the border. Nolan was pacing the tarmac, his head down, hands on hips.

I'd lost my comm link when the Black Wing had scooped me off the road.

"Shit, Nolan. It's Harker!" Bellamy jumped out of the passenger side of the van adjusting his cap. The guy never went anywhere without it. It was a relic from the outside with a strange symbol none of us recognized. Bellamy claimed he'd found it blowing down the road by the turnaround forest. The damn patch of tree-land was a favorite place for kids to play simply because, no matter how far they ran or what twists and turns they took, it would undoubtedly spit them out back on the road to Arcadia. No one ever left the city, although people did enter. I was living proof of that.

Nolan looked up, his anxious expression

smoothing out as I raised my hand in greeting. I crossed the border.

"You made it." He stared down at me from his lofty height, his piercing gray eyes shrouded and unreadable, and then he yanked me into a hug, almost squeezing the life from me.

Bellamy let out a surprised squeak.

Yeah, Nolan was not the touchy feely type. Eleven years my senior, he'd been my mentor forever. He'd recruited and trained me, and he was my go to guy for pretty much all my work related issues. And, shit, was I getting all teary eyed?

He released me. "You're okay." His tone was gruff. "You could have been killed."

I almost had been, but if I told them that I'd have to tell them about the Black Wing and that was something that needed to stay under wraps, because if they investigated why a Black Wing was doing the Protectorates' job, my little brush with his arm might come out and that was something that could never, ever happen.

I lifted my chin. "I doubled back and lost him."

Bellamy sighed. "He went under, didn't he?"

"Yeah."

"Fuck."

We stood beneath the forever sunset for

a moment longer, watching the midnight sky in the distance, swirling with darkness and highlighted by the rays of a moon we would never bathe under.

Nolan clapped a hand on my shoulder. "Come on. We should get back and write this up. It's getting late."

I glanced at my watch. Damn, it was gone five p.m. Jesse would be getting dinner ready soon. But there was no getting out of report writing. Nolan was a stickler for protocol.

Bellamy stepped back to let me ride shotgun. I guess my brush with Midnight was enough for him to give up his throne for me. Aw, boy feel the love.

"Don't get used to it," he said as I climbed up.

I shot him a grin. "Really? But, the butt print you've left is so warm and comfy."

He narrowed his eyes in mock annoyance and climbed up back.

The van roared to life and we did a three point turn and headed back into Sunset. Back to base.

The words wriggled around on the paper, refusing to stay where I'd put them. Gah! This sucked. Why did it have to happen now? I'd fed dammit. Ah, but then I'd used the juice to ride the roofs out of Midnight. Exhaling slowly, I closed the unfinished file and headed out of my office, down the corridor to the cells. It wasn't often we held any scourge, but it just so happened that we'd picked up a stray bloodsucker two days ago. The handover to Protectorate happened once every two weeks and only Nolan ever went, taking the cell van and returning all somber and shit. Made me wonder what the heck happened at these handovers.

So yeah, the bloodsucker was curled up in a corner of his cell, all skeletal, and pale and gross. I could never make up my mind what was worse, the rippers or the bloodsuckers, and rumor had it there was much worse in Midnight.

I closed the door to lock up behind me, heart pounding partly in fear, partly in anticipation. The sucker glanced up, his beady red eyes tracking my movements.

He sniffed the air and moved closer to the bars. That's it, come closer. I grasped the metal, knuckles white and waiting. He'd lunge soon. Attack and hope to latch on. But he hadn't fed in days, and I was faster. A mere touch was needed to get what my body craved. Damn, I hated this. Hated that I needed to do this. Nausea mingled with need as I lowered my shields in preparation. The dark craving in my solar plexus wriggled and writhed. I pressed myself against the bars and exhaled. The sucker's eyes rolled in his head, and a low moan drifted up from his parted, blackened lips.

"You want some?" I held out my hand. "It's hot and thick and delicious."

It watched me almost warily. Shit. Why wasn't it attacking? It shouldn't be taking this long. One of the other officers could come in to check on the prisoner at any minute.

"Come on." I wriggled my fingers. "You want a taste." My tone dropped to something, low, seductive and inviting.

The wary expression fell away and the bloodsucker fell forward onto all fours.

"That's it. Good boy. Come here. Closer."

He began to move slowly toward the bars, eyes half closed. My pulse was a jackrabbit in my throat. And then the fucker lunged. I grabbed his chin, and inhaled. Energy poured into me, sips, and slurps, so fucking good, but not enough. Just one more sip. One more draw from this irresistible pool.

The bloodsucker made a strangled sound, part pain, part ecstasy. My eyes snapped open and my heart slammed against my rib cage at the thing I was clasping. Its eyes were red pebbles in its sunken sockets, its cheeks were sallow hollows, and the body, oh god, if the sucker had been thin before he was positively skeletal now. I released it, and it slumped to the floor and lay unmoving.

Shit, shit, shit.

Was it dead? Had I killed it? Oh god. What had I done? Wiping my hand on my jeans, I backed up and then the thing gave a shuddering breath, raised its head and smiled.

The door slammed behind me as I strode back to my office, my stomach a writhing pit of nausea.

I finished up the report on autopilot, my mind whirring. It wasn't as if the bloodsucker could tell anyone what I'd done. Scourge didn't speak. At least not any language we understood. There was nothing to worry about. But the whole thing left a bitter taste in my mouth, stirring up memories I'd prefer remain buried. Memories of twinkling blue eyes and dimples, memories of Jonathon — my first crush and first sexual encounter. I'd almost killed him. Turns out shields didn't work so well when you were in the throes of an orgasm. I'd slammed them down in time, but not before I'd tasted something so pure and delicious it had almost made me lose my mind. If I hadn't been so fucking infatuated with him, I'd have carried on feeding. But my feelings for him had pushed back the darkness or I'd have killed him. Turned out because humans had no supernatural power, the only thing left for me to siphon was their life force, and, man, that shit was intoxicating.

That was my first and last relationship. Just couldn't risk losing control like that again. Ever. Ten minutes later, report done, I was headed for the exit. Henry, one of the officers, was chatting up Julie, our receptionist, and Bellamy was busy pulling fliers off the corkboard.

I grabbed a scrunched up sheet of paper. "Join the silvered and be saved." I snorted. "Fucking tossers."

"Yeah." Bellamy shoved the balls of paper into the wastepaper basket. "I keep taking them down and they keep showing up." He shook his head. "If I catch who's been pinning these, I'm gonna rip them a new one."

Bellamy had lost his wife and son to the White Wings less than a year ago. Hannah had fallen prey to the propaganda after their son had been born. Maybe it was a postnatal thing, maybe just a mother thing, but she'd become obsessed with saving her son from all the possible nasty fates that awaited him. What if the magick of Arcadia got to him? What if he went scourge? What if he didn't and one of the bloodsuckers or rippers got hold of him?

The White Wings provided the perfect answer. A completely safe haven for all humans in the district of Dawn. It wasn't even expensive, not really. Not like the house prices in Sunset. No. All you needed to do to get into Dawn was hand over your free will and become silvered.

Yeah, a pretty silver chain that made you their puppet. As far as I was concerned, the White Wings were monsters. They had the perfect sanctuary, a place where the scourge couldn't enter, where the magick of Arcadia couldn't warp and they kept their gates closed, accepting only humans who'd happily agree to be their slaves.

I screwed up the flyer and lobbed it into the bin. "Have you heard from Hannah?"

"Not in three months."

The White Wings allowed minimal familial contact. Two or three visits a year, but not out of compassion. It was in an effort to recruit more slaves. Maybe the families left behind in Sunset would miss their loved ones so much they'd sign up to be pearly gate prisoners too. The visits didn't last once you made your resistance clear. Once that happened, you were unlikely to ever see your loved ones again. Once you were silvered, there was no going back. No one had ever returned to live in Sunset. Sorry White Wing,

I changed my mind, being a yes man sucks and I'd like my free will back now, please.

Nope. That didn't happen, and yet every year, more humans packed up their belongings and left for Dawn.

"This is *them*, you know," Bellamy said. He pulled off his cap, smoothed back his hair and then shoved it firmly back onto his head again. "Those bastard White Wings have us trapped here. This is them."

A popular theory. "We don't know that for sure."

His lip curled. "They're the only ones getting anything out of this." He dropped the bin and lifted the barrier. "There has to be a way out."

This was dangerous talk. Crazy talk. Talk that often preceded going scourge. "Bellamy, babe, I know you're hurting, but you can't think like that."

The barrier slammed shut and he turned to me, eyes red rimmed. "If people can get in, then there must be a way out."

He was talking about me—one of the few people to end up in this town with no memory of a time before. Me with a handful of others, all gone now, taken by the scourge or lured into Dawn by promises of sanctuary and peace. There would be more. There always were, every twenty years or so the stories said. Outsiders would wander into

Arcadia and our ranks would swell, a little.

Except this time, the twenty years had come and gone and no outsiders had walked out of the turnaround forest.

"Bellamy, I—"

The entrance bell beeped, and I turned to find Mrs. Carlson standing on the welcome mat, her eyes behind her Coke bottle spectacles.

Oh shit.

"I called and called and the line is engaged. Why is the line engaged for so long?" she asked.

Julie reached for the phone and cursed softly. "Dammit, I had it on busy."

"Did you see him?" Mrs. Carlson asked. "Did you see my boy? Is he all right? He didn't mean to hurt those kitties. He doesn't know what he's doing."

Julie and Henry exchanged panicked glances. This was the part every officer hated—telling a parent their child was lost to them. Going scourge was one thing, but it was when you went under that you truly died. To some, it brought comfort. They even held funerals for their lost loved ones. But for Mrs. Carlson, it would only bring grief. It was no secret that Romeo had been hanging around Sunset due to his attachment to his mother. The neighbors had even reported sightings of him in their back yards. He'd found a way back into Sunset each time we'd chased him out. Each time we'd thought the Protectorate would find him. But he'd come back a few weeks later. It had been a year and Romeo had held on, fighting going under. It was a testament to his mental strength, and no one could truly blame Mrs. Carlson for encouraging the visits. But her son was gone for real now.

She looked up at me. "Serenity, dear. Did you speak to him? You know he always adored you."

Oh, man. I so did not want to be the one to do this. But she was here, and I was here and damn it. "Mrs. Carlson I—"

"Harker, what the heck are you still doing here?" Nolan's voice boomed down the corridor leading up to reception. He strode down the hall, his long stride eating space. "Get your arse home to your sister and take tomorrow off."

I looked from Mrs. Carlson to Nolan and he jerked his head toward the exit. This was him giving me an out and, with the fucked up day I'd had, I was grateful for the reprieve.

Nolan lifted the barrier. "Why don't you come with me Mrs. Carlson?"

With a final confused glance my way, Romeo's mother followed Nolan into the depths of the SPD.

It was my cue to make a getaway.

The smell of lasagna hit me as I entered my house. It was a neat bungalow on a nice street with neighborhood watch and way too many electrified fences. Sunset was a place for the affluent and the skilled. Humans in here were highly educated or could offer a special skill essential to the running of the district. To stay on this side of the border, you needed to fit into the machine, and you needed to make money. Money didn't take away the fear, though. Nor did it make Sunset as safe as Dawn. But this was home, and I loved it.

The clang of pots and pans filled the air. A quick peek at my watch told me I was over an hour late for dinner. A glance at my mobile phone showed ten missed calls, but the damned thing had been on silent.

Crap.

Okay, so Jesse was going to be pissed.

I'd made a huge song and dance about family time a couple of weeks ago, moaning that she spent way too much time working, grading papers and doing after school activities with the kids. I'd pouted and done the whole, me, me, me, thing, and when she'd finally caved and promised to do family dinner at least two nights a week, I'd turned up late for the first one. Yeah, I deserved a verbal bashing.

I stepped into the kitchen perfectly prepared for her wrath. "Hey, I'm so bloody sorry I—"

She whirled round, dropped the spatula she'd been wielding and flew at me. I backed up, but not fast enough, because she had me in a crushing hug before I could get my foot back over the kitchen threshold.

"Oh god, oh god, oh, god."

Her slender body trembled in my arms.

"Jesse babe. What the fuck?" I stroked her back. "Shit, are you crying? What happened?" I pulled back, gripping her shoulders tight. "Jesse, what's wrong? Did someone hurt you?"

She shook her head vehemently. "You were late and I couldn't get hold of you, and the office phone was engaged, and I thought... I thought you were dead." Her face contorted in a silent wail, and I pulled her against me, rocking her back and forth.

Dammit. I was an idiot. A total fucking

moron. "Jesse, baby girl." I kept my tone soft. "Jesse, you know if anything were to happen to me, Nolan would have called you. Heck, he would have come down here to see you himself."

She pulled out of my embrace and nodded. "My head knew that, but my heart..." She pressed a hand to her chest. "My heart was so scared. I thought they'd gotten you, like they got Mum."

My mouth was dry. "I'm sorry, babe. I didn't mean to scare you."

She slumped into a seat at the table. "It's stupid. I know it's stupid but...You should have called."

"I know. I'm an idiot. But, babe, you know my job. You know I have to work late sometimes."

"But you *always* call," She insisted.

Did I? Yeah, I guess I did. Probably why she'd succeeded in hiding her fear for so long, her terror that she'd lose me, that one day I just wouldn't come home. I'd thought I'd created a safe secure environment for her, that I'd chased away the past with my commitment to our family.

At twenty-one, Jesse was three years my junior, and had never known a world without me in it. She'd been barely a year old when Mum and Dad had taken me in — the four-year-old child that had walked out of the forest and into the Arcadia. Where had I come from? Who were my real parents? These were questions I'd never have answers to, but it hadn't mattered because the Harkers had become my family. They'd loved me and nurtured me, and Jesse had been the perfect little sister. When Dad had gone scourge, it had almost crippled Mum, but she'd soldiered on. I'd been barely thirteen then, and Jesse had just turned ten. We'd slowly rebuilt our world, and just when we'd finally healed, Mum had gone to the shops and never returned. They never found her body, just bloody scraps of her favorite floral skirt up by the border to Midnight, at the edge of the forest. At seventeen, devastated and broken, I'd taken on the responsibility of looking after Jesse. I'd pieced myself together for her and it had been just the two of us ever since.

"You should have called," she said in a small voice.

I pulled out the chair beside her, sat, and took her hands in mine. "Jesse, I am not going anywhere. Not ever. You get me. It's you and me against the world, babe."

She swallowed and lifted her chin to look me in the eyes. "Jimmy Wright went scourge today."

My hand went to my mouth. "No..." He was only ten years old. It never happened that young.

She nodded. The motion was jerky and stilted. "His parents have petitioned the district council to keep him until he goes under. They're requesting special privileges. A cell in their basement." Her eyes shimmered with tears. "Why is this happening to us, Serenity? Why are we being punished this way?"

She said it as if she assumed there was still a higher power at work, but everyone knew that God had packed up and left. He'd abandoned us to the White Wings and the scourge and the nephs. This fucked up city was our world, and we needed to do what we could to survive, and it wasn't *so* bad. It was home, except right now she was upset. She was coming down from an adrenaline rush and she wasn't thinking straight.

"Don't you wonder what's out there?" Jesse said in a hushed tone, her eyes wide. "*They* say we used to be part of a world that's still out there."

My heart skipped a beat. "Who says?" I squeezed her hands. "Jesse, who have you been talking to?"

She lowered her lids and gave her head a shake. "No one."

She'd just lost one of her pupils, and then I'd been late home, it was enough to throw anyone for a loop, and if she hadn't emphasized the word *they*, then I'd let it go, but there was only one group of people I knew who made such claims to knowledge. But they couldn't be in Sunset. Not without an official permit, and the SPD would have been alerted if that had been granted. Still, I had to ask.

"Jesse, have you been speaking to the Order of Merlin?"

She looked up sharply. "No. I mean not intentionally. They just, they came by the school a couple of days ago wanting to speak to the children and their parents. We called security of course, but...I was curious."

Shit. How the heck had they slipped into the district? "You spoke to them?"

She winced.

"Jesse, come on, you know better than that. Those fanatics thrive on curiosity. Look, promise me you won't engage with them again, please."

She gave me her most earnest look. "I promise."

Ignoring the thud in my pulse, I smiled reassuringly. "I'll speak to Nolan. They shouldn't be on this side of the border without a permit." We'd have to do a sweep, find the troublemakers and chuck them back over the border. "You know they're not entirely human, right?"

She gnawed on her lip. "He said they

were witches able to harness the magick of Arcadia, that if you join them you *never* go scourge."

Oh for fuck's sake. I pressed my lips together. "Babe, they're just as bad as the White Wings. They just want mindless followers to do whatever shitty nefarious thing they want to do. If they have all this harnessed magick then what the fuck are they still doing in Arcadia, why not channel that shit and blast their way out, huh?"

She sighed and pinched the bridge of her nose before tucking her blonde locks behind her ear. "You're right. Of course you're right. Let's just eat. I'm starving."

Jesse busied herself with plates and cutlery and I sat back, my heart still thudding too hard in my chest.

The reason Sunset thrived was because we had no illusions. We accepted our world and we lived life to the fullest. Clubs and bars and theatre, we had it all. Yet people still left, lured by the prospect of a different kind of security offered by the White Wings—the sanctity of their souls. No one wanted to go scourge, because going scourge meant eventually going under, and once you did that, your soul was lost.

As we sat down to a home cooked meal my stomach quivered with a strange sense of dread, because if the Order *had* infiltrated

Sunset then things were going to get messy. And messy made keeping my secret that much harder.

The coffee room was teeming with activity. The aroma of freshly brewed coffee was potent on the air, and someone had brought in donuts too. Yum.

"Did you hear?" Henry said with a nudge to my ribs. "We've had three Order sightings today." He winked, eyes twinkling.

"Three? What? This morning?"

"No. They were reported this morning, but timeline-wise the earliest was around a week ago." He rubbed his hands together. "We're finally going to get some action."

There was no denying the leap in my pulse. This is why I'd joined the SPD, not just to protect humans, but to have the opportunity to beat the shit out of stuff. Of course, aggression was a poor substitute for what my body really needed, and all the physical activity tapped me out, heightening the need to feed, but the momentary high it gave was irresistible. The Order was on our turf without permission. Surely, some ass-kickery would be permitted.

Nolan clapped his hands. "Everyone. Please, calm down and take a seat."

Coffee was being poured and officers were hiking up their trousers. Yeah, this was exciting stuff. The SPD was merely a figurehead for law enforcement in the District. We dealt with petty crime, the odd domestic abuse case and, maybe once or twice a month, a scourge sighting. Once the scourge we succeeded in catching were handed over to the Midnight Protectorate, that was us done. We trained hard, but rarely got to utilize the skills we learned. Nolan had been heading up the department for over a decade, and despite the lack of real crime, he insisted we keep fit and sharp. So, this was big for us. The Order was in our midst—lurking in the sleepy district of Sunset. Whoop-de-doo. Ha.

Chairs scraped against lino and butts kissed plastic. Mugs were set down, and the buzz died as all eyes found Nolan. He stood, arms crossed, legs slightly apart as he scanned the room.

"Three reports of the Order spreading their word," he said solemnly. "The school, the Sunset Coast Club, and the bowling alley.

They're hitting public areas, places with families and kids and we know why, right?"

"Because parents are easy targets," Bellamy said, his tone laced with bitterness.

"Yes." Nolan tucked in his chin. "Now, they didn't apply for an official permit, because the council would have no doubt turned it down, so we have authority to evict them. However, this *is* the Order of Merlin, and they have access to magick that we can't comprehend, so we must proceed with caution. I've contacted the Protectorate, and they're sending a couple of representatives with unique abilities required for interaction with the Order."

The room began to buzz with conversation again. The Protectorate were coming here? Wow. That had happened like...never. No one I knew, aside from Nolan, had ever directly interacted with the Protectorate. There was a general air of excitement in the room which ratcheted up a notch with this revelation, but my stomach clenched in anxiety. Protectorate were nephs. And nephs were demons. And demons had abilities. I couldn't be around when they showed up. I couldn't risk them finding out I wasn't entirely human. Okay, so I'd fake being sick and go home, hide under the duvet until this was over, I'd—

"Serenity," Nolan said.

My head whipped up, eyes wide. "Yeah?"

"I want you to run point on this one."

My mouth went dry and my throat closed up. Did I just squeak?

Nolan frowned. "Are you all right?"

No, I wasn't. I was sick. Terribly, horrifically sick. Not just with fear but with a taint I didn't fully understand. My mouth worked, but the words failed to make it past that dastardly lump in my throat.

Someone slapped me on the back. "She's lost for words, Nolan." Bellamy chuckled. "Come one Harker. You know you're the woman for the job. If anyone can keep those trumped up Protectorate in line, it's you. This is our district and they better not throw their weight around."

"Serenity?" Nolan was watching me cautiously.

He'd made a bold call by putting me in charge. Henry was my senior on staff by two years, if anyone should be running the case, it was him, and, from the stormy look on his face, he thought so too. This was Nolan saying he believed in my training, my commitment and just, well... in me. If I turned tail and ran, claiming illness, he'd end up looking like a twat for picking a weakling. He'd been my mentor, my supporter, my shoulder for the better part of seven years.

There was no way I was letting him down. I'd just have to strengthen my shields and hope for the best.

I fixed a cocky smile on my face. "You got it, boss. When do they arrive?"

His shoulders relaxed and he grinned. Tires screeched outside the window.

"About right now."

Seats were pushed back and the window was suddenly the focus of all attention. Everyone's except Henry's.

"You sure you can handle this, Harker?" he asked snidely. "I'm happy to step in for you. I know Nolan has a special spot for you in his pants, but..." He shrugged. "This is business."

"What the fuck are you implying?"

His lip curled in a knowing smile. "Nothing the whole department isn't thinking."

This was news to me. He was lying. He had to be.

He chuckled. "Oh, man. You really didn't know, did you?"

The urge to punch his stupid smug face was almost overwhelming. Instead, I clenched my fists and offered him a close lipped smile. "No. I didn't. Thank you so much for enlightening me. Now how about you piss off and let me do my job. After all, I have *worked* so hard to get this far."

His expression shuttered and I turned on my heel and headed out of the room.

The office had two washrooms, one for the ladies and one for the gents, and even though there were only three females working for the department, they'd given us the larger washroom. Magnolia tiles, clean linoleum floor and toilets that actually flushed. Nolan had even had them install those sanitary towel dispensers. Nolan...shit, why had I said that stuff to Henry? He'd probably twist it and take it as some kind of admission to an affair that never happened. Urgh. It made me sick how he'd taken something so innocent and turned it into something sordid. And did everyone really think I was banging Nolan? Probably. Especially because they knew I certainly wasn't banging anyone else. A woman my age who didn't date, didn't have a special someone... Shit. They were probably thinking I was saving myself for trysts with Nolan.

The water from the bathroom tap was cool on my fevered skin. My face, bathed in the orange glow of the setting sun, was drawn and tense.

Pull it together Harker, you can do this. Just batten down the hatches and act natural. Forget Henry and his stupid jibes. Focus on the Protectorate. If only I'd had some in depth knowledge of these nephs, then maybe I'd know what to watch for, what to shield against. The door to the washroom opened and Julie clipped in on her four-inch heels. She paused and looked me over as if she was assessing me.

"You okay, babe? You look flushed." Her brows shot up and she gave the toilet stall a quick glance. "Flushed, get it." She snickered to herself.

I shook my head and sighed. "Seriously, Julie. You need some new material."

She plonked her purse on the counter by the sink, fluffed her auburn hair, and rifled through the bag for her lipstick. "I don't need any new material." She applied the plum shade and then pouted. "I look like this." She winked, her thick dark lashes casting shadows on her cheeks. "Besides, men love it when you make them feel superior intellect wise." She leaned in conspiratorially. "And then you can control them without them suspecting a thing. Make them think that everything they do is their own idea, when in reality, you're the one planting the seed." She tapped a perfectly manicured nail to the side of her head. "It takes work."

Her face was suddenly more angular, her gaze more focused and shrewd. This giggling ball of fuzz who was constantly telling dumb jokes and getting in a tiz so the guys had to help her out was an act. So who was the real Julie?

She zipped up her purse. "But this isn't for you, is it? Some of us are meant to be taken care of and others are meant to do the heavy lifting. Good luck out there, Serenity."

"Wait."

She arched a perfectly waxed brow and sighed. "Don't worry about what the big lug said. Henry is an arsehole, and so is anyone else who thinks you're sleeping with Nolan. But," she said. "I'd doubt that Nolan would be averse to the notion. He wants you, Harker. Wants you balls deep. I can't believe you haven't noticed the guy has a serious hard-on for you."

Blood roared in my ears and my cheeks heated. "No."

She snorted. "You may be kick ass in the field, but, hon, you have a helluva lot to learn about men."

She clipped out of the washroom leaving behind a trail of floral perfume.

Nolan...No. I shelved the thought and pulled my reddish auburn hair up into a ponytail.

It was time to get out there and rally the troops.

It was time to meet the Protectorate.

The reception was ogle center as I strode out to meet the Protectorate representatives. Two huge males stood by the notice board, their massive bodies eating up space. So, it was true what they said about nephs being giants. And, damn, did they have a penchant for leather or something because those trousers should be banned. Julie was practically drooling all over her keyboard and Henry stood, stiff and stern by her side, his hand on the small of her back as if protecting his investment.

My attention was captivated by a pair of awesome butts, broad shoulders and hair that I'd die for.

I cleared my throat. "Hello?"

They turned in unison and the term heart in mouth was suddenly a reality. The blonde haired dude with blue eyes stared steadily at me and then blinked rapidly and averted his gaze. The dark haired, dark eyed one glanced at his companion and then graced me with a sexy smile.

"Well, hello there. You must be our escort for the day."

Escort. Yeah. My shields quivered under his heated assessment. Careful Harker. "I'm Officer Harker. You'll be on my team. Officer Bellamy and Fulstrom will be joining us. If you come through, we can formulate a search plan."

The dark haired neph's smile widened, showcasing perfect white teeth. "I like it. Straight to the point. I'm Drayton. his is Ryker. He doesn't talk much."

"Is that because you do enough talking for the both of you?" Shit where had that come from? I coughed. "Sorry, that was uncalled for." I lifted the counter barrier. "Please, come through." I stepped back to allow the neph entrance and then strode quickly down to the corridor to our special ops room. It was probably in need of a good dusting, the damned space was rarely used.

I pushed through the double doors to find Nolan setting up the projector. A map of the city flashed up on the white screen.

"Thanks." I smiled. "I can never get that damned thing to work."

"I know." His gaze was soft. Intimate.

Shut it! No, that was Henry getting into my head. This was Nolan—my mentor—who'd never been inappropriate to me in his life. But that didn't mean he didn't like me. Urgh. Damn Julie and Henry with their stupid theories.

The room swelled with the presence of the neph, and I realized with a start that our seats would probably be like kids chairs to these guys. Matchstick chairs that would smash under their muscular bulks.

Fulstrom, an aging operative with heaps of experience and a penchant for paperwork, joined us, followed by Bellamy, cap in hand. The nephs took a stand, leaning up against the wall at the back of the room, and Nolan stepped back to give me the floor.

Shields tight, I took the limelight and flicked through the reports of the sightings that Nolan had handily fetched for me.

"Okay, so they've hit one school, the bowling alley and the Sunset club by the coast. It's Saturday today so the schools are out. But I have a list of other public family spots they might hit. I say we split up into two teams and check them out."

Drayton raised his hand, an amused smile tugging at the corners of his mouth. "Ryker and I come as a package. We do not split up."

"Um, okay. Bellamy can go with you.

He knows the city inside out."

Bellamy's eyes widened a fraction. His knuckles tightened on his cap and then he nodded. "Sure thing, Harker."

Drayton shook his head. "I have another suggestion."

I cocked my head. "Go on?"

"You ride with us."

His colleague, Ryker, shot him a disgusted look.

What the heck was going on here? "Why me?"

He grinned, flashing his dimples. "Because I work better when surrounded with eye candy, and between you and Ryker, I should be set."

Was he serious?

Nolan stepped forward, but I held up my hand to stall him. He'd given this case to me and I was gonna handle this idiot.

I placed my hands on the table in front of me. "Is this a joke to you? Huh? We have a serious problem here. It may not be a big deal to you where you come from, Midnight is probably crawling with crap and you've gotten used to stepping in it on a daily basis, but this is my district and we keep our streets clean. The Order is your shit, so stop pissing around, roll up your sleeves and get to cleaning it up."

Nolan made a choking sound, but I

barely registered it. I was too busy vibrating with rage. How dare this neph belittle our investigation with his sexist comments.

"I will ride with Miss Harker," Ryker said. His voice was gruff, almost hoarse. "You go with the others."

Drayton blinked in shock, his mouth parting and then he let out a bark of laughter. "As you wish."

My shoulders unknotted. "Okay, let's get to it." I handed Bellamy a list and took the other.

"Bellamy, is it?" Drayton said. He slung an arm around Bellamy's shoulder dwarfing the man. "You want to drive or shall I?"

Fulstrom looked from me to Drayton. "Go with them. I'll be okay." There was something solid and safe about Ryker, gut instinct and all that. I didn't mind getting in a vehicle with him.

"I'll be in the van," Ryker said and followed the others out of the door.

I sagged against the white board. "Well, I wasn't expecting nephs to be so..."

"Rude?" Nolan supplied.

"Yeah. And Normal. I mean they're big and look pretty intimidating but...yeah, they're just guys."

Nolan shrugged. "Guys who happen to have Black Wing blood in their veins."

Yeah, there was that. That blood

unlocked abilities. The back of my neck prickled with the reminder of what I was. What I didn't want to be. I wasn't sure how it worked, and I didn't care. Their world wasn't mine, and the quicker this hunt was over the better.

The van idling outside was a monster in itself. The wheels were almost as tall as me, and I'd have to jump to climb up into the passenger seat. The door swung open and Ryker held out a hand. I reached up and then faltered. Checking my shields were tight, I placed my hand in his huge one and allowed him to tug me into the vehicle. Whoa, he was strong.

Door closed, I buckled up. Ryker waited, his sun-shaded gaze fixed on the road, fingers drumming a rhythmic beat on the steering wheel. It was sunset, not high noon, definitely not bright enough for sunglasses.

"Can you even see with those shades on?"

He snorted. "I live in Midnight."

Huh? Then the penny dropped. His eyes were used to the night, to the pitch black depths of Midnight. Sunset to him must be the equivalent of midday.

"Sorry."

He pulled onto the road, the ride

smooth and silent.

I unfolded the sheet of paper with the list of locations we needed to scope. "We'll hit the shopping center first. It's a Saturday. Families will be out in force today."

He nodded. "Directions."

"Drive to the end of the road and take a left."

And we were off. We drove in silence for ten minutes, aside from my barking out directions. But even with the lack of conversation, there was something soothing about Ryker's presence.

"It's serene," he said softly.

"Yeah. I guess it is."

"It's...nice."

Damn, what was life like for him in Midnight? I'd always thought of the MPD as stuck up. Looking down on us, but maybe I'd been wrong. What had they got over us really? Special abilities and super strength? But they lived in a district where danger stalked every corner. I couldn't even begin to imagine what kind of stuff they had to put up with. We had the sun, even if it was always setting. We had relatively safe streets and we had community. There was nothing for them to look down upon.

We'd entered the strip that led to the mall. Salty sea breeze filtered in through the vents and tickled my senses. The ocean was still a mile or so out but the breeze was strong.

I waved a hand at the windscreen. "Just drive along this road, the mall will be on your left."

The blonde Adonis inclined his head, his cerulean eyes sincere and solemn. "Forgive my colleague, Drayton. Beautiful women are his Achilles heel."

Had he just called me beautiful? My neck heated "Oh. No. That's okay. I just can't be dealing with all the cocky macho shit, you know?"

His lips twitched. "Yes. I know."

He pulled into the car park, and slid into a spot. The engine died. He stared at the vast building before us. "This place is for shopping?"

"Um, yeah."

"The building is huge. How many things do you humans need?"

I studied the mall, as if for the first time, as if through his eyes — a three story monolith stretching east and west with a thousand doors swallowing people and spitting them out. It was something I'd always taken for granted, and yet, to Ryker it seemed like an alien concept. For the first time since living in Sunset, I felt a pang of shame for our excesses. The fact that even with all this at our disposal, people chose to upgrade to Dawn.

I unlocked my door, needing to get away from the reflective thoughts. "It's not always about need. It's more about want. I guess having stuff makes people feel safe."

He nodded slowly as if digesting the fact. "Does it make you feel safe?"

Did it? "No."

We exited the vehicle and headed toward the shopping complex. Ryker, in his leather and kick the shit out of you boots, drew every eye in the parking lot. Women pulled their children closer, men stepped in front of their wives and teenagers gawped, and for those few minutes, I was utterly and completely invisible.

We pushed through the glass doors into the air-conditioned interior of the mall.

I turned to him. "Why all the leather?"

He paused and glanced down at himself. "This isn't leather." And then he was striding off, cutting a path through the wide eyed humans. "Come, this place is vast we must work fast."

He wasn't wrong and it took the better part of two hours to check out the first two floors. Ice-cream parlors, restaurants, the kids zone filled with arcade games and mini-golf. No Order of Merlin here.

I parked my butt on the edge of the ornate but useless waterless fountain on the second floor. "I don't think they're here."

"No. I agree."

"Why are they here?"

He glanced at me, his brows meeting in confusion. "I thought we agreed they weren't here."

"No, I mean here, in Sunset. It's not like we have it as bad as the humans of Midnight. You'd think they'd have their hands full recruiting there, where people actually want to leave."

Ryker smiled thinly. "Midnight has its charms. We have our community just as you have yours. We may not have huge shopping malls, but we have other diversions."

Riiight. "So people *don't* want to leave?"

"What do *you* think the Order wants?"

Answering a question with a question? What was he hiding? Never mind. I shrugged. "I don't know. To fool people into believing there's a way out of Arcadia."

"And what makes you think they're lying?"

Now he was toying with me, but he wasn't smiling. Damn, I wish I could see his eyes, read what he was thinking. "You're saying there *is* a way out of Arcadia? That by joining the Order humans can seriously be free?"

"No. I'm not saying that." He glanced to his right, at a young woman in the wedding boutique window fingering a cream embroidered wedding dress. "We should move on."

Well that was confusing, but he was right about the fact we needed to move on. "Yeah, let me check in with the others."

I dialed Bellamy and he answered almost immediately. His tone was barely above a whisper. "Harker, thank god. We found them. They're here at the Dip in the Sea Mot—"

The line went dead.

I held the phone away from my ear. Full battery which either meant that Bellamy's battery had died or that he was in some kind of trouble. An icy finger of dread ticked the back of my neck.

"We need to go. Now."

But Ryker was already on the move.

The Dip in the Sea Motel was actually a mile away from the sea. Tucked up on a rise with an ocean view, it was a favorite place for business conferences and events, and pretty empty this time of year. The Order must have taken it over. God, please don't let them have hurt Mrs. Goodwin, the owner. She was old, like almost eighty and still going strong. If they'd hurt her, I'd find a way to make them pay. Using my ability was out of the question, but I could kick some Order arse.

"Is this the place?" Ryker asked as we drew up at the bottom of the steps that led up to the motel.

Bellamy's car was parked up a meter or so away. "Yes it is." I jumped out and drew my taser.

Ryker stared at it for a long beat. "What's that?"

"A taser." I made a zapping motion.

"You stun the perpetrator with it."

"*That's* your weapon of choice?"

"Choice? We don't get a choice. This is standard issue fare. It's either this or the baton. I mean the baton is okay, but you can't disarm someone from a distance and..."

He'd walked off round the van. The back door slid open, but he was out of view, so no idea what he was doing. He returned a moment later clutching a... was that a fucking battle axe?

"Whoa!" I pressed my hands to his torso, Oooh, hard. Focus. "You cannot go in there wielding that thing."

He cocked his head. "I'm Protectorate, and we're dealing with the Order."

"Yeah, but this is my jurisdiction, so put the damned battle axe down."

He slowly lowered his weapon. "You believe your taser will disable a member of the order?"

Okay, so he had a point. "I'm hoping that maybe we can talk them into leaving of their own volition. And, if not, then we go to plan B."

"Which is?"

I allowed my lips to curl into a sadistic smile. "Kicking some Order arse."

He let out a bark of laughter. "Well. This I have to see." He tucked the axe into a sheath at his back. "Lead the way."

My carefully cultivated smile slipped. Why did I suddenly feel like the butt of an incredibly funny joke?

The steps were steeper than they looked, but I reached the top un-winded. Going in guns blazing was a bad idea, best to circle the building first, get a lay of the land. I indicated we do an outside sweep and Ryker nodded. I set out, low to the ground, body in a half crouch.

I turned to speak to Ryker. "We can double back and—" He was gone. "Shit."

Someone screamed. A loud thud followed and a body came flying out of the dining room patio doors. It scrambled to its feet as Ryker came striding out of the building. Drayton was right behind him, the cocky dark haired neph's face was twisted in fury.

The guy who'd just been bodily expelled, obviously a member of the Order, locked gazes with me, his hand shot out and then I was flying through the air toward him. His wiry arms closed around me, locking me against him by the throat and the waist.

"Stay back." His voice was steady and sure, vibrating with command and laced with something that fizzed and popped. Magick?

"Oh, come on, Daryn. Do you really want to fight us?" Drayton asked. His tone was easy and chilled even though his face told a whole new story, one of murder and mayhem. "You don't belong here. You're not wanted here."

Daryn gripped me tighter. "We belong everywhere and the humans need to know the truth. They need to know which side to join. The truth will set them free."

"Where are the others?" Ryker asked.

A ball of energy smashed into the ground beside Ryker. I jerked in surprise, but Ryker merely sighed and craned his neck to look up at the first floor.

"Hello, Marika," he said. "Why don't you come down here so we can speak?"

She snorted. "So you can cleave me in two with that axe of yours, you mean." The woman, slender, pretty in a haughty way, crouched on the edge of the upper level balcony.

"You have no jurisdiction over us here in Sunset," she said. "Let the SPD deal with us. Why come all this way for a fight that isn't yours? We're no longer the MPD's problem, so why do you care?"

Drayton arched a brow. "She does have a point."

Ryker shot him a stern look. "You're breaking the law and that's enough. Sunset is out of bounds and you know it. Besides, what makes you think the humans here will listen to your claims any more than the ones in

Midnight?"

"Because, here in Sunset, the humans are closest to nirvana, they can almost taste it, and we can offer it to them without a silver chain to bind them. We can set them free."

Drayton rolled his eyes.

Several figures appeared to our left and right—more Order members. Where the fuck was Bellamy and Fulstrom?

Ryker's jaw tensed. There had to be about twenty members of the Order. Twenty witches with access to the arcane, all poised to let fly with the magick.

"You're surrounded, Protectorate scum," Marika said. "And I, for one, am glad you came out all this way. Away from your buddies at the MPD, away from your territory." She leapt down, landing lightly on her feet a few meters to my left. "You think you're better than us just because you have Black Wing blood in your veins? Well, we don't need the filthy blood of the fallen to have power. We have the arcane, and with it we will be free of this prison."

"Marika," Daryn said. "We can't let them live. We can't have them bringing back reinforcements."

This was my cue. "Reinforcement will come, though,"

Daryn cut off my words with his arm.

But I'd caught Marika's attention. "Let

the human speak."

I licked my lips. "You kill them and more will come looking for them. If they didn't care about you being in Sunset before, they will now. They'll hunt you for vengeance and they won't stop until they get it."

A shadow of doubt flitted across her face, but then she smiled, wicked and sharp. "That's just it, human. They'll have to find us first. This district is large, filled with hidey holes and sympathizers. So many humans just want to be free. Sunset is rife for the reaping, people looking for another kind of safety, a freedom that a silver chain from Dawn can't provide, but we can. And while you hunt us, we'll reap and pick you off one by one for the Order is vast and the Protectorate is…" She held up her pinky and flexed it, bottom lip sticking out in a faux sad face. "But most of all, I just don't give a fuck."

The Order members raised their hands, ready to let fly. My stomach cramped, and my pulse tried to break free of my veins. They were going to do it. They were going to kill us.

Ryker locked gazes with me. And I swear he winked, but with the shades it was impossible to be sure, and then he was moving so fast he was a blur. The axe was a toy in his hand, cutting a swathe through the air, *whoosh, whoosh, swish*, and Drayton had a bloody sword. He moved, easily deflecting the magick that was thrown at him as if he was out for a morning stroll. The Order was going down, blasted by the deflected energy balls. Marika made a break for it and Drayton ran after her.

All this action and less than a minute had passed. And then the arm around my throat tightened painfully.

"Stop. Stop or I kill the human." His arm flared with electrical energy stinging my skin and bringing water to my eyes.

Ryker froze with a sea of unconscious and wounded bodies at his feet. Daryn began to chant. Words I'd never heard, but yet understood as if I'd invented them myself. It was an incantation to kill, a curse to drop Ryker where he stood. How the heck did I know that? Wait, that wasn't important right now. Focus in the main issue. I couldn't let Ryker die to save my arse.

There was only one thing to do, to incapacitate him. I gripped the arm at my throat, ignoring the burn and dropped my shields. Power rushed into me, Daryn's power, the arcane power the Order commanded. Glorious and filling and—oh, fuck—I wanted to scream in ecstasy as it rushed through my limbs, pooling in my belly and setting every nerve ending alive.

Wait, there was something else, something even thicker and purer. Drink, drink, drink. I couldn't stop, didn't want to. Why should I? This was good, too good, and, damn, I'd been hungry for so fucking long.

The arm slipped and the body holding me captive fell away. My eyes snapped open and locked with Ryker, his shades were off and he was squinting at the floor, at the empty husk that had a moment ago been a member of the Order.

No, this couldn't be happening. He couldn't be dead. He was supernatural, right? He had magick. But the pure delicious stuff I'd devoured...Oh God, he was pure human. A human who could wield magick. Not a neph, not scourge. I'd drained what little arcane power he was hoarding and then moved on to his life force. This is what could have happened to Jonathon if I hadn't stopped. I staggered back, turned my head and puked on the grass. Oh God, oh hell.

There was movement in the periphery of my vision as Ryker took a wary step toward me.

I straightened and wiped my mouth with my sleeve. "Please. I didn't mean to. I didn't know he was pure human." My shields slammed back into place. "I can't...you can't."

Drayton came strolling around the side of the building. "The bitch got away, but I doubt she'll stick around Sunset now that we've taken out her cell."

Ryker rushed over to me and scooped me up into his arms. "Be unconscious, let me speak."

I closed my eyes and slumped against his hard body. But my heart was jack hammering in my chest.

"What the fuck happened to him?" Drayton asked. "Wait... Damn that looks like..."

"His spell backfired," Ryker cut in quickly. "It knocked the human out in the process. The damn fool was overreaching with his magick."

Drayton was silent for a long beat. "*Is* that what happened, Ryker?"

His tone was saturated with sarcasm, doubt, an opening for Ryker to spill the beans. He suspected something. Drayton suspected. Shit. There was a long beat of silence, the only sound the steady thud of Ryker's heart against my ear. Was he going to tell?

His biceps flexed and his chest rose and fell in a sigh. "Yeah, that's what happened."

"All right," Drayton said slowly. "I'll check on the other two humans. Daryn knocked them out when we arrived. Fucker knew we weren't alone. He wanted you to come so he could kill us both."

"I'll get her into the van and see you back at SPD."

Oh, God. He knew. Ryker knew. I remained unconscious as he loaded me into the back of the van.

"You can open your eyes now?" he said.

I did so to find him hovering over me, his shades were off again and his eyes, the clearest blue, stared deep into me, as if attempting to touch my soul.

"What are you?" his asked softly.

"I'm human." I blinked back tears, biting down on my quivering bottom lip and despising this moment of weakness. "Please. I'm human."

His exhale was warm and sweet on my face. He nodded slowly. "Be careful little *human*. Sometimes what we think we want isn't always what's best for us." He scooted back and jumped out of the van. "Strap in."

The door slid shut and I dropped my head into my hands.

What had I done? What the fuck had I done?

My hands shook as I poured coffee into my mug. It sloshed over the side and onto the counter. I'd killed a man. A man who'd wanted to kill me, but still. I'd killed him, sucked the life right out of him. I was a murderer, and Ryker knew I wasn't human. My stomach roiled and quivered with nausea, and my eyes burned with the pressure of holding back tears. The Protectorate was gone, thank goodness. They'd taken the bloodsucker we'd had in lock-up with them and jetted for Midnight. Ryker had kept his mouth shut. He hadn't even looked at me, but Drayton had and there was way too much speculation in those glances.

A shadow fell over me and a large hand clutching a tea towel mopped up the mess for me.

"You all right?" Nolan asked.

I nodded, wanting desperately to lean into him, to draw from him to quell the shakes. They knew. Two members of the Protectorate knew.

"How are Bellamy and Fulstrom?"

"Recovering." He cupped my shoulder and turned me to face him. Looking down on me with the concerned expression I was so used to, and something else, something dark and new I'd never noticed before. "Tell me you're all right."

I nodded, breaking eye contact. "I'm fine. Just shaken up. It was crazy."

"You could have been killed."

"That's the second time this week you've said that to me. Way too much excitement for the SPD." I cracked a smile, wanting to ease the tension.

His fingers flexed against the taut flesh of my shoulder and then he released me. "If you need to talk... If you need *anything,* you come to me."

What I needed was to run. To fuck like a jackrabbit and expel this excess power thrumming inside me, but personal relationships were a no go area for me. Aside from Jesse, there was no one close — no one except Nolan, my mentor, my rock.

He wants you Harker. Wants you balls deep. I can't believe you haven't noticed. Julie's words reverberated inside my head, kicking up my pulse and heating the base of my neck.

I cleared my throat. "How did they get in?"

"What?" his voice was rasp.

I glanced up at my reflection in his dilated pupils. My mouth went bone dry. I licked my lips and he tracked the motion. Something stirred inside me, that part of me that just didn't give a damn about right and wrong, the part that just hungered and wanted. The part I worked to keep locked down all the fucking time.

Exhaling through my nose, I took a step away from him. "We need to check out the fence. Do a full perimeter sweep. They had to have got in somewhere."

His lips tightened. "I have Henry and a couple other guys on it."

"Good."

"Go home and get some rest. The report can wait."

"The report can wait?" I placed my hands on my hips. "Okay, who are you and what have you done with my boss?"

His eyes crinkled and the weird dynamic melted away. "Shut it, cheeky. Go home and get some sleep. I'll see you Monday."

"Monday? You don't want me in tomorrow?"

He arched a brow. "You have the day

booked off for the fete remember?"

The Fete? Oh crap. The Fete. Stalls and smiles and cakes to be sold to raise money to buy the materials to fix our fences. Dawn was our provider and the materials weren't cheap. The bastards probably put the prices high on purpose. They wanted us vulnerable and exposed so that more people would become silvered.

"Yeah, good times." My tone was flat and he let out a bark of laughter

"Save me one of Jesse's brownies."

"I'll save you a whole batch."

His eyes twinkled. "You always do."

Did I? Yeah, I did. "Well, someone's got to take care of you." I jabbed his taut abdomen with my index finger teasingly. But he didn't smile, instead his gaze took on that intense vibe again and my stomach did a flip.

Fuck Henry and Julie and their weird ideas. Nolan was just...Nolan. Then why was I backing up so quickly. "Look, can we just keep the details of the mission under wraps? You know how worried Jesse gets."

He nodded. "Of course."

"See you Monday."

I turned and strode out of the coffee room leaving my coffee behind.

Fetes sucked. Okay, not the actual fete

but working a fete sucked. While everyone also milled around on the green, eating burgers and cotton candy, playing games and taking spins on the Ferris wheel, I was stuck at a stall selling cute cupcakes and delicious brownies. Urgh. This so wasn't my forte, but Jesse loved it all. Here, amongst her peers, Jesse was in her element.

Although, right now she was giving me the cold shoulder. My scalp pricked with unease. Had someone said something to her about yesterday? Nolan had promised to keep the details under wraps but still...

A group of older kids from her school came strolling past our stall, must have been around thirteen or fourteen.

"Teenagers, eh?" I nudged Jesse. She glanced up from covering the lemon drizzle cake she'd baked that morning.

"Kitty, Derek, how are you this fine morning?" she asked.

The kids paused and their blasé expressions melted into smiles. "Morning, Miss Harker. Great, Thanks, Miss Harker."

Jesse smiled indulgently. "Care for some yummy cake?"

The kids walked over eagerly and began picking out their treats. Jesse spoke to each of them, adjusting her tone to suit the child and they were putty in her hands. She was good with them, good with kids in general. It's what made her such a great teacher.

The group wandered off, waving bye and Jesse turned her attention to restocking our table.

I passed her the box with the chocolate muffins. "How do you do that?"

"Do what?" She took the box and began to unpack it carefully.

"Remember each face and each name."

She shrugged. "I dunno. I just do." She popped the empty box behind her. "I heard about the massacre at the motel."

I closed my eyes. "That was supposed to be kept on the down-low."

"Yeah. Well, this is Sunset."

True. Gossip was gold here. Considering that not much of note ever happened, when something did blow up, it was all over the district in record time. The motel was probably the biggest incident to hit Sunset in years.

"The Order is gone. That's all you need to worry about."

"You neglected to tell me you were nearly killed."

I froze, cupcake partway to my mouth. "Who told you that?"

"Henry swung by just before you got here."

That prick. "Henry wasn't even there. He knows nothing."

"So, you weren't held hostage by one of the Order?"

Gah. "Jesse. I'm an officer of the law which means sometimes I'm put in dangerous situations. It happens."

She turned to face me, her eyes bright with what I'd come to recognize as her idea face. I stifled a groan.

"There's a job opening at the school for a TA."

I set the cupcake back on the counter. "No."

"But we can be together, and you can be safe."

I didn't want safe. I didn't want to be working with kids. I needed action, any action I could get and the threat of danger, however slim, because without it, I'd go insane. Without it, the hunger would consume me.

"I like my job."

"But you could have been killed."

"I'm seriously going to throttle the next person that says that to me."

The sound of bells filled the air. Crap. Seriously? They were going to do this now. Here at the charity fete?

Jesse undid her apron. "Are you coming to watch?"

"No. And neither are you."

Her jaw set stubbornly. "Stay here if

you want, but you can't tell me what to do."

"Pot calling the kettle black, much?"

Her lips twitched. "Oh, come on. Aren't you curious what they'll say?"

"No. Because it's always the same shit." But I was on my feet regardless, because there was no way she was going alone.

The tinkle of bells intensified as we exited the back of the stall and joined the other humans making their way across the green toward the spectacle.

"Did you see Gerry's girl? Yes, she's one of them," someone said.

Gerry ran the supermarket on main street. His twenty-five-year-old daughter had run off to join the silvered with her six month old baby in tow after her husband had gone scourge. Gerry, a widower, was left devastated. And she was here? Damn. Let's hope Gerry hadn't decided to come today.

The silvered came into view over the rise. Humans dressed in gold and white robes that fell down to their ankles. Their feet were clad in silver sandals and around their necks glinted the silver chains of the White Wings. There were ten silvered today. They strode purposefully onto the green, silver bells at their waists jingling, ready to spread the word.

Jesse gripped my hand, and stood on tiptoe to get a better look. She was tiny, barely five foot four inches, there was no way she was getting a good view, and even though I hated her seeing this, if she wanted to, then I needed to make sure she got a good spot.

"Hey, excuse me." I pushed my way through the crowd using my five foot seven height and SPD authority to get to the front of the mass.

Jesse stifled a giggle and then we were upfront with an unobstructed view of the spectacle. Two district councilmen were standing either side of the silvered, their expressions tight. Yeah, this hadn't been on the agenda. This little demonstration had probably been requested by Dawn last minute, leaving our district little time to prepare for it. But a request, however late from Dawn, could not be denied. Dawn provided most of our goods and services through export between the districts — things such as vegetables and fruit, things that didn't flourish as well in Sunset. They also held the monopoly on technology, and the power plant that ran Arcadia was located within their borders. Our electrified fence was only running because of the high tax the citizens paid, another reason why not every human could afford to live in Sunset.

The ten silvered came to a standstill. They formed a line and began to sing. It was a song of praise to the White Wings for their benevolence and mercy, and it made me sick.

Jesse's grip on my hand tightened. A quick glance showed her to be enraptured, mouth slightly parted as she absorbed their words. A sick, queasy feeling squirmed in my belly and the urge to shake her was almost too much. Instead, I fixed my attention back on the silvered as the designated spokesperson stepped forward to deliver the speech. It was Clara, Gerry's daughter.

"There is safety and comfort and peace beyond the gates," she said. "There is a home for all who wish to follow. There is love and joy and everlasting happiness."

Really? Because that face sure didn't look happy.

"The decision is forever in your hands." She delivered the final words in a monotone.

Yeah and it would be the last decision you'd make. I bit the insides of my cheeks to stop the words popping out.

"Clara, come home, baby!" Gerry stepped out of the crowd. He took a step toward her. "Sweetheart. I miss you so much."

Clara didn't even blink. Her expression remained neutral, her attention straight ahead.

"What have they done to you? Tell me?" His voice rose, trembling with a cocktail of emotion.

He began to walk toward the silvered. Shit. Accosting a silvered was a criminal offense.

"Serenity..." Jesse urged.

But I was already striding into the clearing to cut him off. "Back up, Gerry. You know the rules."

He blinked at me, his dazed expression clearing, and then his jaw clenched. "You think I give a damn about the rules? That's my baby girl there. Get out of my way."

He tried to sidestep me, but I blocked him again. "Gerry, stop. I don't want to hurt you."

The crowd was buzzing with murmurs.

Gerry rushed me, but came up against a wall. Yeah, stronger than you thought, huh? I twisted, grabbed his arms and kicked the back of his knee bringing him down.

"Out of the way! Move!" It was Henry's voice bellowing above the crowd.

Great the cavalry had arrived.

I looked up as my colleagues strode toward me; Bellamy, Henry and Fulstrom.

"Hey, guys. It's okay. It's just Gerry. He'll be fine in a min..." My glaze slipped past them to the five-man extraction team. Suited and armed with guns. Guns. They circled me.

Me.

My heart went into freeze frame and then lodged in my throat. "What is this?" My voice was a croak because damn it, I already knew.

"A mistake," Bellamy said. "Harker. It has to be. But you need to come with us now 'kay."

They knew. They knew what I was. I could see it in Bellamy's sorrow filled gaze, and Henry's triumphant one.

"Serenity?" Nolan appeared to my left. "Are you coming?" He said it casual and soft, as if he was asking me to dance, but the nullifying cuffs in his hand said different.

I swallowed hard, and carefully released Gerry. "Don't touch her, Gerry. Just make the right choice." He sobbed into the grass as I pulled myself up and faced Nolan.

"There's no need for those, Nolan. You know me."

His gaze flicked to the extraction team. "I know. But it's protocol." His left eye twitched.

"We'll get this squared," Bellamy said again, but this time there was no conviction in his tone.

I held out my wrists and locked gazes with Nolan. "Do it."

His strong hands cupped my slender wrists. "I'm sorry, Harker. I really am." He cuffed me.

My body went numb, my ears buzzing with the inevitability of it and then Jesse's scream tore my resolve in two.

"Serenity? Let me go. That's my sister." One of the extraction team guys had her in his grip, his arm like a vise around her waist, holding her back.

My control snapped and tears blurred my vision. "Jesse, calm down."

But she was a wild thing, clawing at the arm that held her back, kicking and screaming as her worst fears were brought to life. As SPD began to lead me away.

"No! Stop, you're hurting me."

I spun to see Jesse pinned to the ground her arms hiked up her back in an incapacitating position. Rage, hot and potent, coursed through my veins.

"Let go of her." I took a step toward the guy.

"Serenity, don't." Nolan made a grab for me just as the extraction guy, pressed a knee to my sister's back.

Jesse cried out and my shields fell. "Get the fuck off her now!" The power I'd absorbed from Daryn, the power I'd stored up and squirreled away blasted out of me and slammed into the officers, knocking them flying. Jesse was suddenly free and sprinting toward me. My knees buckled and I went down, too weak to stay upright. Drained. I was fucking drained.

Jesse pulled me against her, her face in the crook of my neck, her tears smearing against my skin. "No. Please don't let them do this. Don't let them take you."

There was no shock, no confusion as to why they'd come for me, just fear that they'd be taking me.

"You knew?"

She nodded. "I don't care. I don't care because I love you."

My chest ached with sorrow, and my shoulders shook with sobs.

"Jesse," Nolan said. "It'll be okay. Everything will be okay."

But it wouldn't. Nothing would ever be okay again.

My legs were finally working properly, but my head still throbbed dully. I'd never done that before—expelled power like that. This was something new, another clue as to what I could possibly be and to who I was.

The cell was a reprieve from prying eyes. My friends, my colleagues, people I'd known all my life were looking at me warily, as if afraid I'd attack at any moment. Being locked in a cell was better. Head cradled in my hands, I studied the cracks in the stone floor—a network of tiny fissures, kinda like my life. Jesse had known, or suspected at least. Why hadn't she said anything? Would they let her see me before they shipped me off to Midnight? How long before I was expelled?

The door to the cell block clanged open, and Nolan strode in, his boots clipping against the floor.

"Serenity, I brought you some tea and something for your headache," he said.

My eyes misted. "How can you be so nice to me now that you know the truth?"

"Doesn't change who you are," he said. "You're still the feisty, determined woman who walked into the recruitment drive five years ago and stole my heart."

Had I heard right? I looked up slowly and met his steadfast gaze.

His throat bobbed and he ducked his head. "I can't believe I just said that."

Yes, I'd heard right, and now my insides were doing all kinds of squirmy fucked up shit. "You never said anything."

"No point. You didn't feel the same way. You respected me and cared about me. I was your mentor, but that's where the line was drawn."

The words, *we could have been more* were on the tip of my tongue but I bit them back, not wanting one of the last things I said to him to be a lie.

He entered my cell and pulled the door to.

I offered him a watery smile. "Aren't you worried I'll jump you and make my escape?"

He handed me the tea and pills then crouched in front of me. "If there was somewhere for you to run, I'd take you myself."

Dammit. Now I was crying. I put the mug and pills on the bench and buried my face in my hands.

"Don't." His tone was harsh, reproving. "You're stronger than this."

I sniffed. "No. I'm not. I'm fucking terrified."

The bench creaked as he took a seat beside me, and then he tugged me against him and lifted me onto his lap. He cradled me while I sobbed away my fear and despair. After what seemed like forever, the sobs subsided, leaving me spent and despondent.

"Are you done?" he asked.

I nodded against his chest. The steady thud of his heart was a channel for calm and resolve.

"Now listen to me, Serenity. You were made to protect the weak. It's in your blood. Neph blood, and that ain't a bad thing."

I leaned back to look into his face. "How can you say that?"

He scanned my face. "Because the nephs are all that stand between us and *them*—the White Wings and the scourge. The neph are stronger than us, more powerful. You think if they wanted to take Sunset we could stop them?"

I blinked up at him. "But the treaty..."

"A piece of paper to make us feel safe. It's all an illusion, Serenity. The neph choose to stay in Midnight. They choose to protect humans who live there and prevent the scourge from spreading into Sunset, and now you're one of them. You get to do what you were born to do."

His words should have made me feel better, but they barely chipped away at the sadness. "I don't want to be a hero. I want to stay here with my friends and Jesse. This is my home."

He sighed into my hair, his fingers caressing the back of my neck and running down my back. Touching, touching, as if making up for all the times he'd held back, and I allowed it, greedy for the affection and eager for the comfort the contact provided.

"If I had my way, you'd get to stay," he said. "But we must maintain the illusion of control. You have to go."

I pressed my forehead against his shoulder. "How long before they come for me?"

"I made the call a half hour ago."

So, maybe another half hour or so. Depending on how busy they were. "Can I see Jesse?"

"You know the rules, Harker."

So I was back to Harker now. "Those are for scourge."

"Any non-human entity, Harker. Besides, even if I could, I wouldn't"

"What?"

"She wants to go with you."

"What!" I jumped off his lap. "No. She can't. She mustn't try and follow me."

He nodded. "I know. Midnight is no place for someone like Jesse. It would chew her up and spit her out, but you...you can handle it, Serenity, but not if you have Jesse to look out for. In time, she will move on and build a new life."

It was why contact between citizens of Sunset and Midnight was prohibited. The only line of communications ran between law enforcement and district councils.

I pinched the bridge of my nose. "I promised to protect her, to keep her safe."

"And you can do that from Midnight. You're an excellent officer, Serenity, but you've always held back. Run a little bit slower and pulled your punches. Now you get to realize your full potential. If the Protectorate won't have you, then maybe the MED will."

The Midnight Enforcement Department dealt with all the minor crimes in Midnight. They were like the SPD, but on the other side of the border. Working for either organization would be better than not taking any action at all. Yes. I could still keep Jesse safe by controlling the scourge infection in Midnight.

"Promise me you'll keep an eye on her. Promise me you'll watch out for her."

He smiled, but his eyes didn't light up. "Always." He stood, towering over me again and reached out to cup my cheek. "I know it's presumptuous and highly inappropriate, but for the last five years I've dreamt of kissing you. I just don't want to—"

I grabbed the back of his neck, yanked him down and pressed my lips to his. His mouth parted and his tongue met mine. Heat coursed through me, shooting out from the hungry dark part of me that usually lurked behind my shields. My fingers tightened on the nape of his neck, body pressed up against his. I deepened the kiss, and a raw moan rattled at the back of his throat.

"Ahem!"

Nolan pulled back, his cheeks flushed, his eyes bright.

"Sir, the Protectorate are here." Bellamy kept his eyes on the ground shifting from foot to foot.

Nolan ran his thumb over my bottom lip and then pulled me in for a hug. "Thank you." He whispered in my ear.

The cell door clinked shut, but neither Nolan nor Bellamy bothered to lock it. Like Nolan had said, there was nowhere to run.

It was the walk of shame. The brown and cream corridor seemed extra long, doors open on either side as officers peered out to watch the neph who'd hidden among them all her life be evicted. My cheeks burned with the shame of it, but I held my head up high, and kept my stride even.

Reception loomed up ahead, and through the glassed off upper half of the double doors I caught site of the neph sent to collect me.

Ryker stood, arms loose at his side, damned shades firmly on the bridge of his nose. He was in that damned not-leather outfit again, his black t-shirt hugging his biceps lovingly.

The darkness slammed against my shields wanting out, wanting to rage. This was his fault. He'd told and now I was losing the only home I'd ever known. The lump was back in my throat, but I'd be damned if I'd let anyone know how devastated I was. Nolan pushed open the doors and stood back to let me through. Julie stared at me wide eyed as I ducked under the barrier.

"Why isn't she cuffed?" Henry demanded from his position on the customer side of the reception counter.

"She's one of us," Nolan said.

"No, she's a fucking neph," Henry said.

Ryker's head whipped round to spear Henry with his shaded gaze. There was something completely disconcerting about someone staring at you through a pair of sunglasses, as if the shades somehow gave him super vision, the ability to burrow into your head and find your soul.

Henry held up his hands. "Look, I meant no offense."

"Then maybe you should keep your mouth shut," Ryker said.

Henry's jaw ticked, but even he knew better than to take on one of the Protectorate.

"Are you ready?" Ryker asked me.

"Do I have a choice?" There was way too much hope in the question, and I bit the insides of my cheek wanting desperately to take back the tone while hoping that he'd say, *of course you have a choice, Harker.*

"No." He held open the door. "Van's

parked round the side of the building."

With a final glance over my shoulder at the people who'd been my family for the last five years, the people who, with the exception of Nolan and Bellamy, were looking at me as if I was a freak, I stepped out into the sunset.

We drove in silence getting ever closer to the border and farther and farther away from Jesse and home. My pulse was a bird trapped in my veins. What was she doing now? How would she cope?

"I didn't tell them," Ryker said. His tone soft.

"What?" My voice was hoarse, as if I'd been crying a lot. I hated that.

"I didn't tell them about you. That you were one of us."

The knot in my chest eased a little, no idea why. "You didn't?"

"No. But the bloodsucker scourge we picked up did plenty of talking." His fingers tapped against the wheel. "He said you drained his energy?"

"You can speak to them?"

"Not me. But Bane, the head of MPD can."

I pressed my head back against the seat. "Well, shit."

"But right now, I can't sense you. I

mean, you feel human to me."

"Yes, I'm good at that."

"How?"

How could I explain this to someone when I didn't even understand it myself? "I'm not sure. Ever since I can recall, ever since this...hunger woke up inside me, I've had this wall. Walls, sorry. I call them my shields."

The border came into view, and the electric hum of the fence filled the air.

"You have them up right now?"

"Yes."

"Can you open them?"

"No."

"You can't?"

"I don't want to."

He sighed through his nose. "I just need to see."

I turned to him. "Isn't it enough that you're taking me from my home, from my sister, from everything I've ever known? Do you have to test how freaky I am too?"

He lapsed into silence for a long beat. "I get it. This sucks for you. But there are worse fates."

"Like what?"

"Like never experiencing anything, like never having loved or been loved, or like being dead."

Okay, maybe he had a point. I still

didn't want him to poke around in my head though. I crossed my arms.

"When we get back to the MPD we'll need to gauge you. Find out how strong the neph blood is."

"Why?"

"Because there's a hierarchy in Midnight—rules we live by, and a set up for the community. We need to know where you fit in."

Okay, now I was intrigued. "What kind of hierarchy?"

We slowed as we slipped over the border, and my heart lurched. The sky began to darken as we left Sunset behind. As I left Jesse behind.

Breathe, Serenity, just breathe. "Tell me about the hierarchy. Please." Anything to take my mind off what was happening to me.

Ryker slipped off his shades and shot me a sidelong glance with his baby blues. "On one condition."

"What?"

"You drop your shields for the boss."

"How long is the drive?"

"Forty-five minutes."

Great almost an hour to kill. I couldn't keep the bite out of my words. "Fine. Deal."

The corner of his mouth curled up. "You have a temper, don't you?"

"My temperament isn't up for

examination. Hierarchy. Please."

"Okay. So you know that nephs have Black Wing blood in their veins, right?"

"Descended from the bloodlines of human and Black Wing unions."

We slipped into darkness, sailing beneath a full moon.

"Right. But there are different levels of neph," he said. "In some of us, the Black Wing gene has taken stronger root, our bloodlines have had more than one Black Wing in them, and possibly several nephs making us powerful and giving us extra abilities."

"The Protectorate."

"Yes, the Protectorate are all primary nephs. But not all primary nephs are Protectorate."

"I'm confused. What makes the Protectorate special?"

"We each command an element."

"Like earth, water, fire and stuff?"

"Yes."

"So, only primaries that command an element are allowed to become Protectorate?"

"Yes. But we do command a small force of regular primaries."

We passed amber lit stores. People milled about, shopping and going about their day. But it was night, just as it had always been sunset for me.

"It will take some getting used to," Ryker said.

"Are they safe?"

He chuckled. "The scourge don't attack constantly. They have a cycle of their own, not due for another couple of weeks, and the residents of Midnight are pretty savvy."

I guess you had to be to live here. But wait, that didn't make sense. The rippers had attacked me a couple of days ago. "You're telling me that the scourge never attack outside of that time frame?"

His jaw tightened. "There have been the odd instances of late. We're looking into it."

Was the Black Wing who'd saved me looking into it too?

"Back to the nephs and our deal," he said. "You have the primary nephs and then you have the minor nephs. The ones who have abilities like telekinesis or pyrokinesis, maybe telepathy, or it could just be the ability to read auras. The minor neph population is high."

"So, while the Protectorate keep the humans safe, what do the other primaries who aren't part of the MPD do?"

His jaw tightened. "They build their mini empires and play tug of war when it comes to power. Not all nephs have humanity's best interests at heart. There are things in Midnight that the MPD is struggling to keep in control. A breed of neph that wants to break all the rules."

Gooseflesh broke out across my skin. Nolan had said the nephs were the good guys, but the tick of Ryker's jaw told me we had it super wrong, and then the memory of my recent jaunt into Midnight reared its head again. The rippers had me surrounded and then those guys had shown up and they'd asked me...

"What's a house?"

His gaze flicked my way again. "What did you say?"

"Look, a few days ago I was here chasing a ripper and I got surrounded by a pack and these two guys came up and kinda scared them off but then they attacked me. But before they did, they asked me what house I belonged to."

He exhaled sharply through his nose. "They attacked you? So, they didn't sense what you were? Damn your shields are good."

"Not answering my question."

"Later. You'll get a rundown of the lay of the land later."

"Why later?"

"Because we're here."

A set of wrought iron gates loomed up ahead of me, so high they reached for the moon. They swung open, silently and smoothly as we glided closer. My hands went cold and clammy and I pressed my thighs together to combat the need to pee.

The van crunched down a gravel laid drive and rolled toward a dark, hulking shape made of stone and shadow.

I'd thought he was taking me to the MPD, this looked like a haunted house. "What is this place?"

"This is my home. The home of the Midnight Protectorate."

The building was a dead husk from the outside, and it wasn't much better inside. Unkempt and gloomy, dust motes danced in the air, illuminated by shafts of moonlight lancing in through pointed arched windows high up on the wall. A wide staircase, which at some time must have been grand, swept up to the first floor. It was like stepping into a gothic fairytale. Any moment now, a beast would come bounding down the stairs and —

A huge shadow leapt across the wall to the left of the staircase. I stumbled back almost losing my balance.

Ryker pressed a hand to the small of my back to steady me. "Don't be afraid. He can smell it."

He? Who was he? The shadow? My question was answered a moment later when the shadow caster appeared at the top of the staircase.

A beast.

It *was* a beast. I stepped back, but Ryker's hand was still there holding me firmly in place.

"Calm," Ryker said.

It began to climb down the stairs. No, not a beast, but a man. A beastly man. I'd never seen anything like him. He was a giant, his hands so big he could have twisted my head off my neck with them. His hair was dark, pushed back from his face to curl beneath his ears and his face—oh, God that face—fierce, and primal and predatory. He was wearing a black T-shirt stretched so tight across his shoulders that I expected to hear a rip at any moment.

He stopped a few steps above the ground floor and glared at me. His eyes flashed violet and then dimmed to a purple hue I'd never seen before.

What the heck kind of neph was he?

"Human," he said.

His voice was like a caress, penetrating deep and stroking parts of me I didn't even know existed. I suppressed a shudder. How could such a monstrous creature have such a voice?

"No, Bane. She's not human," Ryker said. "This is Serenity Harker, the woman the bloodsucker was babbling about."

The beast, Bane, studied me for a moment longer. His lip curled in derision. "Wrong."

Ryker leaned in toward me. "Remember our deal? Drop the shields."

Breath tight in my lungs, gaze still locked on the monster on the stairs, I let my guards down completely. It was like pulling off a pair of uncomfortable shoes, or yanking off your bra at the end of the day. The relief was a sigh and a stretch.

Bane closed his eyes. His nostrils flared and his head swayed as if inhaling the most delicious aroma. "Yes. Not human." He opened blazing violet eyes and locked onto me. And then he leapt, bridging the distance between is in one bound.

"Fuck!" I turned to run.

Huge arms wrapped around me, and I was hauled up against the hard expanse of Bane's chest.

"Get off! Get the fuck off me." I kicked and squirmed succeeding only in rubbing up against him, in feeling every hard plane and dip of his pectorals and abs. His arms were unyielding bands, and his scent, fucking hell what was that? It was dizzying and intoxicating. The darkness inside me pulsed and stirred, and the hunger rose.

"Bane, what the heck are you doing?" Ryker asked. "You're scaring her."

Bane growled in warning, and the vibration of his chest ran over my back and a sharp throb of need shot my core. His lips brushed my ear sending a shiver down my spine. "You want me to release you?"

"Yes." Why was my voice so husky and breathless? Afraid, I was afraid, that's what it was.

He ran his nose up the side of my neck. "I don't believe you."

No. Neither did I. Oh, fuck. I was throbbing now, in all the right places. What was happening to me? It had never been like this before. The darkness was in my veins, in my blood, taking over with the need to feed.

"Dammit, Bane," Ryker said.

"What's going on?" It was Drayton, his tone lazy and almost bored.

But it was all peripheral because I was wrapped in need, holding on by a thread. "Let. Me. Go."

His chest rumbled in a chuckle. "Make me."

I gave in to the hunger, grabbed his arm and inhaled with my aura. Oh sweet, sweet, fucking hell. Honey and cinnamon, and man, this was something else. It poured into me, over me, filling me.

And then I was free. My knees hit the floor, my head spinning from the intoxicating flavor of his power. My body thrummed and fizzed and buzzed with the need to move, to take action, but I was damned if I could stand.

There were raised voices, then murmurs, but all I could do was hold up my hands and stare at my fingers as my vision blurred and then snapped into high definition.

"Serenity? Serenity. Are you all right? Can you hear me?"

Ryker? I slowly lifted my chin to look into his beautiful face and grinned. "I'm soooo good."

Someone snort laughed and Ryker's brows snapped together in annoyance. Was he annoyed at me? I didn't want him to be mad at me. He was so pretty.

I reached up to stroke his chin. "You are soooo pretty."

A bark of laughter. "Looks like you have an admirer," Drayton said.

"Shut it, Dray." Ryker reached for me. "Come on. Let's get you settled." He scooped me up as if I weighed nothing, and I curled against his chest as a wave of warmth seeped into my limbs.

Sleepy. I was so sleepy.

"So what is she?" Drayton asked.

"A cambion," Bane said. "She's a fucking cambion."

Cambion. She's a fucking Cambion.

I bolted up and cracked my head against something hard.

"Shit." Ryker sat back rubbing his forehead.

I pressed a hand to my own head and massaged the skin. We were in a room, a bedroom if the bed I was laid on was anything to go by. The decor here was slightly less gray and gothic with magnolia walls and even a carpet. Heavy red drapes covered the windows, blocking out the night, and several lamps cast a cheery amber glow.

"How are you feeling?" Ryker asked.

How *was* I feeling? Refreshed, energized. "I feel...great."

He smiled. "Oh, good. Saves me having to kick Bane's ass."

I arched a brow. "Really? You could do that?"

He cleared his throat. "Okay, maybe I'd have given him a severe talking to."

I snorted. "What happened?"

"According to Bane, he was testing you."

"Seemed more like he was having a grope," Drayton said.

How'd I missed him? He was lounging on a chair by a dresser.

"I'm telling you that dude seriously needs to get laid," Drayton continued.

Ryker's lip tightened. "Bane was needling you, pushing you to use your abilities."

"He could have just asked."

"Yes, but sometimes we don't know what we're capable of until put under duress. So, he made you feel threatened."

Threatened was the last thing I'd felt, but there was no way I was telling Ryker that. My hunger had been my dirty secret for way too long, and it had never been so sexual before. This was new.

"He said I was a cambion. What is that?"

Ryker looked to Drayton.

Drayton's lips curved in a half smile. "Oh so *now* you want me to step in?"

"For fuck's sake Dray, you were busy, so I went to pick her up alone. Deal with it."

Drayton pressed his lips together for a moment and then shrugged. "Fine." He fixed his gaze on me. "A cambion is the offspring of and incubus and a human."

"What's an incubus?"

Drayton grinned. "You're looking at one."

"O-kay."

He shrugged. "Most incubi need to feed off sexual energy, but there are some who prefer the life force of their victims, and they drain this through sexual encounters."

"Which kind are you?"

"I'm all about the sex baby." He winked.

"Drayton." Ryker warned.

He sighed. "Fine. Most incubi are sterile but the few that aren't who do impregnate female humans produce offspring called cambions. But there haven't been any cambions in centuries."

"But I'm one?"

He nodded. "According to Bane. And Bane is never wrong. Every cambion has slightly different abilities, and yours are intriguing."

I snorted. "Hardly."

Ryker smiled. "You drew power from one of the most powerful nephs in Midnight, Serenity. While he fought back. That is no small feat."

"He fought back?"

"You didn't feel it?"

I shook my head.

Drayton chuckled. "Well, that'll put a dent in Bane's mammoth ego."

"There's also the question of these shields of yours. We've never seen anything like it. It's fascinating."

They'd been my safety net all this time. They were up now, protecting me from myself, keeping the hunger in check.

"How often do you need to feed?" Drayton asked.

I swallowed hard, and licked my lips. "I can go a few weeks without, but then it gets hard to focus." Although recently. the craving had been getting stronger. "If I don't feed, it gets harder to keep the shields up. I usually get lucky and manage to get hold of one of the scourge we pick up."

"And if not?"

I clenched my jaw. "Then I go hungry."

Drayton sucked in a breath through his teeth. "Have you any idea how dangerous that is? You deny yourself and you risk losing complete control."

"I have my shields."

"Which you just admitted are harder to control if you don't feed for too long. Your hunger is inherited from your incubus father, and trust me if it's denied that darkness will take over."

There was way too much conviction in his words for them just to be an empty warning. Was he speaking from experience? I was about to ask but he interrupted.

"Have you ever fed on a human?"

Ryker tensed and the dried up husk of the member of the order came to mind.

I blinked back the heat at the back of my eyelids. "Yes. But I didn't know."

Drayton slapped a hand on his thigh. "I

knew it! You killed Daryn." He jabbed a finger at Ryker. "And you covered for her."

"You didn't exactly push the question either did you," Ryker said. "You suspected."

Drayton sighed. "Fine. I'm a soft touch, okay. Who wouldn't want to live in Sunset if they could."

"I didn't know. I promise. I'm not a murderer."

Drayton let out a bark of laughter. "Baby, you need to grow a thicker skin. You're a neph, and killing to survive comes with the territory. Daryn would have snapped your neck without a second thought. Trust me. He was a piece of scum."

Did his words make me feel better? Not really. The image of that dried husk played on my mind. "He was human. I ended up sucking on his life force as well as the magick he was channeling. There is nothing right about that."

"Not all humans are worthy of being saved," Drayton said. "We do it anyway, but trust me, there are some pretty fucked up humans out there and Daryn was one of them. You acted in self-defense. Give yourself a break." He paused and studied me speculatively. "There is a way to control it you know. So you wouldn't have to have the shields up all the time."

"How?"

He sat forward in his seat. "Feed more frequently."

I crossed my arms under my breasts. "Not an option."

"Why?"

"Because I hate it."

His eyes narrowed. "No, you don't, princess. You love it, and that scares you."

Fuck him and his insights. "There has to be another way. I can feed a couple of times a month and store the power."

His eyes lit up. "Store power? Interesting."

"Why? Can't you do that?"

His dark eyes grew even darker. "No."

Ryker stepped in. "Here in Midnight you'll burn through that power pretty quickly. You'll need to adjust, Harker."

"There has to be another way. I can't... I don't want to lose control."

"So, let me train you," Drayton said.

Ryker's lips tightened. "No."

Drayton shot Ryker an irritated look.

I glanced from Ryker to Drayton. "Why not?"

Drayton caught his bottom lip between his teeth and then slowly released it. The action was so blatantly sexual, so hot that my body tightened in response.

Man it was obvious. "You'd have to have sex with me, wouldn't you?"

His lips tightened. "No. No sex. I can teach you some breathing exercises to help you pace your feeding and stop before you hurt someone...that is if you mean them no harm. You can siphon off me, no sexual contact required. Wouldn't want to sully our working relationship...unless you want to, that is?"

Ryker's snorted.

Had he been worried Drayton would want to get freaky with me? Why did he even care? Wait what? "Working relationship?"

"Cambions are considered primary nephs," Ryker said. "And Bane has asked if you'd like to stay and join the Protectorate as one of the officers we command."

Join the Protectorate. That was the first thing anyone had said that felt right. Nolan's words rang in my ears. His conviction that I could have a place here, and even though I'd give anything to be back in Sunset with Jesse, that was no longer an option. "Yes. I'd like to stay."

Where else would I go? Out into Midnight to find my own way, to become a no one? Nolan had said I was born to protect the weak. If I was going to stay, I needed to learn how my new home operated, and I needed to learn to make the best use of my abilities.

I touched Ryker's hand. "I need you to

tell me everything about Midnight."

"Of course."

"And Drayton, I'd like to take you up on your offer to teach me how to use my abilities."

His lips curled in a seductive smile. "Wise decision."

I arched a brow. "No sexual contact, right?"

He sobered. "Right."

"If I feed off you, then I'll be absorbing your power, your incubi seduction and that's gonna get messy," I transferred my attention to Ryker, "so if you don't mind I'd like to siphon off you while Drayton instructs?"

Ryker's expression shuttered completely. "No. I can't. I'm sorry."

Drayton's expression hardened. "Look, I know you don't know me at all, but when I give my word I mean it, and I give you my word, there will be no sexual contact during our sessions." His eyes gleamed. "At least none initiated by me."

I looked from Ryker to Drayton. Why was Ryker being so weird about my siphoning off him? I opened my mouth to ask but Ryker stood up and cleared his throat.

"I should go check in with the others," he said. "I'm due on patrol in a bit. Dray, can you show Serenity around the base?"

"Sure," Drayton said. He dropped me a

wink.

"I'll find you later and we can talk about Midnight," Ryker said to me. His expression was impassive as if he'd shoved his shades on, except he hadn't.

He left us to it, eager to get away from me.

"What just happened?"

Drayton pulled himself out of his seat and stretched, his t-shirt rode up exposing tanned abs and the tempting V that sat above his low slung jeans. My cheeks heated. Dammit. Stop staring, woman. I raised my gaze to his face to find him smiling smugly.

Great.

He held out a hand. "I'm starving."

My brows shot up.

"For food, princess." He chuckled. "You should see your face." His tone dropped low and seductive. "Are you hungry for food?"

My tummy grumbled. "Yeah, I guess I am." I slipped my palm into his and allowed him to haul me up. He yanked a little harder than necessary sending me stumbling against his solid frame. I braced myself, hands against his pecs, and looked up into his face, startled and stupidly aroused.

"Turn it off, please."

His brow crinkled. "What?"

"Your mojo or whatever you're doing."

His gaze softened and he scanned my

face. "I'm not doing anything, Serenity."

Oh, fuck.

I pulled back, out of the circle of his arms. "Steak, or chicken. I need protein." I strode toward the door and yanked it open, and then realized I had no idea where the kitchen was. "Lead the way."

He breezed past me, an amused smile playing on his lips.

Behind my shields, the hunger stirred.

11

Drayton walked with a sensual stride that was kind of hypnotic. Were all incubi like him?

I gripped the banister as we took the steps down to the ground floor. These weren't the main stairs. These were a narrow set with sconces on the stone wall to light the way. "Where did Ryker go?"

"He's heading a patrol tonight with Rivers. How much did he tell you about our hierarchy?"

"The primary and minor neph stuff, and the elemental thing."

"Yes, there are only six primaries at the MPD with elemental affinities. Ryker, Bane, Rivers, Orin, Cassie and myself. Patrols are done in groups of four, two head primaries and two regular ones."

"So the elemental primaries are the

heads?"

"Yes. We set up this base. We recruit, we train and we patrol. We also live here in the main house."

"What about the non-head primaries? Do they live here too?"

"No. There are two large guesthouses on the grounds where they live. We have about twenty officers in residence there."

"Soooo, how come I get to live here?"

He shot me a grin. "Bane obviously *likes* you."

My brain stuttered. "What? What do you mean by that?"

He laughed, a full belly laugh. "Oh, God. You should see your face. I'm joking." His tone grew serious. "You're a cambion. Unique, rare and you have those shields and this amazing ability to siphon power with a touch, and use it." He paused at the bottom of the staircase. "You *can* use it, can't you?"

"I'm not sure. I did release the power I'd siphoned off Daryn and knock some people out at the fete."

He blinked at me. "Why did you do that?"

"Gee, I don't know, I thought it would be fun."

He was still staring at me with that perplexed look on his face.

I made an exasperated sound. "They

were arresting me, and they hurt my sister, so I blasted them, okay. It wasn't exactly intentional. I just wanted them to stop."

"Another thing to work on then," Drayton said. "Impulse control. Come on." He led me though the foyer and under an arch, down spooky dark corridors lit sporadically by candelabra's while I avoided staring at his perfect butt. We climbed down another flight of stone steps and stepped through a set of double doors into a huge warm space decorated like the perfect country kitchen. Pots and pans hung off walls and two massive stoves sat against the wall. A long table took center stage surrounded by eight seats. And on the far side of the table were a man and a woman engaged in some kind of game.

"Piss off Orin, the last scone is mine." A slender fiery haired female leapt up trying to reach something clutched in the tall, lithe guy's hand.

The guy, Orin shook his head. "I'm doing you a favor, Cassie. You'll get fat and then none of the boys will wanna kiss you."

Cassie stopped jumping and placed her hands on her hips. "Do you want me to scream?"

Orin's eyes widened and then narrowed. "You wouldn't dare."

Cassie's shoulders rose as if she was

filling her lungs in preparation to let loose.

"Dammit, Orin. Give her the fucking scone," Drayton barked from the doorway.

It was the first time I'd heard him lose his chilled tone and the guy, Orin, quickly held out the baked goods.

Cassie stared at it for a long beat and then shrugged. "I don't want it anymore."

"What?" Orin looked incredulous. "You just kicked up a huge fuss."

"Yeah, well now it's got all your roan germs all over it."

Orin took a menacing step toward the female, and my body tensed, ready to defend her. Drayton held out his arm, blocking me, as if sensing my intention. And then Cassie was in Orin's arms, and they were kissing so deeply it looked like they were eating each other's faces.

Drayton sighed. "You have rooms for this shit."

Orin came up for air. "You're just jealous your incubus seduction doesn't work on her." His attention fell to me, and he gently released Cassie.

She turned to us. "Is this the new recruit Bane was talking about?" She addressed Drayton but her gaze was flitting all over me, part assessing, partly just curious.

"Yes. This is Serenity Harker," Drayton said. "She used to be with the SPD, so she's already trained in combat. You'll just need to give her an upgrade."

Upgrade? My confusion must have shown on my face, because Cassie relaxed, her face breaking into a grin.

"Don't worry, Serenity. It's nothing sinister. I'm responsible for making sure you're ready for the field, finding you your perfect weapon, assessing your kick butt moves, that kind of thing. I'll take good care of you. Plus, it'll be nice having another woman around in this den of testosterone."

"Um, thanks, I guess."

"You hungry?" she asked.

"God, yes."

Orin held out the scone. "You want it?"

I stared at the partially squished item. "I think I'll pass."

Orin shrugged and then shoved the whole thing in his mouth. He chewed a couple of times and then swallowed.

"Pig," Cassie said.

"You love it," Orin retorted.

And then came the goo goo eyes.

"Sickening, isn't it?" Drayton said.

It was kinda sweet actually, stirring up a longing for something warm and intimate that I'd worked hard to deny for years. "So, what is there to eat?"

Ten minutes later and Drayton and I were tucked up at the table digging into the most delicious chicken casserole I'd ever tasted. Orin and Cassie had already eaten so they joined us with two mugs of coffee.

I swallowed my mouthful. "This is so good. Who made it?"

"Bane," Drayton said. "He's the only one of us who can cook half a damned."

I tried to imagine Bane's massive bulk pottering around the kitchen. Would he wear an apron? A soft laugh escaped from my lips.

Cassie bit back a smile. "Your imagining him in an apron, aren't you?"

Shit. How did she know? "Don't tell me you read minds."

"Goodness, no. That kind of stuff is Ryker's department, although to be fair, he's more empath than mind reader."

Ryker was an empath? That explained how he could be so sensitive to my moods. "And you? What abilities do you have?"

"Cassie is a banshee." Orin said. "She can usually sense when something fucked up is going to happen."

"Her scream can also rupture your eardrums," Drayton said.

Well, that explained earlier.

"Anyway," Drayton continued. "We have a rota for cooking. Cassie isn't too bad and Orin's the baker. Rivers just grabs takeout on his night and Ryker always makes spaghetti."

"Orin, you need to make more scones so Serenity can try them," Cassie said.

Orin nodded. "Tomorrow. I promise."

"Can you cook?" Cassie asked me.

"Not really. My sister would do most of the cooking at home." My throat seized up and my eyes burned.

Silence fell, thick and heavy.

"I'm sorry," Orin said. "I can't imagine what you must be going through having to leave everything you've known behind, and here we are acting as if you were voluntarily recruited to MPD." His hand slipped over mine. "If you need anything, please don't hesitate to ask."

Cassie drained her mug and stood. "Come find me in the training room when you're done. We can chat about what you know and where we need to focus with your training."

Orin's hand was still resting on mine.

Cassie sighed. "Orin, are you coming?"

He pulled his hand away and stood. "Yeah. Course."

They left, and I turned in my seat to face Drayton. "What about you?"

He looked up from his plate. This close up, his chocolate brown eyes were flecked with hazel and green. His attention dropped to my mouth. "What about me?"

"Can you cook?" And why were my

lungs so tight?

His mouth quirked. "Are you vetting me, Harker?"

And there was that throb again. Damn him and his incubus vibe. "No. I was just curious."

"I cook. Mainly pasta dishes though. I'm all about carbs and the activity that goes with burning them off."

"How often do you feed?"

He pushed his plate away. "As often as I can." He leaned in, his fresh zesty scent tickling my nostrils. "You're curious aren't you? You want to know what it feels like to just let go and gorge. To take pleasure in what you are."

Did I? The pulse at the base of my throat was throbbing like crazy, screaming, yes, yes, yes.

He sat back, taking his charismatic pull with him. "It's normal to feel that way. You're cambion. You're part incubus, and like calls to like. We are creatures of hunger, desire and need. In my opinion, you've done fantastically in curbing your impulses all these years."

So this connection I felt toward him was all due to my cambion genes. Good to know.

His expression was deathly serious now, and sincerity dripped from every word. "I know Ryker is wary about me training you.

I feed off sexual energy and you...there's something intoxicating about you that I'm sure even Orin, with his tongue down Cassie's throat, must have picked up on."

Was that why she'd left with him so quickly?

I cleared my throat. "I don't feed off sexual energy."

"Are you sure?"

I rolled my eyes. "I think I'd know if I did."

He ran his tongue over his teeth in thought. "Then you must exude it. Even with your shields up, it's strong."

"Trust me. I'd know if I was exuding sex appeal. I mean, I haven't had a date in like, forever."

His brows shot up.

Maybe I shouldn't have admitted that. "Look. I'm not like you."

"You've lived amongst humans all your life. You're among nephs now. Our senses are stronger. I'll help you control your abilities, and I'll keep my incubus in check."

Why was he selling himself? Crap, I hadn't actually agreed to him training me. "I can control myself fine."

"No. You can suppress. That's what you've been doing all these years. Denying and suppressing. I bet you've never had a full meal have you?"

My mouth was dry.

"You let me train you, and once we're done you'll be able to feed without draining, and take without hurting yourself or another."

"Why do you care so much?"

"Because there hasn't been a cambion in centuries and because I don't believe in chance."

He thought my existence was some kind of omen? "Look. I'm just a neph who ended up on the wrong side of the border."

"No. You came with the last batch of outsiders over twenty years ago. And there have been no outsiders since."

"You think that's my fault?"

"I think that there is more to your existence than meets the eye. So, what do you say? Will you allow me to help you?"

Where was the drawling, relaxed Drayton of earlier? He really meant all this shit, and frankly I was intrigued. "Okay."

He grinned, slipping back into the cocky skin he wore most of the time. "Superb. Let's get you to Cassie so she can run through the boring stuff, and then you're mine."

Wait, had his sincerity been...sincere, or had I just been played?

Gah! I trailed behind him leaving the cozy homey kitchen in our wake. It was time to find out what skills I needed to protect

Midnight.

Drayton left me at the entrance to the hugest room I'd ever seen. The ceiling was so high it was lost to gloom and shadows. Pillars dotted the room, holding everything up. Once again, the lighting was all muted, but this time there were sconces fixed to the wall.

"It used to be a ballroom," Drayton said. "At least I think it did."

Now it was filled with mats, targets, ropes and tall frames probably used for practicing jumping and climbing. Some of the pillars were padded with faces drawn on them.

"The MPD owns this building?"

"No. Bane does. He found us and brought us together."

"What is Bane?"

"Now *that* is a question I can't answer."

"You don't know?"

"I doubt even he knows for sure. All we do know is that his neph blood is strong, like super concentrated genes. The guy is a tank."

Yeah, I'd felt that tank up close and personal and the memory sent a spike of terror through me. Yep, definitely terror.

Cassie was in the middle of some kind of kata in one corner.

I reluctantly stepped into the room. "Shouldn't there be more illumination for training purposes?"

Drayton snickered. "Really? We live in Midnight. We fight in the dark. This is perfect."

Point. "I guess I'll see you later?"

"No question about it," he said.

Cassie finished up her moves and waved me over. "Great timing."

Taking a deep breath, I walked toward the banshee. "What was that you were doing?"

She tucked an errant strand of hair behind her ears and adjusted her topknot. "Just a cool down exercise." She sashayed over to a bench and picked up a bottle of water and took a long swig. "That's better." She parked her butt on the bench. "Sit and tell me about your training?"

Training was safe ground. I sat down and ran through my SPD training.

"That's pretty much what we cover

here. The rest just kinda comes with on the job training. You siphon right?"

I nodded.

"So, if you get into hand to hand you can draw power and juice up."

I'd never done it but... "Yes, in theory."

"Wow," she shook her head. "Your enemies can be your battery."

"What else can you do?" she was watching me carefully, almost suspiciously.

Wait, was this about what Drayton had said about the sexual vibe I gave off? "I'm not like Drayton if that's what you're asking. I don't crave sexual energy."

She smiled. "Perceptive. I like it."

"Yep, it's a curse."

"In our line of work, it's a bloody blessing, trust me."

"I can expel the power once I have it. I'm not sure what else because I've kinda kept it locked up all my life."

"What about elements? Any affinity? Are you drawn to anything? Earth, water, air, fire?"

"Not really, no."

"That's all right. Well, we can start training first thing tomorrow. In the meantime, let's pick you out a weapon."

I widened my eyes. "You mean I get more than a taser?"

She pursed her lips. "Oh, honey you

have no idea."

The vault door opened with a creak and a rumble.

"Damn it. Rivers was supposed to oil the door," Cassie yanked, and the thick metal door swung all the way open.

I stepped over the threshold behind her. "I'm kind of expecting some creepy music to start playing,"

"Right? I said that to Orin last time we were here and he was like pfft, women."

"No imagination."

"Yep."

She flipped a switch and the vault lit up, so bright it made my eyeballs ache. "Whoa, can we turn it down."

She gave a breathy chuckle. "One sec."

The lights dimmed and I caught sight of the trove for the first time. Racks lined the walls all hung with whips, and maces, swords and daggers. My eye was drawn by a pretty pair of daggers with gold hilts and a gold and cream sheath. I reached out to touch them but something else caught my attention. Farther along in a slab fixed to the wall sat twin daggers nestled in the stone.

"What's that?"

"Those?" She chuckled. "They're not for you. They're not for anyone. They're called the daggers of Aether. Legend has it they can cut through anything. Like, literally anything. They say Merlin enchanted them into the stone after Arthur died. Some even believe they belonged to Arthur himself. You can't get them out. No one can. Believe me, we've all tried."

"Even Bane?"

"Even Bane."

I'd read about the legend of Arthur. The stories in our great library were abundant. Children born in Arcadia were brought up to believe that there was nothing outside of the city. That this was all there was. But as they grew, when every twenty years outsiders came, that illusion was shattered. Every child went through that phase, the burning need to learn more about the outside world. And Sunset library held that knowledge—stories of places beyond Arcadia. If the White Wings were really responsible for trapping us here, it was a cruel twist to leave such evidence of a bigger world behind.

My fingers itched to touch the daggers but the darkness inside held me back. "He had five weapons didn't he?"

"Yes. The two swords, no wait. Three swords."

"Excalibur, Clarent, and Caliburn."

"Yeah, and the dagger, I can't recall the name."

"And a spear."

We grinned at each other, satisfied we'd identified them all.

"So Merlin crafted these daggers? That's not in any history book I've read,"

Her eyes darkened. "Not everything makes it to the history books."

In that moment, she looked older, much older. It was easy to forget that nephs aged much more slowly than humans. If I took her at her appearance, I'd say early twenties but she could easily be twice or three times that.

Cassie rolled her eyes, snapping out of her little reverie. "Honestly, if you're into Merlin and his history you'll need to speak to the Order. They have everything, and I mean everything on Merlin."

Was she telling me to go speak to them? "Aren't they dangerous?"

"Yep. Completely cuckoo. So, best steer clear. If they knew we had these daggers, we'd have a fight on our hands so," she held a finger to her lips, "*shhhh*, no blabbing to anyone outside of the MPD head primary neph circle." She beckoned me. "Come over here."

She was standing in front of a pedestal which held four bowls. One was filled with dirt, the other was empty, the third had a little water in it and the final one held a matchstick.

"You want to test for elemental affinity?" Cassie asked.

"What do I do?"

"Just take your time and focus on each bowl. See if anything calls to you and then just follow your instincts."

"And if nothing calls to me?"

She shrugged. "It doesn't matter. You're still a neph either way. But don't you want to know for sure?"

Did I want to know? I mean, it would be pretty cool to be a head Primary, but what were the odds of that happening? Still, I took my place in front of the pedestal and closed my eyes.

Cassie stepped back and the space was mine. Just focus on each bowl she'd said. Earth first...earth, dirt, moist, fragrant and

Psst. You, girl. Stop standing by the stupid bowls and get your ass over here.

What the fuck?

Over here, follow my voice, pretty girl.

Yes. What a wonderful idea. My feet were moving of their own accord, and the world suddenly blazed bright through my closed eyelids—a beacon guiding me forward. Somewhere, in the distance was an urgent voice. But it was so far away, inconsequential really.

Closer, yes. Do you see? Do you see me?

The voice was crisp and impatient. Light

dimmed a fraction and twin blades flared in my vision. The ornate handles begging to be gripped. My hands throbbed and ached to hold them.

It's time, girl. Together we are invincible

I reached out and picked them up and then the world shattered in a brain splitting scream.

My eyes snapped open and the world came rushing back. The scream was an alarm, and the vault was bathed in a red flashing light. Someone was shaking me.

"Serenity! Damn it! Snap out of it." Cassie's eyes were wild, her hair half out of her top knot.

"I'm okay. I... what happened?"

She stared at something to my left, her mouth parted in shock.

"What?" I turned my head to see the stone slab fixed to the wall. But the blades were gone. "Cassie, where are the daggers?"

"Serenity..." Cassie was looking down now, down at my hands—my hands which were gripping the twin daggers of Aether.

A roar filled the vault and then there was no room to move, no air to breathe, because Bane was bearing down on me, his eyes blazing with indignation.

"Put them back," he said menacingly. "Put them back. Now."

The last word was a bark. Knees trembling, I tried to shove the daggers back onto the slab but they clung to my palms like glue. "I can't. I can't do it."

"Put them down. Just drop them, damn you."

His tone, which had been terrifyingly seductive in the foyer, was now fire and brimstone, squeezing my bladder and turning my bowels liquid. The terror nudged the darkness, and my temper flared and lashed.

I turned on him, fingers curled around the daggers. "Stop fucking yelling at me!"

His head snapped back as if I'd hit him.

"Oh, shit." Cassie pressed herself to the wall.

Violet flames flickered in his pupils as he took a slow, deliberate, step toward me. "Put. The. Daggers. Down." The word were tiny bites.

I grit my teeth and faced off against him. "Enunciating. Won't. Make. A. Difference."

"Oh, boy," Cassie said.

"What the heck is going on?" It was Drayton, but Bane's mass blocked him, denying him entry. "Bane. Calm down."

Bane's ferocious face swam closer, his massive body squeezing into the confined space, pushing me back against a rack loaded with swords and other pokey stuff, but fuck if I was gonna let him intimidate me.

Well done. Do not back down. He wants to assert his authority. Do not let him.

My pulse skipped. That voice, where was it coming from?

Focus girl.

I locked gazes with Bane. It was like locking horns with a bull, or what I'd expect that to be like—pure unadulterated terror. He could probably crush me with one hand, and man, did he look like he wanted to do just that.

"Why did you touch the daggers? Did Cassie tell you what they were? Was it the challenge?" His hand came up lightning fast to wrap around my throat.

"Dammit, Bane. Let her go." Drayton's tone was ice, but Bane didn't even flinch.

My breath caught in my lungs as I waited for the squeeze, but it didn't come. He held me captive, his calloused skin against my delicate flesh. His feral face drifted closer. His eyes were at half-mast as he studied my mouth waiting for the words to fall. His thick dark lashes cast shadows on his flat high cheekbones and, from this close up, the beginnings of stubble in the dip above the cupids bow of his lip was clearly visible. His breath rasped against my face, minty and fresh.

"Are you one of them?" he asked, coaxing, soft and cajoling. "Are you a spy little woman? Tell me, what magick are you wielding?"

It was that tone again, he was playing confidant, potential ally. Hey I'm not gonna hurt you if you fess up. But those fingers around my throat belied his words. He could snap my neck with a flick of his wrist. So, where was the dread? It was taking a back seat to my irritation.

I took a couple of slow shallow breaths. "I have no idea what you're talking about? Get your damned hand off me. Now."

He looked up. Right into my eyes. "Or what?"

It was something I'd never done before. I'd only ever drawn power using my hands, but my hands were occupied with blades that didn't seem to want to be dropped. Maybe it was about time I experimented. I dropped my shields and allowed the hunger full reign. His power rushed into me, hard and fast, but I didn't allow it to settle, there was no way I was letting it incapacitate me this time, instead I shoved it back outward. Back at him.

His nostrils flared, and a low rumble lit up his chest and then he was stumbling back, and I was free.

Good girl

We stood like that, him and I, chests rising and falling, neither of us willing to back down.

"Serenity, are you all right? Cassie, is she okay?" Drayton asked.

"Are you working for the Order?" Bane asked me, soft and lethal.

What? "No!" I shook my head. "What the hell gave you that idea?"

"It's all right, Dray," Cassie called out. She stepped away from the wall. "She was testing for affinity, Bane. Then she went into some kind of trance and picked up the daggers."

Bane's left eye twitched. "What happened?" he asked me.

"What *happened*?" I snorted in disgust. "*Now* you ask me, what happened? Maybe lead with that next time?"

He exhaled heavily. "Just answer the question."

"No. Not without an apology."

Cassie made a strangled sound.

Bane glared at me aghast. "An apology?"

"You know. The thing you do when you've done something wrong, say like attacking someone for no valid reason." I placed my hands on my hips.

Banes gaze dropped to my waist.

"Where did they go?"

"Where did what..." My hands...they were free. The blades were gone. I examined my palms and then turned in a circle searching the ground. "Where did they go?"

"Serenity, your wrists." Cassie reached for my arm and yanked up my sleeve. "Shit."

I stared at my creamy skin, now marked with ink in the shape of a dagger.

Bane gently gripped my other arm and slid the sleeve up to expose a twin tattoo.

This couldn't be happening. This was crazy.

Bane released me and walked to the entrance of the vault. "Come with me."

"What's happening? How is this happening?"

His jaw tightened. "I don't know, but maybe we can find out. Together."

Okay, that wasn't an apology, but it was a start.

Bane stepped out the room.

"What the fuck, Bane," Drayton said. "You need to control your temper."

Bane ignored him and tried to push past, but Drayton pressed a hand to his shoulder.

"I respect you, and we're friends, but you could have hurt her."

Bane's lip curled. "Yes. I could have, but I chose not to."

There was a double edge to his words, and as soon as he said them, he snapped his mouth closed as if wishing he could take them back.

Drayton dropped his hand, shaking his head. "Low blow, bro. I'm coming with you."

"No. You're not."

"Why not?"

"Because we're going to the roost."

Drayton's eyes flared and he stepped out of the way. "If you lay a hand on her..."

Bane leaned in close. "Don't forget who you're speaking to." He pushed past the incubus and this time Drayton didn't stop him.

I had daggers inside my skin and a voice in my head. Hello voice? Yoohoo? Silence reigned.

"What's the roost?" I climbed the steps behind Bane.

His shoulders brushed both sides of the corridor and his black shirt blended into the darkness, making it look as if a pair of denim clad legs were scaling the steps.

Where did he get his jeans? I mean they had to be custom made for sure because the guy was huge.

"Yes, they're custom made. Now stop thinking so hard."

"How did you know what I was thinking?"

"Your thoughts aren't always shielded."

Fucking hell, a mind reader.

"Only sometimes," Bane said.

We reached the top of the steps and Bane opened a door. Cool crisp air slapped my cheeks and then we were outside with only a parapet to provide shelter. A couple of wide marble type benches acted as seating and a huge iron bell hung from a metal frame by the balcony.

"What is this place?"

"The roost. Now sit."

"God, you're bossy."

"That's because I am the damned boss," he snapped.

Blowing out my cheeks in exasperation, I lowered myself onto the bench and winced as the chill from the marble seeped hungrily through the fabric of my jeans into my skin. Damn it was cold out here.

Bane gripped the rope attached to the bell and pulled. I waited for the clang of the clapper but nothing happened.

Absolute silence.

"Um... I think your bell is broken."

He tilted his head to the moonlit sky. "Wait."

I pulled up my sleeves and studied the daggers. The voice was gone. But my gut told me I hadn't heard the last from it.

The air stirred and a shadow flitted across the moon. Something was coming. Something big.

Bane stepped under the parapet and a moment later a figure landed on the balcony. Its huge wings flexed then snapped closed, vanishing from view.

Of shitting hell, it was a Black Wing.

He stepped forward and the moonlight highlighted a familiar face. It was the Black Wing who'd saved my arse when I'd been surrounded by the rippers. I was hidden in shadow, not bathed in moonlight like Bane, and he hadn't seen me yet.

"Why have you summoned me?" the Black Wing asked Bane.

"The Daggers of Aether are no longer in the stone slab," Bane said.

The Black Wing's face froze for a fraction of a second. "The Order?"

"No." Bane jerked his head in my direction.

The Black Wing's gaze scoured the shadows and then fell on me. His lips parted in surprise. I opened my mouth to say something: hello, hey great to see you again, thanks for saving my life. But his expression hardened and he shook his head infinitesimally. What?

He dismissed me and turned back to

Bane. "A human has the daggers?"

"Not human," Bane said. "Drop the shields woman," he said to me.

I did so automatically, too flustered by what was going on to get all defensive. The relief was immediate, like a band releasing and allowing me to really breathe. I exhaled then inhaled, savoring the sweet Midnight air.

The Black Wing flinched and then slowly approached. He crouched in front of me and his wings flared out, shielding us from Bane's view.

"Hush," he said. "He must not know."

Know that we'd met before? Huh?

"Look at her wrists," Bane instructed.

The Black Wing arched an enquiring brow and then held out his hand. God, he was beautiful, alabaster skin and raven's wing hair, and his ice blue irises. I rested my wrist in his hand, palm up and he carefully pulled back my sleeve. The inked daggers were exposed, jet black against my pale skin. He sucked in a breath and slowly traced the dark lines with the tip of his index finger. Heat trailed in the wake of the contact and my hunger lurched outward, eager to taste what he had to offer again.

I pulled my arm back and pushed my sleeve down. I licked my dry lips. "Do you know what's happening to me?"

He stood slowly, towering over me, and drew his sword. "I'm sorry. But I cannot allow you to live."

"Abbadon?" Bane said. "What are you—"

But the sword flared to life, silver and magnificent, and then it was arching toward me. I was going to die. My brain went into panic mode, body flooding with adrenaline. I instinctively brought my hands up to shield myself, forearms crossed. My wrists burned and then weight settled in the palms of my hands. The sword cut through the air with a whoosh but never made contact.

"Look, Bane. Look at that." Abbadon said.

I raised my head, blood roaring in my ears and stared at the daggers in my hands.

Bane was on his knees before me. "Are you all right?" His tone was gruff but tentative.

I shook my head. "No. No I'm not all right. What the fuck is going on?" I stared from Bane to Abbadon. "Can someone please explain this shit to me?"

"The daggers reacted to what you perceived as a threat. They materialized when I attacked you."

I stared at the wicked sharp blades still clinging to my skin. He hadn't meant to kill me. It'd been a stupid test. Panic was a live thing burning its way through my airways.

"I want them out. I need you to get them off me." I shook my hands desperate for the blade to be gone. They blinked out.

Gone? Were they gone? I tugged up my sleeve and let out a growl. I'd been expelled from my home, taken from my sister, and just when I'd convinced myself being part of the Protectorate might not be so bad, I had daggers stuck under my fucking skin.

"Abbadon. What is going on?" Bane asked. His body heat wafted toward me, bathing me in warmth I desperately craved now that the adrenaline rush was abating. "You asked me to keep the slab safe. To keep it out of the Order's hands. You told me no one could remove the daggers from the stone."

"The daggers are all we have left of Merlin," Abbadon said. "Creating them was his last act before he vanished, and the Order, with their insane ideas, must not get hold of the relic."

With my shields down it was weird, but it was almost as if I could taste the evasiveness in his response, and man it was suddenly crystal clear. "You're afraid The Order might know something you don't, aren't you?"

His eyes narrowed, and he pressed his lips together.

I stood up. "You have no idea what these daggers are, do you?"

My tone was slightly more accusatory then intended, but then did I really give a shit? He was hiding stuff from not only me, but Bane as well. Pretending to know shit when he was as clueless as we were. Not cool.

"They are rumored to cut through anything," Abbadon said.

"Yeah, even I know that, and I've been here for five minutes. But how can you know for sure? You've never tried them, because they've always been stuck in the stone."

"That's right."

"And you have no idea why they chose me." I rubbed the tattoos through the fabric of my shirt.

He smiled, and it lit up his face. "Oh, that I *can* answer. These are daggers of *Aether*, which means they can only be wielded by someone with an affinity for Aether and void." He paused to let that sink in. "They chose you. Which means you've found your elemental affinity."

An affinity... "I don't have an affinity for anything."

"You obviously do. Problem is the Aether affinity is so rare we have very little information on how it manifests."

This was too much—revelation on top of revelation with no time to breathe or get my feet under the table. Not enough time to adjust.

"What happened?" Bane asked. "Cassie said you were in a trance."

Okay, a rundown of events was a good idea. It was a chance to focus and hopefully fix this thing. "I heard a voice calling me. I followed it and the next thing I knew I had the daggers and alarms were blaring."

"A voice?" Abbadon said. "What kind of voice?"

"A man's voice. I don't know."

"And what did this man say?" he asked.

What had he said? "Just stuff like, come here, do you see me and... Oh, together we are invincible." Invincible. I pulled up my sleeves again. "I'm stuck with them aren't I?"

"For now," Abbadon said. "But we *will* find out more, and we will find a way to unbind you."

Unbind me, because I was bound. Of course, I knew that was what had happened, but hearing him use the word brought it home. My heart sank and the darkness inside me stretched and sighed. Wait...the shields were still down but the crazy desperate hunger was gone. I didn't need to feed. How was this possible? Could it be the daggers? Were they somehow soothing the need or was it the feast that Bane had given me on my arrival—the honey that had knocked me for six but had left me energized and refreshed. Too many questions without answers.

"Serenity," Bane said. "I promise you, we will find answers."

"I'm fine. Cassie said we needed to pick a weapon, right?" I flexed my hands. "These daggers will have to do for now."

His chuckle was like gravel over syrup.

"No." Abbadon said. "If the Order finds out what you're wielding it could be dangerous."

"So, what are you saying? I have to stay indoors until you fix this?"

Bane and Abbadon exchanged glances.

Abbadon locked gazes with me, his expression solemn. "No. You'll come with me. You will be a guest of the Black Wings."

My stomach did a flip. Guest was just a polite way of saying prisoner. Well, that so wasn't happening. "Does the Order even know these daggers exist?"

"We don't know," Abbadon said.

"Let me get this straight. You want to take me prisoner—"

"*Guest*," Abbadon said. "You'd be free to roam the mansion."

I shot him an arch look. "As I was saying, you want to take me prisoner because you're worried that the Order *may, possibly* know about the existence of these daggers, and could *maybe* recognize them if I used them. Never mind the fact that no one is supposed to be able to pull them from that slab, or that fact that Aether affinity is super rare."

"She has a point," Bane said. He moved slightly, enough to obstruct Abbadon's access to me.

A chill skittered up my spine. Would the Black Wing take me by force? Could he best Bane?

Abbadon's eyes were speculative slits as his gaze slid from Bane then back to me. "We cannot take the risk," he said.

"Fuck that!" I stepped away from them both. "I am not going to be a prisoner because of a maybe, or a possibly. I didn't want to be here, but now I am, and there is no way I'm sitting and twiddling my thumbs while there are humans out there that need saving. That isn't who I am, so if you want to keep me off the streets you're gonna have to kill me." My pulse was hammering with adrenaline, with the need to flee or fight and my palms burned just like they'd burned when I'd been attacked. They were responding to my fear. "But I warn you, you'll have a fight on your hands."

The daggers slid into my palm in response to the threat, but it looked good, as if I'd summoned them on cue, and my chest heated with gratitude for the display of power.

Good girl

"These things can cut through anything right?" I arched a brow, feigning confidence and met Abbadon's stare head on.

"Talk some sense into your officer, Bane," Abbadon said.

Bane tucked in his chin, hands on hips and then he shrugged a huge shoulder. "They *are* rumored to cut through anything." He looked, up, his lips turned down. "Possibly even wings."

Abbadon pinched the bridge of his nose. "Dammit, Bane. When will you accept that we're on the same side?"

"When you stop keeping secrets from me," Bane said.

"Fine, you can keep her. But she is your responsibility. If the Order discovers the existence of the relic, if they come for her, if they get their hands on the daggers, it will be on your head." He strode toward the balcony. "If you change your mind, you know how to get hold of me." His wings stretched and flapped, and he launched himself up into the air with one powerful leap.

"The others don't know about the Black Wings. No one comes up here but me," Bane said shortly.

"What are you saying?"

"They can't know." He turned on me,

his eyes blazing, lips pulled back to reveal wicked canines. "You breathe a word of this meeting, and I will end you, and don't think those daggers will stop me. I'll catch you while you sleep and I'll tear out your throat."

"Whoa!" I held up my hands. "Look, I think I know a little about keeping secrets. You don't need to get all *grrrr.*"

His lips dropped back over his fangs and his brow furrowed. "You're either incredibly brave or incredibly stupid." He headed for the door. "You must be cold. Let's get indoors."

Goodness he was a mercurial creature. "Thanks,"

"What for?" he said gruffly.

"For taking my side."

He turned his head, offering me his wickedly gruesome profile. His lip curled showcasing a lethal canine. "You're one of us now, Harker, and I take care of my own."

"Wait."

His chest rumbled in exasperation. "What now?"

"What shall I tell them? The others. They're gonna ask what happened up here."

He turned slowly, his eyes glinting in the night. "You could tell them we had a tryst?"

Was he serious?

His regard was suddenly too intimate,

too probing as it raked over me. "No, they wouldn't believe that. If I fucked you, you'd probably break."

My heart slammed against my ribs. Whether in fear or arousal I wasn't quite sure. His nostrils flared and he cocked his head as if listening for something. He was a mountain not a man. He was mean and rude and temperamental. It was fear that was sending my blood rushing to my head, but the daggers didn't materialize.

He snorted and turned back to the door. "Tell them we talked. Tell them I'm looking into things."

"And then she was like: *Enunciating. Won't. Make. A. Difference.*" Cassie's voice drifted out of the kitchen to greet me. It was a pretty good impression of me, I had to say, she had the right amount of jaw clenching going on.

Male laughter filled the air.

"I wish I'd been there to see it," Orin said.

I stepped into the room and all eyes were on me.

"Here she is, the woman of the hour." Cassie held her arms wide in greeting.

Ryker kicked the seat out opposite him in invitation, and I slid into the spot, scanning the faces around me. Cassie, Orin and Ryker I knew, and Drayton wasn't here, but there was a new face at the table — slender, features, an inquisitive mouth and a guarded gaze.

"Hi, I'm Serenity." I held up a hand in

greeting.

The new guy studied me for a moment, his throat worked and then he picked up his cup. The silver cuff on his wrist glinted in the overhead light. "I know who you are." His tone was cold, indifferent.

"Rivers..." Ryker shot him a warning glance.

Rivers pushed back his seat and stood. "Don't worry, Ryker. I'm not sticking around. I have to get ready for patrol. See you around, Serenity." He strode from the room. His wiry form vanishing out the door.

I winced. "I don't suppose he's like that with everyone is he?"

Ryker exhaled through his nose, but Cassie laughed.

"Oh, don't mind Rivers. He doesn't like change. He's inherently suspicious of anything new but he'll warm up to you. You just have to give him time. Rivers is our resident genius. He makes things, and fixes things."

I desperately wanted to ask what Rivers was but it didn't feel right.

"It was dangerous," Ryker said. "Going head to head with Bane like that."

"Oh, come on, Ryker," Cassie said. "Bane wouldn't hurt her."

She didn't sound too sure though, plus hadn't she been pressed up against the wall out of harm's way at the time? I glanced from Ryker's stern face to Cassie's guilty one. But it was Orin who filled the silence.

"Bane is an honorable neph," Orin said. "He believes in protecting the humans of Arcadia, and if you're on his side, then he would never hurt you. However, if in that moment he thought you were a spy, a member of the Order sent to infiltrate and steal from us, he would have killed you."

"And it was her standing up to him that stopped him," Cassie said. "There was no way a spy would have had the balls to do that, not with Bane's fingers wrapped around their throat."

Ryker tensed. "You didn't tell us that."

Cassie shrugged. "It worked out all right." She popped a chip into her mouth and chewed. "So, what happened at the roost?"

Now they were all giving me sly looks. But Bane's voice reverberated inside my head. *The others don't need to know about the Black Wings...tell them we talked and I'm looking into things.*

I repeated his words and shrugged. "So, I just wait."

"And in the meantime we have no idea what those daggers are actually doing to you?" Ryker said.

"Ryker, man. Chill." Orin said.

What was going on here?

Ryker pushed back his chair. "I'm gonna run some laps. I'll find you when I'm done and we can talk," he said to me.

The room was deadly silent for several beats. "What just happened?"

Cassie tapped her empty plate. "Ryker's a worrier, that's all. He cares. He can't help it, and sometimes it twists him up inside."

Orin frowned and opened his mouth to add something but the scrape of Cassie's chair as she pushed it back cut him off. His shoulders slumped as if in defeat.

"There's some left over pie in the oven if you're hungry." Orin smiled disarmingly, his handsome face suddenly boyish and appealing. "I made it earlier."

"Okay, you big lug, let's get some rest," Cassie said. "We have patrol in four hours." Cassie tugged him to his feet and they left hand in hand. For the first time since being brought to the MPD, I was alone with my own thoughts, and, frankly, I had no idea what the heck to think.

In the absence of any constructive thought, pie sounded bloody fabulous. I'd eat pie and wait for Ryker and maybe I'd get some proper answers.

After several wrong turns, dusty, spooky corridors, and locked doors, I found my way back to my allocated room. Someone had laid fresh clothes on my bed, and the wardrobe had been stocked with the black clothes I'd come to associate with the Protectorate. A quick feel of the material confirmed that, yep, they were definitely not leather. They were stretchy, thick fabric that could probably withstand some serious wear and tear—perfect for going up against the scourge.

I sat on the edge of the bed and stared at the dagger tattoos on the inside of my wrists.

"Why me?"

Was I expecting the voice to answer? Kind of, but there was silence. Did the voice only speak when the daggers were out and when I was in danger? Where was it? In my head. Shit. Was it in my head? No. It had to be connected to the daggers which were under my skin. Urgh. It was invasive and unsettling and as cool as it was, I wanted them gone. But they'd picked me, which made me different, special maybe? Could this be a clue to who I was and why I'd been abandoned to Arcadia?

There was a knock on the door.

"Come in."

Ryker entered smelling all fresh and showered. His hair was still damp and curled under his ears, and he was dressed in joggers, a t-shirt and slippers. "Are you tired?" he asked.

Should I be? "What time is it?"

"Almost nine in the evening."

"This Midnight thing is going to take some getting used to."

"You'll adjust. You lived in Sunset all hours of the day. Soon, Midnight will be no different. Your body clock will adjust, in the meantime just rely on your watch." He sat on the edge of my bed. "I'm sorry for running off earlier." He pulled a mobile phone from his pocket and handed it to me. "This is for you. I've pre-programmed it with all the important numbers. You won't be able to call out of the district though." He made an apologetic face.

I popped the mobile on the bedside table and shuffled back up against the headboard. "When we first met, Drayton said you didn't talk much."

He balked. "Are you saying I talk *too* much?"

I chuckled. "No. Gosh, no. I just wondered why he'd say that."

Ryker ducked his head. "Because it's usually true."

"But not when it comes to me?"

He fixed his gaze over my shoulder. "It's impossible *not* to talk to you. You ask so many questions."

"You don't *have* to answer."

He smiled. "I find myself wanting to."

What was it about this guy that made

me feel so safe and at home? I crossed my legs and got comfortable. "Can you tell me about the others? I know Cassie is a banshee, but what about Orin and Rivers."

What about you, I wanted to ask. All I knew was that he was an empath, but my gut told me there was more to his story. Cassie and Orin's weird shared glances when Ryker had left earlier and his own reticence all made that gut feeling stronger.

"I know it's nosey. but I kinda really need to know. It's been driving me nuts."

He shifted to lean back against the post at the foot of my bed. "Orin has an affinity for water. He can breathe under water, and he's able to draw moisture from the atmosphere if need be. He's also a wizard with scones, and anything baked. We think he may have Roan in his family tree somewhere."

"What's a Roan?"

"A first generation of nephs who could shift into seals. When in human form, they'd shed their skin and hide it until they were ready to return to the sea. Orin can't shift though, but he does crave the sea."

"And Rivers?"

"Surprisingly, his affinity is air."

"Why surprising?"

"Rivers is a siren. He has sea dweller in his blood line like Roan so water should be his thing, but it isn't. He can pretty much make anyone do what he wants with a few words uttered in the correct timbre."

"That's disconcerting."

Ryker's smile grew brittle. "Yeah, it is. But he's been forbidden from using that particular ability so you don't need to worry."

It was on the tip of my tongue to ask why he'd been forbidden when Ryker continued.

"And you're probably wondering about me?"

Oooh, interest piqued. "I can't lie. I'm intrigued."

"I'm an empath."

I knew that. "And..." I made a winding motion with my hand.

He shrugged. "That's about it. I can sense emotions, intentions, sometimes I feel others pain. To be honest, it's uncomfortable at the best of times, and so I keep my shields up."

"You have shields too?"

He cracked a smile. "Nothing like yours. I can't mask who I am. But I can block out the unwanted sensory stimuli."

"And what is your elemental affinity?"

"Air." He traced the pattern on the duvet with his finger. "I don't use it much anymore though."

There was more, he wanted to say more,

and I held my breath, waiting, sensing there was something important he needed to say. The urge to drop my shields and taste his intentions was strong but I bit it back. It was invasive and it would probably destroy our budding friendship.

Friendship.

That's what this was. This fresh, safe bond we seemed to share. A secure heat bloomed in my belly.

"I spoke to Bane," Ryker said. "You'll train until you have a handle on the daggers and your abilities."

"I can do that."

"You'll be training with him." He looked up at that moment, capturing my gaze, and absorbing my shock. His brows snapped low over his eyes. "Be careful. Don't test him. Don't push him."

He was asking me to go against my very nature. My smart mouth had a mind of its own most the time. "In that case, you'll need to get me some duct tape."

"What? Why?"

I gave him a flat look. "To tape my mouth closed. What do you think?"

"Serenity, I—"

"Look. I get it. You're looking out for me, and Bane is pretty damned scary, but I am not going to cower every time he raises his voice. That isn't who I am, and I won't turn into some meek little mouse to please anyone. If Bane wants me here in the Protectorate, then he's just gonna have to take me as I am. I'll respect him, but I'll expect the same in return."

"I want to argue with you, but you have valid points. Just be careful."

"I will." I cracked my shields just a tiny bit and his agitation was a soft lapping wave. Cassie had been right about him being a worrier. Time to change the topic. "You never did finish explaining about the house. What were the creatures who scared off the scourge?"

His brow crinkled as if he was taking a moment to arrange his thoughts. "They call themselves the Breed. They're minor nephs who can transform into hyenas and they preyed on the humans of Midnight not under the protection of a primary neph house.

"I thought you said that minor nephs can only do stuff like telekinesis and read auras?"

"The Breed are an exception. They command the power of transmutation and they hunger for human flesh both to consume and to use carnally." His lip curled in disgust. "Being affiliated to a house provides some safety, but even then they've been known to take humans."

"So, what is a house?"

"There are only two in the city: House Mort and House Vitae."

A skitter ran over my scalp. "Death and life?"

You know Latin?

Latin? "Was that Latin?"

His eyes narrowed. "Yes. Mort and Vitae mean death and life."

"Oh...Um...I guess I do then. I must have heard the words somewhere, sometime."

He was looking at me strangely, and I just wanted him to stop. "So, who runs these," I made bunny ears with my fingers, "houses."

Primary nephs. The Sanguinata and the Lupin. The Sanguinata have a serious red blood cell deficiency and require regular infusions of human blood to survive, and the Lupin's females have an infertility issue so they require human females for surrogacy purposes. The only problem is, not many of the humans survive childbirth."

"So, why risk it? Why not just ally with Sanguinata?"

"It's not that simple. The houses have an agreement. They recruit humans once a year and they hold an annual game to determine which house gets to recruit. By my count, Lupin have won two years in a row, and humans wanting protection have little choice.

They either sign up to the available house or remain unprotected and the prey of the Breed. It was even taken to the Midnight district council and made legal to deter any sly recruitment outside the annual drive. If either house tries to recruit without authorization, they forfeit the next year's games."

"What about the scourge? Does affiliation protect from them?"

Ryker smiled smugly. "That's where the Protectorate comes in."

I was beginning to get a better idea of how Midnight operated, but being told wasn't the same as being out there and learning from experience. If this district was going to be my home, I needed to be on the streets.

"I need to get out there, Ryker."

"Just do the training, Serenity. You're strong." He reached for my wrists, and smoothed his hand over the ink. "You have an Aether affinity."

I looked up sharply. "He told you?"

"He didn't have to. The daggers chose you."

"I don't know if that's actually true. I don't know anything about Aether."

"Just give it time. Give yourself time. You were meant to be here. I knew it the moment I laid eyes on you at the SPD, and then you confirmed it with your actions at the motel. Just give it time."

A yawn ripped through me, and Ryker chuckled. "It's been a long day. Get some sleep." He stood and pulled up the covers, indicating I get under them. It felt normal, natural for him to tuck me into bed and turn down the lamp. He smoothed a hand over my head and a sense of calm and wellbeing seeped into my bones. "Sweet dreams, Serenity."

Bane circled me, his huge intimidating frame cutting off any escape.

Two weeks we'd been at this. Two weeks of training, talking and more training. I was ready, so ready to get out there and patrol. There was no way I was bringing him down, and so we'd focused on stamina, evasion and trying to get in the odd hit. The daggers never made an appearance.

I bounced on the balls of my feet. "Look, just let me out there, and let me play it by ear. I'm not a newbie. I know what I'm doing." I grinned, flashing him a dimple. "I've even got Rivers talking to me."

He snorted. "Well, that's it then. You're ready for anything," he said sarcastically.

Frustration stabbed at my brain. "Oh, come on. What more do we have to cover?"

"This isn't Sunset, woman. This is Midnight. There are things out there your sheltered mind couldn't comprehend."

"Really? Like what? I know about the houses, and the Breed and the scourge. I've done my homework, Bane."

He snorted in derision, continuing to circle me, thighs bunching and flexing beneath the material of his yoga pants. My temper flared. "You know what? I think you're working with Abbadon after all."

His body went super still. "Don't say his name."

But my anger and frustration had shoved me into push-the-buttons mode. My agitation made me forget Ryker's warning. "You're working with him, and instead of him keeping me locked up at his mansion, you're keeping me locked up here." The anger was a real writhing thing now, fueled by the relative inaction of the past couple of weeks, and just general fuckedoffness. "You're a liar, Bane. A fucking liar."

And then he lashed out and hit me. Like seriously hit me. The blow sent me flying across the room, and landing hard on a mat. The air smashed out of my lungs and my face throbbed twice before the pain registered.

What the... I reached up to touch my lip and my fingers came away bloody.

"You fucking talk too much." He

ducked his head and barreled toward me.

There was murder in his eyes—the serious desire to do some damage. Hot potent adrenaline flushed through my limbs and the daggers settled in the palms of my hands. I rolled as he lunged. He hit the mats and spun, knuckles grazing the mat, body in a crouch and I saw him for what he was.

A monster.

"Yes," he said. His tone was deadly. "Yes, you see it now. You see the truth." His violet eyes gleamed in triumph, and something else, something that I couldn't define. "I'm not your friend, Harker. I'm not your fucking buddy. You don't get to question me. I'm your fucking boss."

I was already in a defensive stance, daggers at the ready.

He picked up a mat and threw it at me. I lashed out, swiping with my blades. The mat cleaved in two and fell to the ground.

He nodded, and the light in his eyes ebbed.

What the heck?

He pulled out of his attack crouch, and the aggression leached out of his body. His features smoothed out, and a shadow fell across his brutal face. "Go put some ice on that." He turned his back on me and walked away.

I held an ice bag wrapped in a tea towel to the side of my face, and leaned against the kitchen counter. My cheekbone ached and throbbed and there'd be a nasty bruise, but it should be worse right? Bane was strong, his fist could have, should have, broken me.

The clip of boots on stone was followed by Cassie's tousled head. She caught sight of me and faltered in the doorway, and then she was striding toward me, her face contorted in concern.

"What happened?" Cassie pinched my chin and turned my face so she could examine the bruise. "Damn, Serenity. Did you charge a wall?"

"No. I just pissed off Bane."

Her eyes widened. "He *hit* you?"

I rolled my eyes trying to make light of the situation. "We were training, after all. Some bumps and bruises are to be expected."

I pressed the ice to my face, and blinked back tears of pain and shame focusing on my words which had come out strong and level. It wasn't like I'd never been in a scrape before. I'd taken my fair share of blows and given back just as hard, but for some reason, this one stung.

"But... He hit you." She shook her head, her lip caught between her teeth. "I can't believe he'd intentionally hurt you."

"Yeah, and neither did I..." Neither did I! Oh fuck. We'd been training for two weeks and the blades hadn't manifested once, and Bane didn't ask why. He hadn't needed to. It was obvious I hadn't thought he would seriously hurt me. I hadn't felt that my life was in danger. But the daggers were a part of me. They were my weapon. If I hadn't had a chance to use them then the training would have been incomplete. He needed to know if Abbadon's assessment of them coming out to protect me was true. Was that why he'd kept me base bound?

"What is it?" Cassie asked.

"I think he was trying to make me fear him enough to bring out the blades."

She clenched her teeth. "Fuck that. There are other ways to test the bloody daggers." She gingerly touched the side of my face.

"Ouch."

"You need to heal." She gnawed on her bottom lip. "Siphoning power feeds you right? Do you think you can use it to heal?"

"I don't think it works that way. I guess if I absorbed someone's healing power then maybe." I shrugged.

"Go find Ryker. He'll put you to rights."

Ryker's room was a floor above mine. I knocked softly and waited. The door swung open. Ryker took one look at me and his expression went flat. The kind of cold that was deadly.

"Who did that?"

"I was training with Bane."

His jaw ticked. "He hit you? On purpose?"

I held up a hand. "Yeah, but I think he could have hit me much harder. It brought the blades out and that's what he was aiming for, I think. I had to feel threatened for it to work."

He ducked his head, shoulders rising and falling. "There are other things he could have tried."

"Look, it's all good. Can you just patch me up? Cassie said you could."

"Come in." He stepped back, letting me into his inner sanctum. The room was decorated in shades of cream and brown. It was a man space lined with bookshelves stocked with interesting looking tomes.

"You like to read?"

"Books are an escape that I enjoy, yes."

"Um, could I borrow a couple?"

His eyes lit up. "Of course."

"Awesome."

He turned me to face him and raised a hand to hover over my cheek. "Close your eyes."

I did and the sensation of pins and

needles spread across the side of my face. It was an uncomfortable sensation but not painful, and then it was over.

"All done."

I opened my eyes to his smiling face. His fingers caressed my cheek but the motion wasn't sexual, it something else. And there was no pain.

"Thank you. I got to go. I have a session with Drayton."

"Have you eaten?"

"I'll grab a bite in a bit."

"You're tired, Serenity. Tired and fed up, but keeping fueled up will help."

"I look that bad, huh?"

He averted his gaze. "I'll bring you some soup."

It was his empathy thing. He was picking up on my exhaustion, my irritation and frustration. On impulse, I stood on tiptoe and pressed a kiss to his cheek. "Thanks for looking out for me."

His swallowed hard and smiled. "Course. You're one of us now."

I'd just let Drayton into my room when Ryker arrived with the soup he'd promised.

He placed the bowl on my bedside table. "Make sure you drink it. It's excellent soup." He shot Drayton a serious look. "Don't work her too hard. She needs to rest and recharge."

"I'll be fine." I stifled a yawn.

Ryker raised a brow as if to say, see, I told you. God, he'd been like a mother hen the past week. But the truth be told, I liked it. It was nice to be the one being looked out for, for a change. He left us to it, albeit reluctantly.

"You're good for him," Drayton said.

"Who? Ryker?"

"Yes. I actually caught him smiling the other day."

He smiled all the time for me, but maybe that wasn't something Drayton wanted to hear. Wait, did he think Ryker and I were... "We're friends. That's all."

Drayton blinked at me in surprise. "Oh, I know that."

"You do?"

He strolled toward me. "Shall we begin?"

I nodded.

"Drop the shields."

Why did it sound like he was asking me to take my clothes off? I lowered the barriers. His chest rose and fell and he smiled. Then his power slammed into me, and every nerve ending in my body was alive with need. The darkness unfurled wanting to feed, fuck, whatever it took to get the hit it needed. His power, his charisma was a drug.

"You want it." His tone was breathless.

"Yes."

We'd done this before. He would flood me with power, surround me with temptation and I'd resist, training the hunger, training the darkness. I would take but only as much as I needed. Except this time, I was tired. Bane had worn me out and it had been almost a week since I'd fed the hunger. My cambion side wasn't going to be denied.

"Stop." I turned my head to the side, as if that would stop his power from pressing against me, stroking, and stoking a fire that shouldn't, couldn't be set alight.

My heart fluttered in panic as I felt the lethal edge of my hunger for the first time — a razor sharp edge wanting to slice and devour. I needed to put the shields up. I tugged with all I had, but they wouldn't budge.

"I can't, Drayton." Another wave of sexual need hit me. "There's something wrong."

He moved closer, his dark eyes alight with gold swirling flecks. "You can, Serenity."

He didn't get it, he didn't understand. My body bucked as heat flooded me and then my body was no longer my own. It belonged to her, the darker side of me, the one I'd kept locked away for far too long, her sigh was a purr and then her fingers, my fingers were grasping Drayton's shirt and pulling him close. Her lips, my lips claimed his, tongues entwining as I drew, and drew, and drew.

Drayton moaned into my mouth and my back slammed up against the wall, as the full length of his body pressed up against me. He ground into me, his hardness pressing up against my abdomen, fueling the hunger. His power, hot, sensual and core melting, flooded my veins.

And then he was torn off me.

"What the fuck!" Ryker stood like a wall between the two of us. Drayton lay on the ground, his eyes dazed, his mouth bruised.

"That was... wow." He looked past Ryker, and locked gazes with me, and fuck, if I didn't want to shove Ryker out the way and climb on top of Drayton. To rip off his jeans, free him and take him. But the hunger had been sated, these thoughts were all mine. My shields came back on line and I wrapped my arms around myself. What had I just done? I'd practically assaulted the incubus.

Drayton tried to stand but lost his balance and slid back to the ground. "Head rush," he said.

Ryker held out a hand and hauled him up, clinging to him to keep him upright. "I'll be back," he said over his shoulder. He led Drayton out the door.

My face was on fire, my pulse all over the place. So, that's what it felt like, to feed fully. To take what my body needed. How long would it last before I needed another hit? Because after experiencing that I didn't think I could go back to starving myself again. No. This wasn't me. I wasn't the kind of monster whose world revolved around feeding. I'd fought too long and too hard to give in to this darkness now. It would bend to my will. It would wait and be fed when I was ready to fucking feed it. But this, being cloistered wasn't helping my resolve. Back in SPD, I'd had a life, an actual job, action to keep me on my feet and keep the darkness at bay. I needed to get out there. If I couldn't patrol, at least I could get the lay of the land, familiarize myself with the terrain.

Bane had said no patrolling, no sightseeing. With the training and the others ducking in and out on rota, there'd been no time for such trivial shit. But it no longer felt trivial, because if I had to spend another day cooped up within these gray stone walls, I would seriously go insane.

It was time to take a trip into Midnight.

I found Cassie doing crazy leaps in the training room.

I leaned against the door jamb and waited for her to finish her little obstacle course. She was good. Real good. Fast and agile and her whip skills were pretty epic. She landed in a crouch and shot me a grin.

"You want to train more? Damn. You're a glutton for punishment, Harker."

"Nope, I was hoping you'd take me out."

She rose smoothly to her feet, her brows flicking up. "Bane let you off the leash?"

To lie or not to lie. Fuck it. "Nope. But I want you to take me out anyway."

She sucked her teeth. "Now that is naughty."

I pushed off the door frame. "Would you be able to stay cooped up here for two weeks?"

"I get it, Harker. I totally do. But Bane's the boss and until he says you can patrol, I can't take you out."

"I know that. I'm not asking to go on patrol...yet. I want to go out. See the District, get some takeout. You know, get the lay of the land."

"Oh." She shrugged. "Sure, that's actually a great idea. I can show you my sector. Who knows, once Bane clears you, you might end up partnering with me." She walked away toward the bench. "Actually, I was going to come find you. Bane asked me to give these to you."

She strolled over and handed me the gold and cream weapons belt I'd seen in the vault before being distracted by the slab and the enchanted daggers.

"I already have daggers."

"Yeah, ones that only appear when you feel threatened. Sometimes, you need to show force to prevent an altercation, or just like, cut stuff." She held out the belt. "Take them. Use them. At least until you can figure out how to make the Aether daggers appear consistently at will."

Excitement fizzed in my belly as I strapped on the belt. "So, can we go now?"

She chuckled and sauntered toward me. "I have a better idea. It's Drayton's night off.

We'll grab him too. He probably needs to feed anyway."

"Feed as in fuck?" My voice went up an octave.

She slid an arch look my way. "You have a problem with that?"

I cleared my throat. "Course not."

"Good. It's quite fascinating actually. You should see him work. He is pretty amazing. The way he has the women eating out of the palm of his hand."

My stomach twisted. "I'm sure he is, I mean he does."

"Maybe do a little undercover scoping while we're at it." She eyed me up and down. "You'll want to put on something less Protectorate. You'll want to blend in."

"And what does blending in look like?"

"Jeans are good. Come on." She led the way down the corridor and up the flight of stairs to the first floor. "We're about the same build. I have a top that will totally bring out your eyes."

An hour later we were driving out of the iron gates and into Midnight. My pulse did a little hop, skip and jump. This was my new district. Mine to patrol and keep safe. Drayton steered the vehicle, his shirt sleeves rolled up, his strong forearms on show. So far, I'd only ever seen him in his Protectorate get up or joggers and a t-shirt. Tonight, he was slick and suave in a deep green shirt and dark jeans. His jet black hair fell in just got out of bed waves over his forehead and his hazel eyes blazed from beneath dark brows and lashes, and when I was done admiring him, I needed to roll my tongue back into my mouth and wipe away the drool.

Gah. I was so hopeless.

Cassie locked eyes with me in the rear view mirror, a smirk playing on her lips. "Like what you see, Harker?"

"You look lovely," I said sweetly.

She bit back a smile. Yeah, she's caught me checking out Drayton. Thank goodness he was none the wiser though.

"I think Cassie was referring to me," Drayton drawled. "Do you like what you see? Think the female population of Midnight will approve?"

Shit. "Don't you control the level of approval with your mojo?"

"It doesn't work that wa—"

"Yes. I guess I do." Drayton cut Cassie off.

I checked her out in the rear view and her brow was furrowed. Why had he cut her off like that?

"Check out your new hunting ground, Harker. The night is our friend. We hide in the shadows and pick off the nasty shit that thinks it owns the darkness."

We were driving through a residential area, lined with neatly kept houses and white picket fences. It looked like Sunset, except it wasn't bathed in orange.

"The streets look so normal."

"What did you expect? Carnage and mayhem. Blood spurting as scourge fed."

Yeah, actually I kinda had. "So, people just get on with it?"

"They know when to keep close to home," Cassie said from the backseat. "They know when to go into lock-down and batten down the hatches. The scourge runs once a month and we have a strict curfew on those days. Most businesses are closed. All the scourge that have gone under, hunt on mass and it's the only time the whole of the Protectorate are called to duty. Even then, we can't prevent the deaths."

We slid onto a main road chock full of cars and lit up with street lights. Fresh sea air blasted through the vents.

"Are we close to the coast?"

Drayton smiled. "Yes. A half mile to the east. It's the sea dwellers' territory."

"Sea dwellers?"

"Nephs like Orin and Rivers," Cassie said. "But minor ones who can't dwell on land for extended periods of time. They hang out at The Deep. It's a pretty popular club. Some people believe that the sea dwellers are nephs descended not from human and Black Wing unions, but from the Black Wing union with an ancient race from another plane of existence. One that walked this world for a time before retreating back to their realm."

"It's almost impossible to think of different planes of existence when we're stuck in a single city. I'd be happy to see the world outside of Arcadia, never mind another realm."

"I took a boat once," Drayton said softly. "Rowed until my arms ached. Rowed as far as I could. Into the middle of the ocean so the land vanished behind me. For a moment, I actually thought I'd made it out, and then land appeared before me. I rowed like a mad man, my heart in my mouth believing I'd found the outside world and then the sky line became clear and I realized I was back where I'd started." He shot me an apologetic smile. "If there is a way out, then we have yet to find it. The only creatures that know for sure are the winged, and they're not talking."

Shit, that was depressing. I focused on the scenery outside my window, at all the twinkling lights that obscured the moon. "And what is this place?"

"The strip. East side belongs to the

Sanguinata, West side to the Lupin. Their businesses are in constant competition."

"And the Breed?"

His jaw tightened. "We still haven't pinpointed their base of operations. Those fuckers need to be put down."

Cassie shifted forward in her seat and slid a hand onto his shoulder. "We'll get them, hon. I promise."

There was a story here and I made a note to quiz Cassie about it first chance I got. "So, where are we headed?"

"The Deep." Cassie grinned, her eyes gleaming as they caught the street lights. "Aside from being awesome, you can pick up a lot of information about what the houses are up to. The place is gossip central."

We turned onto a narrow road, and began to move away from the strip. The street lights became sparser and then died all together.

"It's been too quiet recently," Drayton said softly. "The scourge is due to run in a few nights, and nasties usually begin crawling out the woodwork the week leading up."

"What kind of nasties? I thought the scourge were the nasties?"

"Yeah, so did we until about a year ago, but we've been coming across new creatures all the time. Bane has Rivers doing the research and cataloguing. We even considered approaching the Black Wings about it. Maybe even trying to get an audience with the White Wing council. But Bane has asked us to hold off until we have more information. If this shit gets worse, then I'm not sure even the Protectorate can keep on top of it, and if that happens it'll spill into Sunset and, eventually, Dawn."

The road spiraled down and land rose up on either side of us creating an open top tunnel, and then we were breaking free, with the ocean up ahead and the twinkling stars above. A dark shape rose up out of the water, the peak of a cliff, and, atop it, a towering black building with tiny amber dots for eyes.

I leaned across Drayton's to point. "What is that?"

He didn't even turn his head to look. "Black Wing manor. We don't go there and they don't come out."

Yeah, they did. But he wasn't supposed to know that. Bane had been pretty clear. "If no one goes there, and they never come out, how do you know they even exist?"

"You can see them sometimes." Cassie said. "Flying around the manor. If you aren't looking too closely you'd think they were huge birds."

The road wound alongside the serene ocean far below. The view was breathtaking.

If I'd thought Sunset was gorgeous, then the ocean at midnight, bathed in silver moonlight, was a sight to capture your breath and stall your pulse.

We traveled in silence until a low long building strung with lights came into view. Cassie let out an *eep* of excitement and even Drayton, who'd been pretty somber since the mention of the Breed, cracked a smile.

It was like a Christmas tree, if a building was a Christmas tree. Green and yellow light bulbs were strung along the guttering and wound up pillars and a blue neon sign flashed the words, *The Deep*.

We swung into the car park and came to a halt. The engine died with a graceful purr and Drayton turned in his seat to look at me. "Stick with Cassie."

My face fell. "Aren't you coming with us?"

His gaze dropped to my lips, his mouth parted and his pupils dilated.

"He needs to get his fix, right, Drayton?" Cassie nudged.

His expression shuttered and he pulled back. "Just stay with Cassie." His tone was suddenly distant, as if he'd already stepped away into the club. As if he was already with someone else.

My chest tightened, and I wanted to kick myself. He wasn't mine. I didn't even want him to be mine. Relationships were off the table for mo. It was all these bloody training sessions with all the sexual energy he'd been blasting me with. Thank goodness I'd fed off him earlier, even though that hadn't been the plan. At least my hunger was in check.

"Watch her," Drayton said to Cassie. "She fed off me earlier, and probably hasn't burned through all the power. It may leak out of her shields and attract unsavory types."

"You can speak to me directly you know. And my shields are perfectly airtight, thank you."

"Good, keep it that way."

I was about to snap back but Cassie grabbed my arm from the back seat and shook her head. Then we were piling out of the car. Drayton strode off immediately, leaving Cassie and I to trail after him.

"What is up his arse all of a sudden?"

"You've seen the playful chilled out Drayton. This is his alter ego, the incubus. And when he's on the hunt, he's a different person. Single minded, intense, and detached."

"How can he be detached when he needs to lure women to him, how can he be detached when...you know, fucking them?"

"How can he not?" Cassie looked at me as if I was a moron. "He is fucking to feed.

Would you get attached to a burger, or a steak when you knew you were about to devour it?"

"No, but it's not like he's about to kill them?"

"No, he's about to make them fall in lust with him and leave them crazy for more. Laying with an incubus is an addiction. Whomever he chooses will crave his touch for weeks to come, doesn't matter if his conquest is a neph or a human. He never hits the same target twice in three months." Her eyes grew dark with sorrow. "Incubi can't fall in love and have long term relationships, Serenity. That kind of connection would drive both the female and the incubus insane. Then love and lust and the need to feed would become entangled. Drayton survives by compartmentalizing his emotions. There is the incubus, hungry, intense and single minded in his pursuit of what he needs, and then there is playful Drayton, sated and chilled."

Was that what had happened to my mother? An incubus liaison? Maybe more than one? Had she gone crazy and abandoned me, leading me to stumble into Arcadia? Had she recovered and looked for me or had she succumbed to madness?

"Why are you even telling me all of this?"

"Because I care about Drayton, and I see the way you look at him, the way he looks at you. I just...I wanted you to know the score."

My neck heated. "Thanks for the heads up, but I'm seriously not looking for a relationship or anything like that. Trust me, I tried it once, and it's just not for me."

She slipped her arm through mine. "Let me guess, you dated a human and almost fed off him?"

I glanced sharply at her. "That obvious?"

"Logical. You're a neph who lived amongst humans all your life. Who else would you have dated? But you see, now you're amongst your own kind. You can drain their power but it will recharge. It would be pretty hard for you to kill us."

Her words clicked into place and a small part of me lit up with hope. Of course, how the heck hadn't I thought of it before? Oh yeah, because I'd been too busy holding on to the rule I'd set six years ago. The no relationship thing had become ingrained in my psyche, and it hadn't even occurred to me that everything was different now. I could date...I could have a relationship.

Just not with Drayton. Not that I wanted to date him anyway.

I fixed a smile on my face. "Well, that's good to know."

Drayton was long gone. Off on the prowl inside. Cassie and I walked toward the entrance arm in arm.

"What did the Breed do to Drayton?"

Cassie's arm tensed. "That's something you'll need to ask him." Her tone was hoarse and saturated with memories.

A knot formed in my belly. It was bad, something really bad.

We climbed the steps and entered the warm confines of The Deep. We'd barely stepped through the door when Cassie's arm was tugged from mine. For a moment, I thought she'd merely pulled away but then she let out a shriek. I whipped round.

"Cassie? Cassie?"

Another shriek and a flash of red hair.

She was bobbing against a mammoth back.

And then the crowd closed on her and she vanished.

Cassie vanished into the throng of clubbers bopping to the music. The whole place was a dance floor. Strobe lights glanced across interesting faces, turning blue hair green and green hair blue and man it was just too much sensory information. I wound and squeezed my way through the bodies. Human and neph, there were so many of them, and everyone seemed to be chilled and having a good time, and if I hadn't been stressing about Cassie's wellbeing, I'd have stopped to study some of the nephs that smelled of the sea. These sea dwellers with large eyes and flat mouths, slightly pointed teeth and ears and skin tinged green and blue, but not by the lights.

The crowd thinned and a squeal cut through the beat, I caught a glimpse of Cassie as she was hauled up onto the bar by an epic creature with rippling arm muscles who had abducted her. I picked up pace, ready to defend her, and then she threw back her head and laughed—a throaty sexy sound that immediately had me faltering.

Her gaze met mine over the nephs shoulder. "Serenity!" She waved me over. "Come meet my friends."

I approached warily, and the guy standing between Cassie's thighs, his hands gripping her hips, turned his head to look at me. His eyes flashed pale grey as he studied me. Damn, he was almost as big as Bane. Long hair hung in seaweed mimicking ropes down his back, green and blue and turquoise. His face was chiseled and proud.

He arched a winged brow. "You hanging with humans now, Cassie?" He kept his gaze on me.

Cassie punched him lightly on the shoulder. "Aha, she had you fooled too, huh? Serenity is a neph, she just has awesome shields."

He scanned me from head to foot as if looking for a crack. "Shields?" he scoffed. "You and your jokes." He dismissed me, turning his attention back to Cassie. "Tell her to go away. She's making me hungry."

Cassie's expression sobered. "Killion, please tell me you haven't..."

He snorted. "You know I can never lie

to you."

"Dammit!" She shoved his shoulder hard. "How many times do I have to tell you—" She broke off and glanced my way. "Um, Serenity, can you give us a minute?"

Drayton had asked me to stay with her, but this guy, Killion, gave me the creeps. "Sure. I'm gonna grab a drink."

I strode off along the bar, found a gap and slipped through to the front. A tall broad shouldered purple tinged Neph was doing the serving. His head was bald, and his green eyes seemed to shine with an inner glow. He poured and slid drinks across the bar to customers, his gaze constantly scanning the floor as if in vigilance mode. Finally, he made his way to me.

"What can I get you?" His voice was a harmony at odds with his physique. He didn't take his eyes off the floor.

"An orange juice, please."

He poured the juice and slid it over to me. "Three fifty."

I placed a five on the counter. "What are you looking for?"

"Trouble."

"What kind of trouble?"

He tore his gaze from the crowd and dropped it to me. "The kind that could get me shut down." His lips twisted. "You see anything, you come tell me."

"See anything? Like what?"

He leaned in. "Anything that makes you feel uncomfortable. Anything that makes you feel unsafe. This place here, it's a sanctuary for humans and neph. A place we can mingle without fear. A place where our differences don't matter."

"Jonah, honey." A woman appeared at his side. Small, blonde, pretty and very human.

The neph straightened. His intensely serious expression softened as he looked down on the woman. "What is it, Poppy?"

"The barrel needs changing, babe."

He nodded. "I'll be right back." He pressed a kiss to the top of her head and then ambled off down the bar.

A human and a neph...together? The thought made my brain hurt.

Poppy's eyes crinkled. "How long have you been in Midnight?"

"That obvious, huh?"

She smiled and dimpled. "I'm afraid so. You'll find we do a lot of things differently from Sunset."

"How long have you two been together?"

Jonah and I have been together for years. We'd get married if it was allowed." She sighed. "He's a good man. This place is our way of spreading the love. It's a place where others like us can find a sanctuary, maybe find love?" She raised a shoulder in a delicate shrug.

"Jonah mentioned trouble?"

Her expression clouded. "Yes. A couple of humans never made it home after their visit. The MED are looking into it. It's probably nothing to do with The Deep, except that both humans were last seen here. Jonah has taken it personally. He prides himself on the sanctity of this place. No violence. No gang rivalry. Once you walk through those doors, you leave all the baggage behind."

"And how do you make sure patrons respect that?"

She smiled sweetly. "Jonah is a gentle giant...most of the time. But he can be brutally persuasive when the occasion calls for it. He protects his property and the people he loves, and there aren't many nephs who could challenge him. Jonah is descended from what the humans used to worship as a sea god. His blood is powerful. Most of the nephs that come here are sea dwellers and they know." She pushed a packet of peanuts my way. "Here, on the house. If you do see anything odd, please let us know."

I nodded. "Of course."

She wandered off down the bar to help serve. There was so much about Midnight I needed to learn—not only the layout but the customs and the people. I downed my juice but left the peanuts—I'd never been a fan. I needed to pee. Where were the toilets? I walked through the thong, past couples dancing, groups of women huddled together giggling, and a couple of macho neph crowd watching. A curvy brunet head in a glittering sequined dress was pressed up against a human male, her tongue licking out his ear while he ground his hips against her body. He stood out because of his ginger hair flashing in the strobe lights.

I followed a gaggle of humans in high heels as they tripped through the crowd of nephs, and was about to push into the ladies when a hand closed over my arm.

"Hello, beautiful." The voice was smarmy and over familiar.

I tugged my arm from the nephs grasp, and studied him. Pale, slim and not overly impressive or memorable, I had no clue what he was. Was he a sea dweller?

"I'm not interested."

I turned back to the loo, and he blocked my path, stepping into me to force me away from the ladies.

"Oh, come now, you haven't even heard my proposal." He somehow had me backed up against a wall. I pressed my hand to his chest and pushed but he was immovable, like stone.

"Back off."

He smiled, showcasing elongated eye teeth. "I'm not going to hurt you. In fact, I want to offer you sanctuary. You're without a house and we can offer you one. Join the Sanguinata and be protected from the Breed." His lips dropped over his teeth. "We take excellent care of our humans. Health plan, home improvements, you name it, we can help. Not only do you get protection from scum like the Breed, but we also provide shelter during the scourge run. Anyone messing with you is messing with House Vitae."

It was a bloody sales pitch. Wait, wasn't recruitment supposed to be determined by house games? I dropped my shields. His eyes widened and he stepped back.

"You're not human."

I cocked my head. "Nope. And you're not supposed to be—"

But he was gone. What the fuck? How had he moved so fast? I'd have to report this to Cassie once she'd finished with her sea dweller friend. Maybe even let Poppy and Jonah know? My bladder twinged, reminding me that I really needed a pee. My hand was on the door when awareness prickled across my scalp, and as if drawn by a magnetic force I turned my head. My gaze fell on a couple hidden in the shadows, bodies pressed together intimately. The woman clung to the man's shoulders, her nails digging into the fabric of his deep green shirt and then trailing up to slip through his dark hair. He pulled her closer, his hands cupping her arse as he ground into her. Her skirt was up around her waist, her panties on display. Heat bloomed in my chest, as their arousal slammed into me. And then the man raised his head and the familiar profile was highlighted by an errant beam from the disco lights. Drayton turned his head and locked gazes with me. He didn't even bat an eye at finding me there, he just smiled, a satisfied smug smile and then dropped his head back to the woman he would probably end up fucking against that wall, dismissing me.

My stomach churned, and I slammed into the bathroom. At least he was having fun. Ignoring the giggling humans preening by the mirrors, I did my business and headed back out. I could see how this place could be fun, but so far it had been a bust for me. It was time to head home. I began to nudge my way through the revelers, intent on finding Cassie and getting the heck out of there when I spotted the Sanguinata by the bar with a human. He had her by the wrist and her face was frozen in shock.

Fuck this. I dropped my shield and sauntered over. "Hey, you, House Vitae."

The Sanguinata looked up startled.

"Are you supposed to be recruiting?" I raised my voice so that the nephs around me turned to see what all the fuss was about.

The Sanguinata dropped the woman's wrist and held up his hands. "I was just offering to buy this lovely female a drink."

The human shook her head as if coming out of a daze.

"Is that right?"

"I... I don't know," she said. "He was...was..."

The Sanguinata smiled slyly. He shrugged. "But if she's not interested then..." He backed off slowly.

The human looked dazed and confused. Had he used some kind of power on her? Damn, I didn't know enough about the Sanguinata to tell for sure. But he'd definitely propositioned me.

"You may not have tried to recruit her, but you certainly tried to recruit me."

"House Vitae recruiting?" A guy to my right said. He was neph, but very minor.

The Sanguinata's eyes widened in panic but then a mask slipped across his features, cunning and sly. "Now why would I try and recruit a neph?"

Shit, of course, my shields were down.

Jonah chose that moment to appear behind the Sanguinata at the bar. "Problem?"

His tone was mild, enquiring, but his expression was intense.

The Sanguinata held up his hands. "Hey, I was just asking the lovely lady if I could buy her a drink."

"Is that right?" Jonah asked the human.

She opened and closed her mouth a couple of times. "I don't remember."

Jonah's jaw clenched and fixed his terrifying gaze on the Sanguinata. "You memory blocking?"

The Sanguinata took step away from the bar. "I meant no harm, Jonah."

Jonah glared at him. "Get the fuck out of my club and don't come back."

What, no. I needed to question him, find out why he was recruiting when he wasn't supposed to be, but the Sanguinata moved so fast he was a blur. And then he was gone.

Shit! "Damn it. He was recruiting for his house. I needed to speak to him."

Jonah shrugged. "Not my problem. The Deep is my problem, and he won't be back."

Which didn't help me in the slightest. The crowd at the bar closed in, blocking him from view.

"Are you all right?" Drayton's voice was like a caress against the back of my neck.

I tensed. "I thought you were feeding."

"I'm done."

He'd fucked the woman. Great. "A

Sanguinata just tried to recruit me."

"What? No. They can't do that. Not until they win the house games."

"Yeah I know that," I snapped. "But he tried anyway, and then I caught him trying to recruit someone else."

Drayton's jaw tightened. "We need to report this to Bane." His brow furrowed. "I thought I told you to stay with Cassie?"

No point in telling him Cassie had asked me to piss off for a bit. "I needed a pee, okay."

Something dark flitted across his face. "You were by the ladies a few minutes ago?"

Was he seriously kidding me right now? "You know I was. You looked right at me."

His brow furrowed for a second and he honestly looked thrown and then he pressed his lips together. "Let's go find Cassie."

He cut a swath through the crowd, as human and neph stepped aside to let him through. Killion's broad back and taut buttocks came into view and Drayton let out a muffled curse.

"Cassie," he said. He didn't raise his voice but it carried across the distance between us and the corner of the bar, cutting through whatever track the DJ was playing.

Cassie peeked over Killion's shoulder and winced. "Hey, Dray. Just bumped into Killion. We were catching up."

Killion's shoulders tensed, and then he slowly stepped away from Cassie, to face off with Drayton. At least it looked like a face off.

"We're leaving," Drayton said.

The words were delivered in that lazy tone I'd grown so used to. The totally unthreatening, chill timbre that spoke of summer breezes and cool drinks, but his body was as stiff as a board, ready to snap at the slightest provocation.

Killion's thick lips curled in a snide smile. "She's not going anywhere. She's having fun."

Drayton ignored him and focused on Cassie. "If you're not out in five, we go without you." He turned on his heel and strode toward the door.

I glanced at Cassie then Drayton's rapidly retreating back.

"Go," she mouthed.

Drayton was standing outside, his hands on his hips, head hanging as he took deep breaths. It was eerily silent under the blue lights from the neon sign. The nephs and humans who'd been hanging around outside were gone. But then there was a chill in the air, sharp and tangy from the sea.

Drayton kept his back to me, and I curled my hands into fist to prevent myself reaching out to touch his back. Something told me my touch would not be welcome right now. "Are you okay?"

He threw the keys at me. "Get in the car."

I pocketed them. "Drayton, who the fuck is that guy?"

"Cassie's ex and a pain in my arse," Drayton said through his teeth.

"He's one of the sea people right?"

"Yeah, leader of the Black Water gang. He's a kelpie and he feeds off humans."

"How does he feed?"

He raised his head and arched his brow. "With his teeth."

A chill swept through me. When he's said my human scent made him hungry he'd been referring to actually eating me. "Why hasn't the Protectorate done something about that? They go up against the Breed, so why let him walk around among humans freely?"

"Because there's no solid evidence against him."

"I think he's still feeding off humans."

Drayton's head whipped up. "What makes you say that?"

I told him what Killion had said and how Cassie had asked me to give them a minute.

"Mother fucker," Drayton began to pace. "If she's covering for him…"

He left the sentence hanging, leaving me to conjure up all the shit that could come out of me telling him this. The last thing I wanted to do was cause friction in the group, but if Killion *was* eating humans, then something needed to be done.

Drayton glanced at his watch. "Her five minutes are up. Come on, we're leaving." He held out his hand for the keys.

"We're not seriously going to leave her with him, are we?"

"He won't hurt her. She's not human. They'll probably just go back to his place for a little catch up."

Was he implying? "Wait, I thought she was with Orin?"

He blinked at me. "Sometimes, yes."

"Sometimes."

He sighed. "Dammit, Harker. How naive are you? Sex, even frequent sex with the same partner doesn't mean exclusivity, it doesn't mean love."

His tone grated and my hackles rose. "Well, I'm sorry, but I was raised to think different."

He let out a sound of exasperation. "Give me the damned keys."

I threw them at him and stormed off toward the car. I'd barely gone three strides when a piercing scream sliced through the air. I froze for a fraction of a second, assessing where it had come from, and then I broke into a run.

I rounded the side of the building diving into the shadows where the scream had come from. The daggers that Cassie had given me were in my hands, ready just in case. Hopefully, now I had those to hand the other ones tattooed on my wrist would stay put. But the scene before me clearly didn't require a weapon. What we needed was an ambulance.

"Serenity, wait." Drayton came up behind me and stopped and stared at the woman on the ground, partially buried in the sand. The face was familiar—the woman from the bar that the Sanguinata had been accosting. Shit. I fell to my knees and checked for a pulse, there was one, but barely.

"She's alive." I glanced over my shoulder at Drayton. "Call an ambulance.

Now."

And then I began to tug, her body slid out of the sand and I pulled her into my lap, cradling her. "You're okay. You're going to be okay."

"Damn it, Serenity. You could be contaminating valuable evidence."

"Sod the evidence. She's alive and I intend to keep her that way."

He turned away on the phone as he spoke to the operator. Someone had tried to bury her alive? Who? The Sanguinata? He *was* the obvious suspect.

"What? No fuck you very much," Drayton shoved his phone in his pocket then leaned down and scooped up the human.

"What are you doing? Did you call the ambulance?"

"They're not coming. You want to keep her alive, then come with me."

We rushed toward the vehicle just as several people came pouring out of The Deep. I caught a glimpse of a familiar sequined dress and the flash of carrot hair, and then we were loading the woman up into the backseat of the car. Cassie was still nowhere to be seen, and although the thought of leaving her behind with Killion was less than appealing, Drayton's lack of concern and the woman in need of dire medical attention lifted my misgivings.

Drayton drove like a demon, which was kinda ironic, and we reached the hospital in just over ten minutes. With the woman cradled in his arms, Drayton strode toward the entrance to the three story brightly lit building. The doors slid open and we were bathed in garish light. Formica chairs lined the room beyond the foyer, a huge semi-circle reception desk jutted out from the wall to our left and corridors snaked off left and right, white, clean and sterile. A woman in a nurse's uniform looked up from a monitor at reception and then came rushing toward us.

"Drayton?" she said. "Is that a human?"

"Yes, and I need her seen to, Emmy."

An orderly appeared with a stretcher and Drayton laid the human on it.

Emmy glanced about. "Damn it, Drayton. You know we don't treat humans here."

"What?" I looked up at Drayton. "This *is* the hospital right?"

Emmy spoke. "Yes, it is a hospital. A hospital for nephs." Her lips were tight. "The humans have their own facilities and they would never allow one of us through *their* doors."

"Look, the human hospital is miles away and you're here, and you took an oath to save lives, so save this one."

"Miles away, huh?" She pressed her

fists to her hips. "Was she at The Deep?"

Drayton nodded.

"Em, we can't turn her away," the orderly said.

Emmy sighed. "Tristen isn't going to like this."

The orderly gripped the bars of the stretcher, and began to wheel her away.

"Stay here," Emmy said to us. "I'll be right back."

She clipped down the corridor after the orderly and round a bend out of view.

I rounded on Drayton. "Why are we here, Drayton? Why didn't we take her to the human hospital?"

"It's too far."

"Really? Emmy didn't seem too convinced of that."

He turned his head away, his jaw working. "Fine. The human hospital refused to come pick her up because she was at The Deep."

"What's that got to do with anything?"

"She was fraternizing with nephs, Serenity, and if I'd taken her there they probably would have refused to treat her anyway."

"They can't do that. They're a hospital."

"It doesn't work that way in Midnight. We may bust our arses to protect the humans but the majority of them would love to see us dead along with the scourge. They not only fear us, they hate us. Hate the fact that we have the potential to attract them, to possibly procreate with them and sully their human blood lines. If we'd taken her to the hospital, she would have been treated like a neph simply for fraternizing."

"So, all the humans at The Deep...they're there on the sly?"

"Yep."

"Well, crap."

"There are two factions of humans in Midnight. Those that work to exist alongside us, and those that want to eradicate us along with the scourge," Drayton said. "Unfortunately for us, many of the humans against us work for the MED or the public services which makes it hard for us to get the cooperation we need on cases. This hospital was built a few years ago after the main hospital began refusing to treat nephs."

So, there was segregation in Midnight, tiny cracks like the ones in my cell floor back in Sunset.

"We have the upper hand because we have power," Drayton said. "Humans need us for protection. They know it, and they hate it. Yeah, they're pretty savvy about walking the line and not openly opposing us."

"Wait, so all the humans that don't join a house...are they the ones against the nephs entirely?"

"Some genuinely wish to live without ties to the nephs and hold no ill will, but the majority, yes."

"And these are the humans we protect from The Breed."

His lips curled in a sardonic smile. "Welcome to Midnight, Serenity."

At least in Sunset the people I'd kept safe had appreciated my efforts, but here I'd be protecting humans who hated me.

The double doors behind us swished open and four men strode in. Two were in plain clothes and the other two in uniform strode into the foyer. The nephs seated in the waiting room, bristled at the intrusion. Humans. These officers were human, and I recognized one of the plain clothed one. Carrot top met my gaze steadily then blinked and licked his lips.

The other plain clothed officer flipped open his badge. "MED. Where's the girl?"

Drayton crossed his arms over his chest and arched a brow. "What girl?"

"Don't play dumb with me, Drayton. Giles saw you put her in your car, and he followed you here."

"I did," Carrot top said.

"Planting spies at The Deep now, Langley?"

Langley's mouth twisted. "The

Protectorate don't have the monopoly on protecting humans. We're investigating a spate of missing person reports originating at The Deep."

This is what Jonah, the owner of The Deep, had been taking about. What he'd asked me to keep an eye out for. It was what Giles was supposed to have been watching for, instead he'd been making out with a neph.

I cocked my head. "So, your little spy, Giles, didn't see anything suspicious?"

Giles pushed up his bottom lip and shook his head. "Nothing."

"Could it be because you were otherwise engaged? Say...grinding up against a neph in a sequined dress?"

Giles's mouth fell open, but he snapped it closed, quickly composing himself. "She's lying," he said.

Langley shot Giles a sharp look but Giles just shrugged in surprise. Damn, he was good.

"This is our investigation," Langley said. "So, just tell us where she is and we can get on with it."

Emmy chose that moment to reappear, but she wasn't alone, behind her trudged a bespectacled man with an inquisitive face.

"Drayton, it's good to see you," the man said.

"You too," Drayton said. They clasped hands.

The man smiled, and pushed his spectacles up his nose. He then turned to the MED officers and his expression dropped to something below freezing.

"Do you have a warrant?" he asked.

Langley rolled his eyes. "No, Tristan. I do not."

"Then get out," Tristan said simply.

"Look, you have a human here. The girl they brought in is human. You probably aren't aware but—"

"Oh, I'm aware, and she's in good hands. Once she regains consciousness and is ready for visitors we'll inform the MPD who are dealing with this case."

Langley's eyes flashed. "Now hang on a minute. This is an MED matter."

"Really? Tristan looked momentarily thrown. He tapped his bottom lip with an index finger. "Because I thought she was found at The Deep, which is MPD jurisdiction."

"She's human," Giles snapped. "And connected to a string of missing persons cases."

"All originating at The Deep, correct?" Drayton asked. "That is what you said, right?"

"Which makes them all MPD cases."

Tristan tutted. "You really need to learn to do your job better."

Langley tucked in his chin and shook his head. "You nephs, you're all the fucking same. Sly fuckers who'll take what they can, when they can."

My neck heated. "And you humans are ungrateful arseholes who use us for protection when it suits you and treat us like shit the rest of the time." I took a step into his personal space. "Have the paperwork for the missing persons sent over by the morning, or we'll be coming to collect."

He met my gaze, the corners of his eyes twitching as we faced off, and then he backed up. "You're playing with fire," he said. "The MED won't take kindly to this."

"Yeah? Well then tell them to find someone else to save their arses when the scourge runs."

If looks could kill, I'd be breathing my last, but then the heat was off as the quartet turned away and headed for the exit.

I puffed out my cheeks and blew out a breath. "How'd I do?"

Drayton let out a bark of laughter.

"Wonderfully," Tristan said with a twinkle, but then his expression hardened. "However, if you put my hospital on this kind of position again, then it will be a different story. Going up against the MED may be incurably satisfying, however, you know the clout they have in the district. Midnight functions on a delicate balance and the less we do to jeopardize that, the better."

"Wait, you were the one who brought up the whole jurisdiction thing?"

He nodded. "Yes. You were wrong to bring her here, and they were wrong to claim this case."

Emmy smiled. "Tristan is a stickler for protocol."

"Which brings me to our young human patient," Tristan said.

"Is she really still unconscious?" Drayton asked.

"Unfortunately, yes. We've sent off for blood tests and are running some labs on her now. She's stable but unresponsive."

"There are no visible ligature marks on her body, no wounds of any kind," Emmy said.

"We'll know more once we get the results back in a couple of hours," Tristan said. "In the meantime, we'll monitor her and treat her as a Jane Doe."

Or course, she had no personal belongings on her, no hand bag, nothing when we found her.

"We'll call you once we have something more," Emmy said.

Drayton ran a hand over his face.

"Thanks, both of you, and sorry for bringing this onto your doorstep."

The corner of Tristan's mouth lifted half in a smile. "I may be annoyed, but I can't deny that you made the right call."

"Excuse me, nurse?" one of the patients in the waiting room called out. "I've been waiting for almost an hour."

Emmy shot us an apologetic smile. "I'll speak to you soon. It was nice meeting you..."

"Serenity," I supplied.

She nodded. "I'll file that away." She hurried off to deal with patients and Tristan walked us to the exit.

Outside, the night air was crisp and fresh against my cheeks. I breathed it in, letting it wash away the panic of the last half hour.

"You did good in there," Drayton said. "I think you'll be an asset to the team."

"We're not done yet though, are we?" I followed him to the car. "Don't we need to do something about the Sanguinata and their unauthorized recruitment drive?"

He unlocked the doors with the key fob and then shot me a wicked grin. "Fancy paying the House of Vitae a little visit?"

We drove in silence, heading east along the coast. The Black Wing residence was visible in the distance, the lights tiny pinpricks in the night.

"Isn't it illegal to recruit outside of the annual drive?"

He pressed his lips together. "Ryker been filling you in?"

"Yes, so why aren't we going in with a warrant. Wait, do you even have warrants. I've been with you for two weeks, and I see you guys go in and out on patrol with the other primary nephs from the guest houses, but you don't actually do any paperwork, do you? Like keep reports and stuff?"

His brows shot up. "No one's showed you the office?"

They had an office? "No."

"Oh, good because we don't have one."

Oh. "Then why'd you say you did?"

"To see your face." He snorted. "It lit up, all hopeful." He shot me a quick look. "This isn't SPD, Harker. It isn't MED. This is Protectorate. We are the boots on the ground and the fists in the night. We spend our time getting our hands dirty. Yeah, if we come across anything super freaky, we lodge it in the events ledger, and we do keep a rota for patrols. Other than that, there is no paperwork. Paperwork means red tape and time wasting and that's the MED's department. They deal with all the human criminal issues, we deal with the supernatural and that usually involves more permanent and immediate action. No paperwork required. There are certain areas of Midnight that are considered outside MED jurisdiction and The Deep is one of those places. Crimes committed there are technically considered supernatural, which is where this gray area has arisen with the missing humans."

"So, what do you do for cases like this?"

"We usually do them by the book. We fill out the necessary warrants for information on the computer in the study and Bane seals them."

"So we *should* get a warrant."

He winced. "Technically, but if we go in with a warrant, the Sanguinata will see it as a threat, and they don't take kindly to threats.

Best to just drop in on a social visit and hope Dorian is in a good mood."

"Is he their leader?"

"Yes, and they call him Lord Dorian. Sanguinata have their own internal power play and hierarchy. Something outsiders aren't privy to. If he's feeling amiable, we may get lucky and get an audience. Otherwise, we'll have to request an appointment and be ready to move at the drop of a hat."

Maybe it was my time with the SPD. Maybe it was all the years I'd spent parading as a human, but this just felt sloppy to me. "I still think we should get a warrant."

He exhaled sharply. "Being able to throw the book at someone doesn't mean it's always the best option. Trust me. I know how to deal with Dorian. Just let me do the talking. The Sanguinata nobility have their quirks, things I don't have time to go over with you now. Tuck away what you see, and file your questions until we get back to base, okay?"

A shiver skipped down my spine. "What am I going to see?"

He tapped his fingers on the steering wheel. "I can't say for sure. The Sanguinata are an unpredictable contradiction."

Now my head hurt.

The stretch of road we were on was

silent and empty, a slip road between the busy part of the district and the residential side. A figure came into view stumbling along the side of the road. There was no pavement here. He was actually on the bloody road. On the road in bare feet!

"Drayton!" I pointed out of the windshield.

"I see him." He continued to drive.

"Wait. Look, he's not wearing any shoes." I tugged on Drayton's elbow. "Stop, we have to help him. He looks lost. Confused."

For a moment, I thought Drayton would actually just ignore me, but then, with a soft curse and an angry tug on the steering wheel, he pulled over a meter or so behind the man.

"Damn it, Murray." Drayton sat with his hands gripping the wheel, knuckles white as he watched the guy in the rear view mirror.

The guy, Murray, faltered in his step for a moment, looking this way and that. His mouth moved but it was impossible to hear what he was saying from this far away. He was dressed in a faded brown shirt and dark brown trousers. He stopped and ran a trembling hand through his wiry shock of white hair.

I prodded Drayton's bicep. "Well, are you going to go speak to him?"

"Wait here," Drayton said.

He exited the car and slowly approached the confused looking guy. Murray smiled, his eyes lighting up as they fell on Drayton. He nodded vigorously and allowed Drayton to steer him toward our vehicle. The rear headlights spilled across him and for a moment I could have sworn he just disappeared, but no, he was back again. The back passenger door opened and Murray slipped in.

Drayton got back in the driver's seat and started the engine. "We're just going to make a quick pit stop and drop Murray home." The words were clipped. He glanced at the clock on the dashboard. "We may need to hold off on our visit to the House of Vitae and go first thing in the morning."

My heart shrank with disappointment. What were the odds of Bane letting me go with Drayton once he found out about the Sanguinata recruitment? And there was no way Drayton was not going to report what had happened to his boss.

We pulled back onto the road.

"Are we there yet?" Murray asked from the back seat.

"Not long now, Murray," Drayton said kindly.

It was a tone I hadn't heard him use before—soft and considerate, as if he was speaking to a child. A quick peek in the rear view mirror showed Murray doing that muttering thing again. He'd seemed confused and wandering around without shoes. It was clear what was going on here.

"How long has he had dementia?"

"A few years. He's a good guy, just wanders off sometimes. He'd have found his way home eventually, but by that time he'd have worked himself up into a state."

"You can't just assume that. Dementia gets worse with time. I can't believe you were just going to drive off and leave him."

"He would have been fine. Trust me, Murray isn't going to get any worse."

What did that mean? And why did he sound so pissed off about it? I was about to ask when we swung left onto a narrow track that cut up an incline, and then an ornate arch rose up ahead of us. The headlights swept over the curly iron letters that graced the curve of the arch.

Respite Cemetery.

What the heck?

Murray clapped his hands together. "Home. Home."

"Um, Drayton, why are we at the cemetery?"

Drayton shut off the engine. "Because *this* is where Murray lives."

My pulse skipped and my heart lurched

as several figures appeared under the arch. Up here, with the light of the moon shining strong you could see right through them all.

Heart hammering, I turned my head to look into the back seat and right through Murray.

A scream lodged in my throat as I clawed for the door handle.

"Drayton grabbed my wrist. "Seriously?" he snapped. "You've faced scourge and Killion and you're running from Murray, a harmless ghost."

His tone was sincerely incredulous. He really believed I was being ridiculous and when he put it that way, then yeah, it was pretty crazy. I slowly peeled myself off the door and loosened my grip on the handle.

"You have ghosts." Man my voice sounded all croaky and weird.

"Yes, we have ghosts. Everyone here is a victim of the scourge or The Breed. Unable to move on, for whatever reason, they seem to be drawn here. They've made it their home." He stared out the window at the gathered forms, his eyes scanning them as if searching for something.

Murray was patting the window, eager to get out.

"You can stay here," Drayton said to me. "I won't be long."

He got out and unlocked Murray's door.

My fear had evaporated to be replaced by curiosity. Ghosts. Who'd have thought? Drayton approached the transparent gathered figures and I quickly stepped out of the vehicle to join him.

Several pairs of eyes skimmed over me, smiles and nods and talking amongst themselves, Music drifted on the breeze and fireflies hovered over the gravestones. It would have been pretty if not for the whole cemetery housing dead people thing.

"Aw, Drayton, thank you for bringing him home," a plumb cheery woman said. "It's been a while for sure since we saw you." There was no reproach in her tone, just sadness. "You know we've missed your visits."

Drayton licked his lips. "I'm sorry. I..."

"Ach, never you mind." She waved her hand toward the stone mausoleum rising up behind them. "Why not come visit with us for a while?"

The doors to the mausoleum were ajar, and, no, it wasn't my imagination, the music was drifting out from inside the stone structure.

"I... No, I need to get back," Drayton said.

The crowd parted and a beautiful ethereal woman slipped through the gathered. Her cupid bow mouth broke into a beaming smile at the sight of Drayton, and his whole body tensed.

"The fireflies told me you were here," she said. "But I didn't believe, didn't dare hope. But here you are."

"Hello, Viola," Drayton said. His tone was flat and dull.

Her joyous expression slipped, and shadows filled her eyes. "You finally came, but not to see me, did you?" Viola asked with a sad smile. "You want to forget."

"How can I?"

Her gaze slid my way and she caught her bottom lip between her teeth. "Time has a way of healing all wounds...for some of us."

"Not me," he said.

Those two words vibrated with pain and longing and suddenly it was clear why he'd been so annoyed. He hadn't wanted to come here, because he hadn't wanted to see her. This woman. This dead woman. He cared for her...she was someone he'd lost. Was this what Cassie had been alluding to at The Deep? Was this something to do with The Breed? Is this why he hated them so much? Did he love her?

A plump woman held out her arms to Murray and he hurried over to her, allowing her to clasp him to her bosom and rock him back and forth. "You, naughty boy. I warned you to stay put, didn't I?" The plump woman said.

She looked about ten to fifteen years younger than Murray.

"I'm sorry, mama," Murray said. "I got lost."

She smoothed back his hair. "That's all right. You're safe now thanks to Drayton." She turned Murray around to face Drayton. "Say thank you to Drayton, Murray."

"Thank you, Drayton," Murray said compliantly.

But Drayton only had eyes for Viola.

She took a couple of steps closer. "Do you want to stay a while?" There was so much hope in her tone, so much longing in her eyes.

Drayton took a step towards her and then caught himself. "I have to go."

"Drayton." She reached for him, but he was already halfway to the car.

She choked back a sob, and focused on me. "Are you two..." She shook her head, unable to finish her sentence.

"Are we? Gosh, no. I'm new to the Protectorate and he's just showing me the ropes."

She sniffed and pushed back her silver blonde hair. "He hasn't been to see me before," she said. "And he probably won't come back. So, can you please tell him...Tell him it wasn't his fault, and if he believes it was, then I forgive him."

Viola faded into nothing, and the specters drifted off, as if Murray's return had severed them from their need to hover at the gates to their home. A horn honked shattering the relative serenity of the night— Drayton was impatient to be gone. With questions battling for dominance in my mind, I headed back to the vehicle.

"Don't," Drayton warned as I got into the car.

"Don't what? Don't get in?"

He kept his eyes on the windscreen. "Don't ask about her."

"Okay. But she asked me to give you a message."

He gripped the wheel tighter, evident by the whitening of his knuckles. "I don't want to know."

A wave of empathy hit me, and no way was I the empathic type, not when it came to just anyone. The only person who I'd felt empathic toward had been Jesse and that had come from years of being siblings, years of shared heartache. This emotion that had me in its grip, this need to somehow smooth the crinkle from his brow and wipe away the tick in his jaw was disconcerting. And the urge to blurt Viola's words out was so strong I had to bite the insides of my cheeks. He didn't know what she'd said. He wasn't ready to listen, but I'd memorize the words and hold them for him until he was.

He started the engine and did a neat U turn.

"What's in the mausoleum?"

"There's nothing in it," he said shortly.

"Then why did that woman, the plump one want you to go with her?"

"It's a doorway to their home. The world the spirits have built using their combined energy. They call it Respite, and it's been growing for over a hundred years." He steered the car down the incline. "Some of the older ghosts never leave, some have forgotten their deaths and Respite has become their Arcadia, except without the monsters that would hunt them." We were back on the slip road which led into the main district. "As time has gone on, as the living that knew them pass on, as time goes by, they have been forgotten, and so they too have forgotten. It's a blessing really."

"What about Viola? What about her family?"

His throat bobbed. "Viola had no family. Her mother died in childbirth and her father was unknown. She kept to herself and lived a relatively unsocial existence. Viola was sweet and shy."

That tone...regret and longing and loss. He'd loved her.

He cleared his throat. "We'll be back at base in five. I'd prefer it if you didn't mention the cemetery to the others."

Was he worried about them asking questions about Viola? "Sure."

"I'll speak to Bane about the Sanguinata recruiter and let him know we'll be headed there tomorrow."

"I can still come?"

"If you're going to be one of the Protectorate, you need to learn how to liaise with the houses. This will be a great *observational* exercise."

"I get it. You don't want me to speak."

"What you did at the hospital was admirable. But it won't work with the Sanguinata. They don't respond kindly to threats or manipulation. They prefer to deal in them. Like Tristan said, there is a delicate balance to Midnight, and we must work to preserve that."

The gates to the Protectorate base came into view, inky lines against a cloudy Midnight sky. The moon winked out, obscured by the dark churning froth and the world was plunged into absolute darkness. The car headlights swept across the gate and it opened with a *creak*.

"Automated?"

"No."

Okay.

Gravel crunched under the huge wheels of the ride and then a shadowy streak cut across our path, low and fast.

I pressed myself back against my seat, hand on heart. "What was that?"

"Sentinels. Nothing for you to worry about. They won't hurt you. They protect the grounds."

"What are they?"

He shrugged. "No idea. I've never seen one up close. They're just there."

We were almost at the top of the drive when movement in the periphery of my vision had my head whipping round just as something slammed into the side of the car, filling the world with the crunch of metal.

The car turned upside down and right-side up, over and over again until it settled with a clang leaving me suspended in the air, staring through cracked glass. Pain exploded in my chest where my seatbelt cut into my torso, pinning me, and squeezing the breath from my lungs.

"Serenity!" Drayton's hands were on me, fumbling for the clasp to my belt.

How had he already come loose? Wait, had he been strapped in? Shit, was that blood on his face? His hands?

The world rumbled and shook.

"Fuck, it's coming. Dammit!"

Something snapped and then I was free. My head slammed against the roof of the car, but there was no time to react to the pain, because Drayton was pressing me against the passenger side door.

"Sorry, so sorry," he said.

My ribs screamed in pain. What the heck. The crunch of metal and the crack of glass covered my strangled scream and then the pressure was gone. Drayton slid out of the car, his eyes wide.

"Give me your hand."

He reached back in for me. "Now, dammit!"

I held out my arm, and pain lanced down my side. My vision darkened.

The car began to shake around me.

"Stay with me, Harker. Come on." He lunged, grabbed my hand and tugged.

My scream was fire racing up my throat and singeing the back of my nose, and then he had me in his arms and we were stumbling back. Oh, God. What had happened? I opened my eyes to a green haze.

Something had hit us.

Something that was stomping toward us now — an eight-foot tall metallic monster with dull red eyes and a jagged mouth — it's movements were jerky and stiff, but its intention was clear. It wanted to hurt us and it was getting closer, moving as if it had all the time in the world. Each stomp of its oversized feet had the ground vibrating.

Drayton backed up slowly with me still clutched to his chest. "Serenity, can you run?"

My body was on fire. I was pretty sure I

had a couple of broken ribs. "Yes."

"Good. I'm going to put you down and you're going to make a break for the mansion."

"I'm not leaving you."

"Noble, Harker, but that's a golem, and we're not going to be able to take it down just the two of us, especially when you have broken ribs and a concussion. You need to get the others."

"They'll have heard the commotion, surely?"

"See the green shimmer in the air?"

So, that's what that was? Not just a side effect of getting my head bashed in. "I see it."

"It's some kind of spell, it's probably blocking sound, or something. Get the others."

The golem, as if sensing our plan, put on a burst of speed. Probably what he'd used to ram us in the first place. Drayton practically flung me to the ground just as the golem swept the car out the way with an almighty crash. I hit the dirt in a crouch and ran toward the mansion, chest aching, eyes watering.

I slammed into the foyer. "Help! Bane. Ryker, anyone!" Another shaft of pain sliced me in half, and I buckled. "Dammit, help."

"Serenity?" Rivers hauled me to my feet. "Where are the others?"

"You need to help Drayton. There's a golem outside."

Rivers released me, drew his sword and ran out the door.

Ryker appeared in the entrance to the lounge. "What happened to you?" He was on me in a heartbeat, his hands probing for injury, and then heat spread across my torso leeching the pain.

"We have to help the others," I grabbed his hand and tugged him out of the door.

Out into the silent night. No. It couldn't be silent, because there, right in front of us, enveloped in a green bubble were Drayton and Rivers, battling the metal monster who refused to be cut down.

Gravel ate at my soles as I skid into the green haze. It was as if someone had flicked on a switch to turn on the sound. The world was suddenly alive with noise. Crashed and thuds, and yells, and the *whoosh* and *whiz* of air as the golem swung his mighty fists. The earth beneath us protested with rumbles. The gravel shifted and bounced as the monster stamped and stomped. Rivers was too close to the metal beast, he staggered back as if realizing his error but lost his footing and fell down on his back. The golem brought its huge fist down in a slow motion arc, and Rivers let out a bellow, the shock waves were visible ripples in the air. Air, he was using the air to combat the golem. It worked, hitting it in the chest and pushing it back a single step.

Drayton leapt up onto the Golem's back.

"No!"

Ryker grabbed my hand. "He's looking for a breach, some way into the metal. We need to get to the earth inside it. If we can puncture it, we can disable it."

Rivers was already up, slashing with his sword.

Ryker joined him, running circles around the golem to distract it from Drayton's ministrations. I grabbed the daggers at my waist and jumped into the fray. I slashed at its thigh managing only to scrape the metal with my blade. The thing was indestructible. It spun toward me ready with a backhand, but I dropped and rolled out the way, coming to stab at its backside.

This time it ignored me and instead reached for Drayton. Grabbing the incubus by the scruff of the neck, he flung him toward a huge oak. The sound of his body making contact with wood was cut off as it was outside the bubble. But his mouth opened in an exclamation of pain.

Rivers and Ryker circled the golem, as it stepped from side to side, as if unsure what its next move should be. Drayton was already back on his feet and diving into the bubble with us.

"What does it want?" Rivers asked no one in particular.

"We can worry about that when we bring it down," Ryker said.

"My blades are useless, there is no way to cut through the metal," Rivers said.

Blades that could cut through metal. My blades. "Wait. I have an idea." I tucked the twin blades Cassie had given me back in their sheaths. "Just back up. Do not help me."

"What are talking about?" Rivers asked.

"No," Drayton said. "She's right. Back up." He'd obviously cottoned on. "Get out of the bubble."

"No way," Ryker said. "Serenity, it's too risky."

I shoved him. "Go!"

And there was no time to procrastinate because the golem was coming at me, the only target left in its bubble of destruction. It was going to smash into me, hurt me, maybe kill me. Come on! The blades of Aether settled into the palms of my hands with less than a meter left between me and the golem. I dropped, ducking his swinging fist and slashed at his legs with all my might. My blades went through him like butter. And then the upper half of his body was sliding forward. Right at me.

A strangled *squeak* fell from my lips just

as a body slammed into me from the right. We hit the dirt together, Ryker and I. He pulled me close, cradling me against him. "Dammit, Harker. That was close."

Around us, the green haze dropped to the ground and seeped into the earth like a bazillion tiny motes of emerald dust. The golem was down, twitching in the final throes of its existence as the dirt packed inside its metal frame spilled out like life blood.

Ryker pulled me up.

The golem let out an inhuman shriek and then its body lay still.

"What in the world happened here?" Bane stood, hands on hips, face contorted in confusion as he took in the scene. He was a hulking distorted figure under a moonless sky, and then the clouds chose that moment to part and silvery light lit up the driveway bringing the carnage into stark relief. The car was totaled, the driveway a churned mass of gravel and dirt, and Drayton... Shit. He swayed on his feet for a moment as if moving to a melody only he could hear and then he dropped like a stone.

The huge stone hearth in the lounge had been teased into an inferno, and a meeting had been called. Cassie was still absent, but Orin was back from patrol. We sat around on chairs and sofas nursing shots of brandy or whiskey. Drayton was pale and his hair was still caked with blood, but he'd refused Ryker's offer of healing. The meal he'd had at The Deep was enough to knit his wounds, and the bruises on his temple were fading already. If only cambions could use the power we absorbed to heal. The only way I'd be able to do that was if I absorbed Ryker's healing ability.

"They were after something," Bane said. "Information most likely. A test of our defenses." His voice was a stormy rumble. "If it had gotten away it would have taken all those details back with it." His gaze fell to me sending a spike of fear racing up my spine. "You used the blades to bring it down."

It wasn't a question, but I nodded anyway.

"You're lucky you succeeded. If you'd missed, if it had gotten away, it would have informed the order of your pretty enchanted blades."

His tone was patronizing, and it rubbed me up the wrong way. "I know how to fight, Bane. I'm not a newborn lamb. I knew what I was doing. And even if it had escaped and made its way back to the order, we don't know that they're even aware what the blades really are." it was on the tip of my tongue to say that not even the Black Wings were sure, but the warning glint in his eye had me biting back those words.

Getting onto the boss' bad side was just dumb. If I ever wanted to have my wings unclipped, I'd need to play it by the book.

Bane snorted in derision. "You think if they'd found out about a pair of enchanted blades that they'd just shrug and drop it? If they find out about a magical item, they'll look into it. Hard. It's what they do. It's who they are. They're arcane addicts, humans who should have gone scourge but didn't. Instead they formed a fucking cult that worships Merlin. If they find out what those blades are, they will come for you."

"And they'll have us to deal with," Ryker said. "No one messes with one of ours."

Everyone began to speak at once, their voices low murmurs, but my brain was doing that going off on a tangent thing it had a habit of doing.

Humans who should have gone scourge? Is that how the Order had gotten hold of their access to magick? "But why?"

Bane broke off in his conversation with Ryker. "Why, what?"

"Why does the arcane affect the Order differently?"

Bane turned his head on his thick neck to look at me. He was standing by the hearth, dwarfing it with his huge frame, the brandy glass tiny in his paw of a hand. And now his entire attention was on me, every hair on my body quivered.

My mouth went dry. "I'm just saying, there has to be a reason, right?"

"If there is then we're none the wiser," Rivers said. "It's probably something genetic."

Bane looked away, releasing me from the deep violet depths of his eyes. I exhaled slowly, and sat back in my seat.

"What I want to know is how it got into the compound in the first place?" Rivers asked. "The sentinels would have noticed it surely."

Bane tipped back his head and downed his drink. His throat bobbed once and then he set the glass on the mantle. "Not necessarily. A golem is made of earth. It's an inanimate object animated by magick, but it is *not* alive. The sentinels may have sensed it, possibly been confused by it, but they wouldn't have viewed it as a threat. This bubble you spoke of that muted the sound of the fight between you, probably affected them too."

"So what do we do now?" Rivers asked. "We can't just let them get away with this. They attacked our home."

Bane flicked his gaze to the siren. "We do exactly that. We act as if nothing has happened and we watch for their next move."

Movement caught my eye, a scuttling thing on the coffee table. A spider. I let out a squeak.

Rivers shifted forward and gently scooped up the crawly. "It's more scared of you than you are of it," he said.

He walked over to the window with the crawly cupped in his hand.

"I highly doubt that. Give me a ripper or a bloodsucker any day, but spiders, urgh." I shuddered.

Rivers cracked open the window and dropped the spider outside before reclaiming his seat,

"There are a couple of other things you need to know," Drayton said. "Serenity caught a Sanguinata trying to recruit at The Deep, and when we left we found an unconscious human female partially buried in the sand around the side of the building."

"Was Cassie with you?" Orin asked quietly.

Drayton's expression shuttered. "Yeah, she was. She didn't come back out with us though. She bumped into an old friend."

Orin dropped his gaze to his lap. "Okay."

Oh, man. This sucked.

"What did you do with the human?" Bane asked.

Drayton filled him in on the hospital visit and the MED showing up. He even gave them a word by word account of my smack down of Giles.

Bane's brow arched. "So, our new member has bite. Good." He cocked his head. "Arrange a formal appointment with Dorian and take Harker with you when you go. We have a Sanguinata recruiting illegally and missing humans, we can't discount the possibility that the cases may be linked, and we need to do everything by the book. If this does go to the district council, we can't risk their legal representatives pulling the case apart. In fact, draw up a warrant and send it to the district council for approval first."

I sat forward. "Shouldn't we wait on the missing persons files before we act?"

Bane didn't look at me. "Harker is right. Chase the files, then send the warrant."

Drayton tensed. "A warrant will just get their backs up, and if they do know something then they'll clam up."

It was the same argument he'd given me, but from the frosty look on Bane's face, he wasn't buying it.

"They're backs should be up," Bane snapped. "This is a missing persons investigation tied in to an illegal recruitment campaign. You tell them that and, trust me, they'll talk. House Vitae does not like scandal. It will be in their best interests to aid our investigation. Take a damned warrant. Do it right."

Drayton clenched his jaw and for a brief moment I thought he'd argue further, but then he dropped his gaze. "Fine."

An icy breeze tickled the back of my neck and the flames in the hearth dropped then rose hungrily. Bane's chin jerked up, his head slightly to the side as if listening for something, and then the click of heels reverberated against stone.

Ryker cursed softly under his breath, but Orin sat up straighter and Rivers tucked in his chin, pressing himself into his seat.

Drayton's body relaxed, as if every knot and clenched muscle had suddenly, spontaneously unwound. He melted back against the sofa just as a stunning raven-haired woman sashayed into the room. Her hair was long and poker straight with a blunt fringe that on someone less striking would have looked ridiculous, but with her cat's eyes and her high cheekbones she was able to pull it off easily. Her lips were rouged deep crimson and her long fingernails were painted to match. She was dressed all in black, accentuating her pale complexion.

Bane, the man who could probably make a mountain cry, looked as if someone had reached into his chest and wrapped a hand around his beating heart. And then his expression smoothed out into impassivity.

"Lilith. You're early," Bane said.

"Merely a day," She shrugged. "I thought we could enjoy each other for that little bit longer."

Her choice of words was weird. Enjoy each other? Surely she meant enjoy each other's company. I looked to Ryker who had his gaze fixed on the coffee table, then to Orin who was staring at Lilith as if he'd spent days crawling through a desert and she was a tall glass of water. Rivers had his head down, silent and tense, and Drayton sat with his arms out on the back of the sofa perfectly at ease.

Lilith strolled over, her gaze rippling over us all. Her attention snagged on me and her eyes narrowed a fraction.

"You have a new arrival." She studied me for a moment longer.

My shields were up, but I felt her testing them, pushing and running her claws down them.

"Oh, my. How delightful," she said. "Daughter of mine." She stepped around the long sofa that Ryker, Rivers and Drayton occupied and came to stand before me. "Bane, you have a cambion."

"I know," Bane said.

How did she do that? How could she see through my shields when the Black Wings couldn't?

She crouched so that we were eye to eye. "And what can you do, little cambion?" she purred.

"Leave her alone, Lilith. She's nothing special," Bane said.

Well, that stung. Lilith pouted, her dark eyes scanning my face. "Oh, but I beg to differ. Cambions are *always* special. We could add some flavor to our tryst. A little red haired spice?"

Wait? What was she suggesting?

"No," Bane said.

She dropped me a wink and stood.

"Maybe next time, love."

She took her time walking back around the sofa, the same way she'd come, and stopped behind Drayton. He grew still, and closed his eyes. She slowly moved her hand to rest on his head. He let out a soft sigh and she smiled. A wicked kind of smile, and then she dug her nails into his scalp.

Bane moved so fast he was almost a blur, and then he'd scooped up Lilith and swept her out of the room.

I jumped out of my seat. "What the fuck just happened?"

Rivers got up and stormed out of the room.

Orin slumped back in his seat. "I fucking hate that woman."

"Really?" Ryker said. "Because it looked like you wanted to fuck her."

It was the first time I'd heard him use foul language, and it was like a slap on the face, even though it wasn't directed at me.

Drayton sat up, blinking as if waking up from a dream. "Has she gone?"

Ryker made a chuffing noise through his nose. "Yeah, you can stop begging for a pat now."

"Fuck you, Ryker." Drayton followed Rivers in the whole storming out the room deal.

Orin sighed. "She's a bitch no doubt."

Okay, I was so lost. "Can someone please fill me in?"

"Hey." Cassie stood in the archway to the foyer, her eyes wide with shock. "What the heck happened to the drive?"

Orin's lips tightened. "You were with Killion, weren't you?"

Cassie rolled her eyes. "Oh, for fuck's sake, Orin. I asked about the damned driveway, if you're gonna go all jealous boyfriend, then please go do it somewhere else."

He snapped his mouth closed, stood slowly and walked right past her.

Her shoulders sagged and she closed her eyes for a long beat before turning on her heel and following him out of the room.

Ryker shook his head. "She needs to sort her shit out."

"Who? Cassie?"

"Yes. Orin is a good guy, but good isn't exciting enough for Cassie."

"But Killion is?"

"Yeah, and he treats her like shit. Thing is, if Killion treated her right, Orin wouldn't have an issue with the whole open relationship thing. He cares about her enough to want her to be happy."

I'd seen it often enough, the whole bad boy syndrome. "She'll figure it out. She's smart."

"Not when it comes to matters of the heart. When it comes to relationships and emotions, Cassie is like a tangled poisonous vine."

"And this Lilith? Who is she?"

Ryker's sat forward in his seat. "Lilith is Bane's cross to bear. She's a succubus, the first of her kind if legend has it right. The mother of all incubi and succubus. Legend has it that she was the first neph. She's a pure blood if I've ever seen one, and if she has any emotions, they're hidden from me."

"You've tried to read her?"

He nodded slowly. "There's nothing. Like just a void."

"And what does she want with Bane?"

He dropped his gaze. "She feeds on him. Once every couple of months she just turns up and takes her fill."

"But why? Why would he let her do that?"

Ryker shrugged. "Some kind of deal, a pact, I don't know. None of us do. Sometimes I doubt even Bane does. His emotions are...complex, convoluted and confused. Almost as if he doesn't know who he should be or what he should be feeling."

"How long has this been going on?"

"For as long as I've been working for the Protectorate, which may as well be forever."

"Forever? You can't be more than

twenty-five."

Ryker's eyes crinkled. "Try eighty-three."

My mouth fell open. Of course neph didn't age like humans.

He laughed. "The more Black Wing blood you have, the slower you age."

Wow, well, that was good to know.

"Anyway," he said. "Steer clear of her. She seems to have a strange effect on many nephs, especially incubi and succubus, so who knows what she can do to a cambion."

"Was that why Drayton went all buttery on the sofa?"

Ryker picked up his glass. It still had half a finger of whiskey at the bottom. He took a sip. "She affects him the worst. He usually makes sure he's out when he knows she's coming. She surprised us today."

"A lot of things have surprised us today. Wait. Don't tell me it's not always like this?"

Ryker smiled. "Don't worry. I won't."

Should I ask Ryker about Viola? It wasn't any of my business, but curiosity was burning a slow hole in my stomach. "We went to the cemetery today."

Ryker stilled. "You did?" he said without inflection.

"We picked up a ghost called Murray and we had to return him. We met Viola."

He let out a low whistle. "This has truly

been a day of surprises for Dray. I feel like an arsehole for being so harsh on him about Lilith now."

"So, what's the story there?"

His gaze sharpened. "Don't. If Dray wants you to know, he'll tell you."

I winced. "I'm sorry. That was nosey."

He closed his eyes and puffed out his cheeks. "It was, but I can't honestly blame you. You've been thrown into the deep end amongst a group of nephs with their own dynamic and secrets, and you're trying to find how you fit in. It will happen, Harker. Trust me."

Behind my shield, the hunger stirred.

"Serenity, do you need to feed?" Ryker asked hesitantly.

I smiled. "I'm good." This was just a pang. I could go days before I needed to recharge.

"In that case, get some sleep." He stretched. "I certainly need it. The Protectorate have a big day tomorrow."

Big day? "The warrant?"

He smiled thinly. "The warrant will take at least a day to be approved by the district office. We have the scourge to worry about. Tomorrow they run."

"I need to come with you guys."

Ryker frowned. "Bane hasn't cleared you for patrol duty yet, there is no way he'll let you go on the run. He is allowing you to work the warrant with Dray, so that's a great sign." He smiled to soften the news. "Just be patient and learn the ropes, and you'll be on patrol in no time."

I returned his smile, and nodded, but I was damned if I was sitting twiddling my thumbs tomorrow.

I was going on that run.

Bed was a good idea, but my feet led me to Drayton's part of the mansion and came to a halt outside his door. Was he all right? He'd been through a lot today, what with Viola and then Lilith taking him over like that. But maybe he needed to be left alone...

I knocked on the door before my subconscious talked me out of it. He didn't answer. Maybe he wasn't there, so why the heck was I turning the door handle, and yep, I was going in. This was the first time I'd been inside his room. It was pretty similar to Ryker's except for the lack of books. Drayton obviously wasn't a huge reader, which was okay. There was a chess board set up on a coffee table by the small hearth. Two wing backs faced each other on either side of the table. It was a game in progress with invisible players.

The ensuite bathroom door opened, and

Drayton stepped into the room, toweling his damp hair. His chest was bare, bronze, taut and smooth, and he was wearing loose pajama bottoms. He stopped, startled, when he caught sight of me, and then the surprise was wiped away by his signature unperturbed expression. The one that could turn wicked and suggestive at any moment. Yep, there it was—the slight flick at the corners of his mouth, and the glint of impish intention in his eyes. He draped the towel around his neck and slowly padded toward me.

"Do you need to feed, Harker?" His tone dropped an octave, reminding me of thick, dark honey—the sweet sticky kind that clung to the inside of your throat on its way down. "Do you need me to feed you?"

He stopped inches away, and the heat from his body mingled with mine. His breath stirred the fine hairs at my crown, a caress that skimmed my hairline and wrapped around my ear. He licked his lips and it was impossible not to be drawn to them. They were perfectly formed lips. The kind of lips that a woman could spend hours exploring with her mouth and her tongue. The kind of lips that any woman would die to have explore her body and her most intimate place.

His chuckle was a low rumble in his chest. "Your face is so expressive. Your eyes tell a thousand secrets." He cocked his head studying me intensely. "Did you know that when you're aroused your lips grow fuller, your pupils dilate and you get these tiny patches of flushed skin on the tops of your cheekbones, and here — he reached out to run a finger across my chest just under my collar bones — you blush here. My breath hitched and caught. What was he doing?

His lids grew heavy. His mouth parted and he leaned in. He was a magnetic force drawing me in and tempting me with delights my body craved — a wanton craving that throbbed at the apex of my thighs. With the desire came a rolling anxiety, familiar and bitter. I took an instinctive step back.

"I'm not human, Serenity," he said softly. "You can't hurt me."

Not human. Of course. I could lose myself with him, abandon the shields and allow myself to let go and just bathe in sensation. I could discard all propriety and let him touch me in all the ways my body longed to be touched. I could explore him in turn. With my hands and my lips, I could wipe away the darkness that hovered at the edges of his smile and chase away the shadows in his eyes. This was the beginning. This was more than a physical attraction. Cassie's words came back to me. *Incubi can't fall in love and have long term relationships, Serenity. That kind of connection would drive both the female and the incubus insane...There is the incubus, hungry, intense and single minded in his pursuit of what he needs, and then there is playful Drayton, sated and chilled.* Who was he now? His tone had been light-hearted at first but now his eyes blazed with resolute hunger. But I wasn't running, in fact I was stepping closer, my fingers itching to touch his skin, to skim across the velvet expanse of his chest and feel his muscles jump beneath my fingertips. I wanted his body to dance to my tune, to hear him moan when I took him inside me. My breath was coming shallow, short and raspy as carnal images and thoughts tumbled through my mind. Was this me or him? Was he Drayton or the incubus?

Incubi can't fall in love

That kind of connection would drive both the female and the incubus insane

Right now, in this moment I didn't care, and that lack of self-preservation nudged my common sense. This wasn't me. I was the level headed, keep the shields up and protect her younger sister Harker. I'd spent my life assessing risks, hiding what I was to protect those I loved. I was a survivor, and if I let him, then Drayton could be the death of me. But his allure, his pull was too strong, and his hands as they skimmed up my arms were like brands igniting a deep fire that my body ached to be consumed in.

This wasn't Drayton, this was the incubus and the incubus cared only about feeding. I needed to step away. No, don't tilt your chin up. Don't let his lips touch yours.

"Viola." Her name was a whisper, a plea, squeezing past my tight vocal cords.

Drayton's hands stilled.

"She said she forgives you. That it wasn't your fault."

The fire in his eyes winked out and his hands slid from my body. "Get out," he said levelly.

I didn't need telling twice.

My body was aching and my veins burned with a strange fire. The mansion, even with its cold stone structure and high ceilings, was suddenly too hot. Its walls were too close and caged in. There were several exits out of the building, but the nearest was through the kitchen, so I took that one. Out on the chilly flagstones, breathing in the icy air, the buzz in my blood dulled to a hum. Yes, this was better. The clouds from earlier had dissipated, and the sky was an inky blanket of twinkling diamonds. The moon sat like a polished silver disc high above—the jewel of Midnight. The gardens were a place I'd neglected to explore. Aside from popping over to meet the rest of the Protectorate at the guesthouse, I'd barely spent any time out here. The cracked flagstones lead away from the house, through the long grass and toward the tree line. The Protectorate used the forest for outdoor training, there were targets pinned to trees, ropes and pulleys suspended in the foliage, and all sorts. The guesthouse was to the east of the forest—two huge buildings linked by a covered walkway. It housed twenty primary nephs. It would be a while until I got to know them all. My heart rate had finally slowed down. Thank goodness Cassie had filled me in on Drayton and the whole incubus insanity thing. Thank goodness Viola's words had been rattling inside my head. The canopy of trees closed in above me and a different kind of silence wrapped itself around me—thick and comforting. The muscles in my back unknotted, and my pace slowed to a leisurely stroll.

What was Jesse doing right now? How was she coping without me? Was Nolan keeping his promise to watch over her? She was strong, independent, but she needed company like a flower needed the sun. How would she cope with living alone?

The earth swallowed the sounds of my footsteps and then a muted *thud, thud, thud*, cracked the cocoon of silence. I froze. What the heck was that? Another golem, perhaps?

Thud, thud, thud.

Dammit. I continued toward the sound, wary now, lighter on my feet and ready to bolt if need be. I made a note of every tree root and stray branch in my path in case I needed to run back this way. The trees began to thin out and a clearing came into view. It was an area of land dominated by the ruins of some forgotten building—a pavilion. White gray stone glinted in the harsh moonlight—an arch here, a pillar there, crumbling steps and a stone bench covered in thick dark moss. Movement caught my eye as a figure emerged from around the structure. Half bathed in shadow, his mammoth form moved easily over the rumble. I shrank back into the cover of the trees. Bane came to a standstill several meters away. His bare back faced me and his breath plumed in the air. What was he doing out here all alone? Had Lilith finished her feeding? Was he simply trying to escape from her?

He bunched his huge hands at his side, and even from this distance the dark stain of blood was visible on his knuckles. He wound back his arm and whipped forward smashing his fist into the pillar. He punched it over and over leaving smears of crimson on the rock and then he slumped against it, his forehead pressed to the stone. His back rippled and his shoulders rose and fell rapidly. He pushed off, stepped back and attacked the pillar again.

This was pain. This was grief. This was his private moment, and I was an intruder, but the urge to walk toward him, to put my hand on his shoulder and somehow sooth his pain was a twisted wave of desire. My mind asserted control over my impulses. The last thing he needed was a reminder of Lilith and, as a cambion, that was exactly what I was. It was time to slip away, back toward the mansion and leave him to this private moment. I took a step back just as Bane finished a round of punch-the-pillar and the snap of a twig rang like a gunshot through the night.

Not me, it wasn't me. The crack had come from my far left, from another part of the tree line. Bane's head whipped round and his harsh profile was highlighted in silver.

A figure stepped out into the clearing. It was Lilith. Her long, dark hair trailed down her back and her body was encased in a thin white nightdress that ended at her knees and left very little to the imagination. She had to be freezing, right? Her nipples were practically poking out through the fabric, but she walked over to Bane, her hips swaying seductively, not a tremor in sight.

"Oh, come now, Bane. Surely it wasn't that bad?" she drawled.

He turned his head away, the muscles in his lower back clenching.

She reached him and slid her hand up his spine. "We're nowhere near finished." She leaned in and ran her tongue up his arm.

His head snapped up as if she'd applied a shot of electricity to his flesh.

She clutched his face and forced him to look at her. "See me." She pressed herself against his side, rolling her hips, so her nightdress rode up. "Want me."

Her voice was a seductive purr that ran through me, shooting to my core and rubbing against that nub of desire that I'd kept under lock and key for way too long. I clamped my legs together and bit back a gasp. But Bane's moan of need would have covered any sound I'd have made.

"Fuck me, Bane." Her hand slipped under her dress, and it was obvious what she was doing by the sounds that vibrated in her throat. "Fuck me like you mean it."

His jaw flexed beneath her crimson talon fingers. "No."

She chuckled sexy and breathy. "No?"

"No." He closed his eyes as if holding on to that word.

Her hand slid from his face. "We have a deal, Bane. Whether you like it or not, for the next few hours you belong to me." She lowered herself to her knees and undid his trousers before roughly shoving him back against the pillar. "You *will* want me Bane. You *will* give me what I want."

He was facing me now, back pressed to

the stone, eyes still closed. And in the moonlight, his savage face was etched in torment.

Lilith took him in her mouth, at least that's what I assumed she was doing, because the back of her head began to move.

"Please..." Bane's voice was a strangled rasp.

It was a plea, but whether for her to continue or stop, I wasn't sure. Blood was pounding in my ears too hard to think straight.

Lilith leaned back. "You're too large." She sounded annoyed and was about to stand when he grabbed the back of her head.

"You want me," he said with a growl. "Then fucking take it." He yanked her head against this crotch and her gags filled the air.

I clapped a hand over my mouth. The sounds she was making were horrific, and then she began to gulp and moan as if she was enjoying it? Bane sucked in a breath through clenched teeth. His body jerking as he thrust his crotch into her face. He was fucking her, but probably not the way she'd expected. He slammed his head back against the pillar.

"Fuck. Fuck you, Lilith. Fuck you."

And then he opened his eyes—glowing violet orbs—and looked right at me. My heart stalled in my chest. I was frozen in place for the briefest of moments, and then my pulse kick-started and I turned and ran.

I was soundless like the wind, leaping over the danger spots as tree trunks whizzed by. I'd always been fast, but never been able to run to my full potential. Here in the forest, for a moment I forgot what I was running from and what I'd just seen. I ran simply for the liberation of it.

And then I slammed into a wall.

No. Not a wall. A warm hard body, with fingers that latched on to my upper arms.

I looked up into dark eyes that seemed to be drinking me in. Movement behind the man caught my eye. Huge black wings.

A Black Wing. Not Abbadon though. This was someone else.

"Hello, little not human." The Black Wing cocked his head. "How are our daggers?"

The heat from his fingers seeped through the fabric of my shirt to singe my skin, I tried to jerk out of his grasp and he tightened his grip in response.

"Let go of me."

His beautiful mouth curled in a seductive smile. "Or what?"

I brought my knee up intent on crushing some balls, but he spun me, and pulled me against him, my back to his chest. His arms were bands of iron. There was no point in fighting him but I could siphon and—

"Don't even think about it." His breath was hot against my ear. "Abbadon may have waived your punishment for feeding from him, but try that trick on me, and I will hurt you."

I sagged against him. "Who are you and what do you want from me?"

"I want to know why the daggers chose you. What is so special about you? Aren't you curious? Don't you want to know?" His tone had softened, persuasive and seductive.

My head grew fuzzy. Yes. Of course I wanted to know. I needed to know.

"Come with me and we can find out together."

Go with him...wait. What the heck was I thinking? "No. I'm not going anywhere with you."

His grip tightened. "I'm the only one who remembers why we are here. We are at war, little cambion, and you are in possession of something vital. You're not safe here and you *will* come with me."

My pulse jumped. "No. Abbadon agreed I could stay here. I can take care of myself."

"Like you did when the compound was attacked by a Golem?"

He knew about that. "Wait, did you

send it?"

He snorted in disgust. "Black Wings have no need of arcane magick. We claim what we desire."

"Bit arrogant, aren't we?"

He shoved me away so hard I lost my balance and hit the ground.

"You nephs have forgotten the purpose of your creation. You are meant to serve us." He strode toward me. "Not to question. Now get up and do not fight me."

Fuck this. I kicked out, connecting with his knee. The impact was jarring and pain exploded in my knee.

My cry was short and sharp, cut off by the palm of his hand. He hauled me up, as tears streamed down my cheeks.

"You will be safe with us." His tone was softer, almost apologetic. The air stirred behind me and the Black Wing tore his gaze from my face to look over my head.

"Let her go, Abigor."

The voice was huskier and worn, but the tone was familiar.

Bane.

Abigor's face tightened. "She belongs with us, Bane."

"No. She belongs to me. This is my land. My place. You do not rule here." His voice gathered in strength, growing louder.

Was he getting closer?

"The daggers belong with us," Abigor said.

"And yet you gave them to me for safe keeping. And yet they chose the cambion to bond with. I'm beginning to think you're hiding something."

Abigor's wings flexed and ice trickled through my veins. He was getting ready to take off, and he still had hold of me. I began to struggle in earnest. No way was I going with this sadistic Black Wing.

And then he was rising, taking me with him. I kicked my legs, clawing at his hand. His wings beat hard and the world fell away. No. I didn't want this, didn't... My hands grew hot and the blades settled into my palms.

Abigor's eyes widened. "Don't—

His plea was cut off as something slammed into us. The daggers winked out, and I was falling, slow at first and then faster and faster as gravity took hold and the ground rose up eager to greet me. Jesse's face flashed before my eyes and her laugh echoed in my ears. Drayton's smile and Nolan's mock frown filled my vision.

I was going to die.

I closed my eyes and braced for the pain of impact, and then arms wound around me and my body jerked as my descent was halted.

"Harker? Harker, dammit!"

I opened my eyes and stared into Bane's violet gaze. How...how was he doing this? The answer rose up behind him in the form of enormous obsidian, bat-like wings. The beat steady and sure.

"You're safe now," he said. Then he cradled me to his chest and rose higher.

It was like being hugged by a giant, all muscle and heat and security. I buried my head in the crook of his neck and his fingers flexed against the sensitive flesh of my abdomen where my shirt had ridden up.

We landed a moment later, and he set me gently on my feet. The world swayed. No that was me, but he steadied me with gentle calloused hands.

"You're all right now," he said again. "What were you doing in the forest at night?"

The question was delivered innocently enough, as if he wasn't really curious and was just making polite conversation, but there was no mistaking the underlying threat to his words. He'd either seen me and wasn't sure I'd caught him looking, or he hadn't, but was wondering if I'd seen him?

I met his gaze squarely and matched his light tone. "I—I needed some fresh air."

He studied me for a long beat, and his left eye twitched. He swallowed and dropped his gaze. "You're lucky that I had the same inclination."

Shit. He knew. It was evident in the sudden tension in his shoulders, in the fact that he would no longer meet my eyes. He knew I'd seen him and he was...ashamed. The knowledge was a blow to my gut. I wanted to reach out and smooth away the tightness around his mouth. To tell him that no, there was no need for him to look away, that it was Lilith that should be ashamed, that she should be the one to hide away for what she was doing to him. But to do so would be to admit I'd witnessed his sexual domination, and that would rip this flimsy charade to shreds. Instead, I curled my fingers into fists, my nails biting into the palms of my hands, and changed the subject.

"Who was that Black Wing?"

He slowly raised his head. "Abigor is an authority unto himself, and he would have taken you by force. I'll speak to Abbadon about this. It won't happen again." His jaw tightened and flexed. He meant it. "The same deal applies, Harker. The others mustn't know."

"But they're Black Wings. What can you do?"

His lip curled flashing those elongated canines, and my insides twisted and lurched leaving me breathless.

"I can remind them that my assistance is a privilege *not* a right." The shadows in his eyes melted to be replaced by a wicked gleam. "I need to remind them that no one takes what's mine." His gaze raked over me sending heat rising from the tips of my toes to bloom on my cheeks. His gaze narrowed speculatively, and he took a step closer to me. "You're hungry. You need to feed."

The dark need stirred. "I'm fine."

He took another step until I was pressed up against the door that exited the roost. "No. You're not. Why do you deny yourself the sustenance you need?"

He was so close now that I could see the tiny stubble hairs on his jaw. "I don't *need* to feed." Damn it, did I have to squeak?

"You still fight your nature?" His voice rose in surprise.

I made an incredulous sound. "Yeah, yes I fight it. I don't want to have to feed off other people's energy or their power. I know I have to, but it doesn't mean I like it. I'm in control and trust me I can wait."

His tone softened. "Harker, you are not in control if you have to fight your nature. The more you disassociate yourself from what you are and what you need, the more power you give the darkness within. But once you embrace it, listen to it and give it what it wants, you'll finally be free."

He had no idea what he was talking about. What it was like to be a power sucking monster. At least here I had willing nephs to feed off, and enough scourge for a feast. But back in Sunset, everywhere I'd gone had been an all-you-could-eat buffet that was out of bounds, because one slip, one moment of letting my guard down would have resulted in someone's death. My shields and my control were what had saved those people and protected me. There was no way I was giving those up for a few inspirational, and yeah, slightly intriguing words.

He was waiting for a response. I cleared my throat. "I'm good. Thanks."

He shook his head, as if washing his hands of me. "If you need to feed, come find me. My power seemed to keep you sustained for longer last time."

My eyes widened at the offer. "Um, thanks." While he was in a good mood. "There is something you can help me with."

"You want to go on the run, don't you?"

My pulse picked up. "I'm ready. I promise I won't let you down."

His lips twitched and then he unlatched the door behind me. "Sleep well, Harker. You'll need to be on full form tomorrow if you're going to be on duty."

"Really?"

He arched a brow. "Go, before I change my mind."

I ducked through the doorway and ran down the steps.

My bedroom door locked, I stripped down, climbed into bed and closed my eyes. I was going on the scourge run tomorrow. Bane had said yes...he'd said yes after saying no to my patrolling for weeks. A horrific though unfurled in my mind. He knew I'd seen him...was he backing down because he wanted to keep me quiet about what I'd seen? *The same deal applies, Harker. The others mustn't know.* I'd assumed he was referring to the Black Wings, but what if he'd been referring to what I'd seen Lilith doing to him? As if summoned by the thought, images of Bane pressed to the stone pillar tumbled through my mind. What kind of deal would have made him agree to this? What could she have possibly done for him to make him agree to be her sexual energy regenerator four times a year? And how could he think I'd say anything to anyone about his private pain.

There was a knock at my door.

Oh, shit. Was it Bane?

"Serenity. It's me, Drayton. Are you awake?"

Urgh. No more. I couldn't deal right now. Burrowing under the duvet, I held my breath. This place and these people who were responsible for the protection of humanity were a mess of wounds and secrets. And with my unknown past, and my auto-aversion to relationships, I'd fit in just fine, but right now I needed to switch off.

"I know you're awake, I heard you come in," Drayton said.

Darn it.

I climbed out of bed but couldn't bring myself to open the door. Lilith's power over Bane and Drayton's hold over me earlier was all mingled together in my mind, and I wasn't sure I'd be able to resist if he tried to get close to me again. If he touched me or looked at me with that ravenous flame in his eyes, I'd buckle. I'd let him take me and I'd be damned.

I pressed my palms to the door. "Who am I speaking to now? Drayton or the Incubus?"

"I'm sorry. I didn't mean to...I wasn't myself."

He sounded so torn. My hand dropped to the key in the lock. Wait, what was I doing? I curled my fingers. "Is this to do with Lilith?"

"She has a destabilizing effect on me. If I'd known she was coming, I'd have made myself scarce."

Ryker had said exactly that. "It's all right. I just need to sleep, okay."

"Do you forgive me?"

What was there to forgive? He was an incubus doing incubus things, why would I expect any different? Besides, if anyone was to blame around here, it was the bitch Lilith. She'd messed with Drayton's head and wrangled Bane into a box. Even though it looked like Bane had taken control at the end, I couldn't help but wonder if that had been her ploy all along.

I pressed my cheek to the wood. "Why does it matter so much to you what I think?"

"Because I... because we have to work together and for that to be effective you need to be able to trust me."

True trust was built with time, but for

now I'd just have to have conviction in them all. "It's fine I'm not mad. I forgive you."

His sigh was audible through the wood.

"Goodnight, Drayton."

His footsteps retreated, and I climbed back under the warm duvet. Exhaling, I willed my body to relax and closed my eyes. Tomorrow the scourge would run, and I'd run with the Protectorate.

It was almost nine a.m., the moon was still hanging in the sky and the world was still dark through the kitchen window. It was still super weird laying my head down to the moon and waking up to it every morning. Somewhere in the deep recesses of my memory there was an image of the rising sun, golden and new and bright. There were noon days and twilight walks and sometimes, when I focused real hard, there was a firm hand gripping mine, along with a sense of complete and utter safety. I'd hold that memory in my head real tight, my eyes squeezed shut, and turn my head, desperate to see her face. But the recollection would shatter into a thousand tiny shards. It had been a while since I'd had a reminder of my unknown past. When was the last time I'd had that dream-like recollection? Two years ago? Maybe more? I wolfed down a bacon sandwich I'd thrown together. It was the breakfast of champions. The piled up plates and mugs in the sink indicated that the others had already broken their fasts and were off doing Protectorate things.

I washed my plate and dried my hands on the pretty yellow flower-print tea towel. Time to find Drayton. There was a warrant to file and we needed to check in with Tristan about the lab results for our Jane Doe. Drayton may already have received those details.

I found him in the study tapping away at the computer. A pile of files sat to his right and a mug of coffee to this left. The room was all dark wood and warm amber lighting cast by candelabras. Tucked behind the long mahogany desk, Drayton looked the part of a hot shot executive, well if you ignored the body hugging T-shirt and just got out of bed hair.

He looked up as I entered. "I'm busy what—" He broke off at the sight of me, and his gaze softened. "Harker, did you sleep well?"

Tiny butterflies bloomed to life in my stomach. "Yeah, like a log." I approached the desk. "Are these the missing persons files?" I picked up the top one and flipped it open.

"Yes. They arrived an hour ago. I also

spoke to Tristan. The labs came back."

I looked up from the photograph of a nerdy looking young man called Ben Hardly. "And?"

"They found traces of an unknown toxin in her bloodstream. They're still analyzing it, but Tristan said he's never seen anything like it. On a positive note, our Jane Doe is no longer a Jane Doe. Her name is Kerry Wilson and she's awake and fine. Only thing is, she doesn't recall anything about last night. She doesn't even remember going to The Deep. Although she says she recalls having plans to do so."

"Shit. So, that means she doesn't recall speaking to the Sanguinata."

His brows flicked up. "Wait. Was it the same woman?"

I winced. "Did I not mention that?"

He gave me a deadpan look. "No, you didn't. Bane was worried there was a possible link between the recruitment and the missing humans, and this actually gives us a link."

"Except for the fact she can't verify he even spoke to her, which makes it my word against his."

He shook his head dismissively. "If we need witnesses there were a ton of people there who we could talk to. I'll speak to Jonah and get him to put out feelers."

"Yes. Jonah knows about the missing

humans. He'll want to help."

"Good, so now we wait for the warrant, which I've just sent off to be signed and returned, once we get it back we can speak to Dorian at the House of Vitae."

Ryker had said it may take a day for the warrant to come back approved and signed, but I had to ask. "Will it be done today, do you think?"

He chuckled. "I love your enthusiasm, but it's highly unlikely. With the scourge running tonight they'll be tied up dealing with requests for sanctuary from humans not bonded to a house."

"Sanctuary?"

He shut down the computer and gave me his full attention. "The district council has several safe houses with a limited amount of space. The service isn't free and its first come, first served. Most humans prefer to lock themselves in their basements and ride it out. Some areas don't get hit and others get flooded. We never know where scourge will run until they actually run."

"Have all the scourge who run gone under?"

"I don't know. We just kill them. Have been doing so for years, but their numbers just aren't decreasing."

Now that was strange. If all the Protectorate were massacring scourge once a month then there really shouldn't be many of them left. "How many do you kill?"

He shrugged. "A lot. At least two or three each, and there are twenty-five of us in total. The rippers run in packs and are hard to bring down, it's mainly the bloodsuckers we cull, but Rivers thinks that unless we sever their spinal columns they're able to regenerate."

That might explain why the numbers weren't going down as fast as they should, but still. "Have you run the figures? Compared the number of humans turning to the rise in scourge numbers and then deducted your kills?"

He stared at me as if I was a strange specimen under a microscope. "No, Serenity, we haven't. We just kill them."

Which was great, but it didn't answer the question as to why they weren't making a dent in the number of scourge. "Do you keep a kill count?"

He snorted. "No. We're not big on paperwork here. We're more about the action."

"If you're killing as many as you say you are then, even with the few who do manage to regenerate, their numbers shouldn't be going back up that quickly. You should have made a dent."

His brow furrowed. "You have a

theory?"

"No. I don't know. It's just weird."

"No, you two are weird," Cassie said from the doorway. "It's scourge run night and you're holed up in the study?"

Drayton leaned back in his seat, a lazy smile spreading across his tanned face. "Has it started already?" he asked.

I looked from Cassie to Drayton. "Has what started?"

"The scourge game," she said with a twinkle in her eye. "Oh, honey, consider it your consolation prize for not being able to run with us tonight."

"Actually, Bane said I could go."

Cassie let out a low whistle. "Well, then we are so on."

Drayton smiled. "Congratulations for getting off the bench, Harker."

Cassie grabbed my hand. "Come and play. Trust me. It'll be great practice for later."

With a helpless shrug in Drayton's direction, I let her tug me from the room.

The outskirts of the forest were teaming with primary Protectorate carrying paintball guns. Rivers and Orin stood chatting to a couple of young officers who looked familiar, and Ryker was crouched on the ground tightening his bootlaces.

He straightened when he caught sight of us and raised a hand. "Are you joining us for the game?"

Cassie put her arm around my shoulder and hugged me to her. "Better than that, Serenity is joining us for the run tonight."

Ryker blinked slowly. "Bane approved this?"

I shrugged and gave him a sheepish grin. "Yep."

Rivers and Orin broke away from their conversation and joined us, both looked psyched.

"You ready to do some tagging?" Orin said. He walked over to a nearby tree and a large crate with a few guns still sticking out. "Grab a paintball gun and load up with ammo. You ever played before?"

I shook my head. "But I'm sure I'll pick it up."

Cassie grabbed a gun and handed another to Ryker. Drayton strolled over and took the last weapon.

"Don't we need protective gear or something?" I'd seen humans play this game all armored up with helmets and stuff.

Rivers snorted. "We don't do the protective gear. We just avoid getting hit."

Okay. "So, do we have teams? How do we do this?"

Ryker grinned and glanced at the twenty odd Protectorate members. "Yeah, we have teams. It's us against them."

A neph guy called Gary booed. "This time the scourge are gonna win."

The scourge, I looked to Drayton.

"Their playing the scourge and we have to tag as many as we can. You get hit you leave the game, simple. So don't get hit."

Gary lifted his gun. "See you on the other side." He turned and with a whoop led the others into the forest.

"We give them ten minutes to hide and then we go in," Cassie said, hand on hip.

The air crackled with excitement as the minutes ticked by and even Drayton's relaxed demeanor tightened into something resembling anticipation. The energy was infectious, a hint of what was to come, and then Orin jerked his head toward the forest and we went in.

My butt ached from where the paintball had hit it. So much for not needing padded clothing. The bruise covered the whole of my ass cheek. I'd twisted in the mirror trying to get a look at it earlier, black and purple and red at the edges. Sitting down would be an issue for a few days, but there was no time to dwell on that now. It was time to gather in the foyer, but I didn't want to go down alone. Nerves and all that.

I knocked on Ryker's door. There was no answer. I knocked again and ducked in. "Hello?"

He'd said to knock for him. This wasn't my first time in his room, but it was my first time in here alone, and it was impossible not to have a proper look around. People's bedrooms were usually a map of their psyche and Ryker's was filled with literature and pillows. The guy *loved* pillows. A glint of gold caught my eye from his bedside table—a photo frame. I crossed the room and picked it up. It was a picture of a woman, but all I could see was the smile because most of her features were obscured by her red hair whipping into her face. Ryker was in the shot too, his arm around her neck as he pressed his lips to the side of her head. It was a beautiful natural shot and I could almost hear the laughter. Who was she? A girlfriend? He hadn't mentioned anyone. Suddenly, being in his room felt too invasive.

I placed the picture back in its place and left. I'd just closed the door when Ryker rounded the corridor.

"Hey, there you are," he said.

"I was just about to knock for you," I lied.

He glanced at my hand on the doorknob

then back at my face. "We should get downstairs."

"Sure."

The foyer was buzzing with Protectorate as they checked the rota and divvied up into their groups. The district had been split into three sectors and the twenty primary nephs had been split roughly into three groups to be headed up by Bane and co.

Rivers strolled over to me in my spot at the bottom of the stairwell. "Um, you did good out there today."

"Thanks, tell that to my butt."

He grinned. "Yeah, that was some shot." His expression sobered. "It's gonna be tough out there tonight, and I think you should feed before we go out."

I offered him a slow blink. "What? No. What makes you think I..." My gaze slid past him to catch Drayton watching us, his bottom lip caught between his teeth. "Oh. Drayton put you up to this, didn't he?"

River's shrugged. "Look, I get that it's awkward feeding off Drayton because of his incubus nature and Ryker doesn't go in for that stuff, but you're one of the team, and I can't let you go out there unless you're at your best."

I wanted to argue that I'd managed fine in Sunset, that I could hold my own without someone else's energy coursing through my veins, but there was no denying the gnawing hunger in my solar plexus or the fact that I'd been holding back a yawn for the past three hours.

I pressed my lips together and nodded. "Thank you. I appreciate that."

He smiled tightly. "Should we..." He jerked his head toward the lounge.

"Yes. That would..."

We both shuffled along the wall and slipped into the empty lounge.

Rivers pulled up his shirt sleeve and held out his arm. His skin was pale in comparison to Drayton. He was slimmer, more wiry than buff, but his arm under my fingers was taut and strong. I closed my eyes and dropped my shields. The hunger lashed out and latched on and then the scent of the ocean filled my head — the salty tang of the sea, the fresh brisk breeze, and the chilly yet satisfying taste of his power as it rushed into me. I breathed even and regulated just as Drayton had taught me in our sessions. Monitoring the intake until...

Enough.

I tried to pull back, but the hunger held on, stubborn and resilient now I'd let her out of the box. Shit. This was not supposed to happen. With a deep breath, I exerted control and peeled my fingers from his skin. My shields were still wide open and Rivers was staring at me in awe.

His hand came up to hover by my cheek. "What is this?"

He was seeing the darkness. He was seeing the hunger. No. I slammed the shields down and stepped back, ducking my head to cover my face.

"I'm sorry. I..."

I slowly raised my head. "It's not your fault."

A gentle frown marred his forehead. "I didn't realize you could shine."

What was he talking about?

"Harker?" Ryker popped his head through the arch. "You okay?" He glanced from Rivers back to me.

Rivers quickly pulled down his sleeve and my cheeks heated in shame. I hated that I'd needed to do that.

Rivers pushed past Ryker and out into the foyer.

"Are you all right?" Ryker asked again.

I cleared my throat. "I'm fine. Rivers was just fueling me up."

He nodded curtly and led me back into the foyer. "Good. We need you on form out there. You can stick with me and Dray. Cassie and Orin usually team up. And Rivers usually goes with Bane."

The slight knot in my chest eased. Yeah, I'd wanted this. The paintball game, which had been brutal, had given me a slight idea of what to expect, but it had been just that, a game. We were about to do this for real, and the atmosphere in the foyer was a mixture of fear and excitement, a heady concoction that reminded me too much of my moments with Bane.

Speaking of the boss, there he was, coming down the stairs. He was dressed in black from head to foot. The material stretched across his chest and over his biceps. His feet were clad in heavy boots and the hugest sword I'd ever seen was strapped to his back. Where were his wings? His glorious smooth glossy black wings?

He eyed the gathered nephs from his vantage point on the second to last step, arms folded across his chest.

The entrance hall was brightly lit tonight by the enormous chandelier suspended from the ceiling. It was the first time I'd seen it lit, and the foyer, which had always been a place of shadows and gloom, was transformed into a place of white marble and gold edged balustrades. This mansion must have been beautiful once upon a time.

"Rivers, you're with Cassie and Orin. Drayton you're with Ryker. Harker you're with me. Make sure your comms are operational and set the frequencies to receive your squad leader commands."

My heart hammered against my ribs. Had I heard right? I was with Bane? A quick look at Ryker's face confirmed that, yes, I had. He shrugged and shook his head. There was no time to dwell because Ryker was hooking a com device to my ear and static filled my head for a moment.

"You're linked to Bane and the alpha squad," Ryker said. "Test it."

I pressed the earpiece. "Testing, 1, 2, 3." It crackled.

"I hear you, Harker," Bane said.

Echoes of the word copy filled my ear as the rest of my squad connected with me.

Cassie had explained the protocol, but Ryker cupped my shoulders his expression intense.

"Stay with Bane and watch for the flare. It will tell us where the scourge is hitting us from."

"And then we head in that direction."

"Yes," Ryker smiled. "The great thing about the scourge is that they always run in a herd to begin with. If we can cut most of them down at their point of entry, we can then pull back and pick off the others one by one."

"Now, let's move out," Bane said. "We do this quick and we do it clean."

Icy air drifted into the foyer. Someone had cracked open the front doors. It was time to move out.

Bane and I crouched on a roof looking down on the residential street below.

"This area has been hit the hardest over the past few months," Bane said. "It seems to be a favorite for rippers. The residents here can't afford to claim sanctuary."

"How many deaths?"

"Too many. But not tonight." He flashed me a grin and my stomach flipped.

His hair was secured in a knot at the top of his head, accentuating the harsh lines of his face, the sweeping angle of his jaw and the aquiline lines of his nose. I'd been wrong before, he wasn't beastly, he was beautifully terrifying.

The corner of his mouth lifted. "Eyes on the street, Harker. Any minute now."

The other nephs had spread out in pairs to cover our sector. We didn't know which direction the scourge would attack from so we'd covered all our bases.

My earpiece fizzed to life. "We have movement eastside. Ripper pack," a voice I didn't recognize said.

Bane pressed his comm. "All units head east."

Bane pressed his fingertips to the roof, his body ready to launch. "Are you ready, Harker?"

I nodded, my heart in my mouth. Now we knew the direction the scourge was coming from, all units would run in that direction and cut down as many as we could.

Our earpieces crackled again. "Movement south side, boss. Another pack of rippers."

"North entrance, we have bloodsuckers incoming."

Bane froze.

"What is it? What do we do?"

"Hold tight, pick them off if you can," Bane said into his ear piece addressing the whole unit. "Westside unit head south as back up. Eastside we're on the way. North, hold your ground best you can." He shook his head. "This isn't right. They always attack as a heard, bloodsuckers and ripper packs."

"So, what do we do?"

Bane reached for his ammo belt and pulled out a flare gun. He stood, held it aloft and fired. The flare shot up into the air and exploded in a spray of fiery red and orange. He was summoning the other squads to our sector.

"We do the best we can."

We rode the roofs, shingle and slate underfoot as we leapt from house to house, cutting over garages and outbuildings as we crossed the sector eastward toward the ripper pack.

He could have flown, could have carried me but he didn't. Was that part of his secret too, or was he forcing me to do things the hard way as part of my training. It didn't matter because it was exhilarating. Rivers's power had reenergized me, and my body was an unstoppable machine ready to take on whatever.

The landscape flew by. I was fast but even with Bane's larger bulk he managed to stay a step ahead. It became a game trying to best him, and then the sounds of conflict, the screech and howl of the scourge drifted on the air to meet us. Bane landed in a crouch on top of a three story building. Below us, under amber street lights the rippers attacked. The two members of our squad who'd been watching this part of the sector were already down there working in a circle to fend then off. Bane leaned forward, his body swaying and then he leapt, his huge body making a graceful arc through the air. I gaped as he hit the ground in the center of the chaos, landing in a neat crouch. He drew his sword in one fluid move and began to swing. It was hypnotic and magnificent, and I needed to get my arse down there. I slipped onto the gutter pipe, clambered down half way and then let go, landing catlike. My hands bloomed with heat as the Aether daggers materialized and then I was sprinting into the action, right toward a leaping ripper. I dropped, bringing my daggers up and stabbing as the beast leapt over me. My blades sliced open its stomach, cutting the tough hide like it was nothing. I rolled, came up and took out another.

Twelve rippers, no, eleven. No, ten. Bane was tearing them down like they were paper dolls. Yes, between the four of us, we could do this. The other two squad members took down two more rippers and we were four to eight. The pack surrounded us, pushing us together. Back to back we circled, our weapons at the ready. And then a howl cut through the silence.

Bane cursed under his breath as another pack of rippers came running at us from down the street. Another fifteen at least.

We were so fucked.

Bane glanced my way, his jaw gritted. "Hold tight. We can do this."

As the fresh rippers attacked, shadows leapt toward us from the roofs, and rushed out from between the houses.

Ryker, Drayton and their squads were here.

"North side is clear," Ryker shouted over the snarls and growls. "The others are covered."

Bane flashed fang. "Let the culling continue."

My arms ached and my legs screamed for relief, but there was no stopping. They kept coming at us, Rippers and bloodsuckers, as if drawn to us like a hot spot. Cassie, Orin and their squad arrived a moment later, and we spread out between the buildings and spilled into the houses, killing the scourge before they could get to the humans. But even then, death stared back at us more often than not in the sightless eyes of a man, woman, and in one case a child. I'd lost Bane a while back and was hanging with Ryker, and now I was solo, cutting through a back garden in pursuit of a bloodsucker who'd strayed from the herd.

Someone screamed. Shrill and terrified. I leapt the fence to get to the source of the sound. A woman was being dragged down her garden path by her bloody ankle. Behind her, the window to the house was smashed, glass and splinters of wood, which she'd obviously used to board it up, littered the patio.

She caught sight of me. "Help. Help my babies please." She reached for the house. "It's inside. Please." The ripper with a hold of her paused, its yellow eyes locking on to me as if asking, *what you gonna do, bitch?*

I took a step toward the woman. and a high pitched wail rose up from the house.

"Save my babies!"

Fuck. I ran for the house, leapt through the broken window and barreled up the stairs. That high pitched wail again, this time accompanied by sobs and growls.

It was coming from a room at the end of the hallway with the smashed door. I sprinted toward it, taking in the scene in quick economic bursts. Two kids sat huddled on top of a large antique wardrobe. The mother must have hidden them up there when she'd heard the crash downstairs. They couldn't be more than four or five, twins by the looks of it.

The ripper turned its huge head to look at me.

I knew those eyes, even with the yellow tinge. "Romeo, is that you?"

The ripper growled low in its throat, but didn't attack.

"You don't want to do this. I know you'd never hurt a child."

Romeo wouldn't have, but this wasn't Romeo any longer. The Romeo I'd known had gone under. This was scourge. Still, I kept talking, because the idea of hurting him made me feel sick.

"Look, just go." I stepped away from the door to clear a path. "Just go, please." One of the others would probably find him and kill him, and yeah, that was how it would have to be because he was no longer human. It just couldn't be me.

He lowered his head. Was he going to comply? His haunches bunched. Looked like a no.

Your life must come first

"Who the heck are you?"

Watch out.

Romeo was sailing through the air toward me, and my brain was in freeze frame but my body wasn't, a tingle ran through me and the daggers took over, bringing my hands up in a defensive slashing motion. Romeo let out a sharp strangled sound and fell to the ground. His body twitched and I stared at my hands.

How did you do that?

But the daggers vanished taking the voice with them.

Boot falls echoed down the corridor toward me.

"Harker, dammit what the—shit, kids." Ryker stepped over the dead ripper and reached for the children. They clung to him like little monkeys, burying their faces into his shoulder. "Where are the parents?"

Damn. The mother. I legged it out of room, back down the stairs, and into the garden. Of course she'd be gone. What the heck had I expected? But there was a trail of blood, and giving up wasn't in my nature. Out of the shattered back gate, into the alley beyond, I followed the smears of crimson. She was alive. She had to be. The smears led out of the alley and into a community park thick with a shadowy mist. Shit, it was impossible to see any blood on the grass. Wait, the grass was long enough to find a flattened trail where the ripper had dragged the body. It ended at a strip of turned over dirt ready to be sown with moonflowers no doubt. They were the only flowers that grew in Midnight. The trees were a mystery to everyone. They never shed and continued to flourish which defied everything we'd been taught in school. Midnight should be a barren wasteland unable to grow anything and yet it went against the laws of science, just like this trail ending here did.

Could the ripper have picked her up in his jaw and made off with her? Sure, then why drag her all this way? It made no sense.

"Harker!" Cassie came jogging toward me. "We're headed back to base."

I glanced up from the flowerbed. "It's over?"

"Yeah." She gave me a tired smile. "Ryker said you saved a couple of kids and then ran off?"

"A ripper dragged their mother this way. But the trail just stops here."

Cassie crouched and examined the tracks. "Weird."

"Cassie, Harker, we're moving out," Orin called from the other side of the park.

The mother was gone. For some reason the ripper had dragged her here, and what? Picked her up and made off with her? eaten her? No, there would be scraps, as gross at that sounded.

"Come on, there's nothing more we can do here." Cassie steered me toward the street.

With a final look at the bloody grass, I followed.

It was an after-run tradition, Cassie had said. A cleanse and perfect ritual—facials and manicures—and so here we were, cross legged on my bed with all her beauty treatments laid out before us.

She handed me the hand cream. "Use this to soften your hands. It smells awesome too."

I squirted and rubbed the melon fragrance into my palms. "Are the kids okay?"

"They're fine. Bane made sure they got to their grandparents."

I twisted my hair up into a knot. "Good."

Cassie lathered her face with a creamy mask. "So, you and Drayton..."

"There is no me and Drayton, and you know why."

She nodded curtly "Just checking, but right answer."

"I'm not an idiot. I have a strong sense of self preservation." Why did it sound like I was trying to convince myself? His face came to mind now. His warm brown eyes and that teasing smile. I blinked it away.

"Just..." She gnawed on her lip. "Just be wary. Drayton's incubus is strong. He commands it well, and they are usually in accordance with each other, but sometimes things happen to put everything out of whack. Remember, I told you that incubi can't fall in love?"

How could I forget? "Yes."

"That isn't strictly true. The problem is they can, and when they do the incubus can take over. The feelings, the intense emotions, act like a magnet to the incubus and it makes it harder for Drayton to remain in control."

Is that what had happened the night Lilith had come? Had it been Lilith's presence that had made him lose control in his bedroom, or something else? No, I was reading too much into it.

"I'll be careful. I haven't fed off him either. Rivers offered instead."

Her brows shot up. "Shut up! Rod up his arse Rivers let you siphon off him?"

I nodded slowly, taking in her horrified expression. "Is that a big deal?"

"Hell, yeah! Rivers is like the most closed off person I know."

I shrugged. "He seems to be warming to me."

She caught her bottom lip between her teeth, and looked away.

I knew that look. It was the shall-I-tell-them-shit look. "What? You're hiding something? Just spill it."

She picked at her cuticles. "I really shouldn't."

She so wanted to. "Please..." I pleaded.

She rolled he eyes. "Okay, but you cannot tell Ryker I said anything,"

"Ryker? I thought we were talking about Rivers?"

"It's kinda all connected, and it happened before I joined the Protectorate, so no idea how much is true, but Orin filled me in when you joined us."

Okay, I was so confused.

"I got all huffy with him that day in the kitchen when he was paying you loads of attention, and then we had an argument and he told me why he'd been so focused."

"And?"

"It's because you look a lot like Ryker's sister."

I stared at her. "Ryker has a sister?"

"*Had*. He *had* a sister. She died a few years ago. She used to be Rivers's patrol partner, but Orin hinted that she was also a different kind of partner, if you know what I mean."

"Yeah, I got you. So I look like Ryker's dead sister."

Cassie shrugged. "Apparently, she died horrifically, like sooo badly, but Orin wouldn't go into details. He did say that Rivers had been with her at the time, and things between him and Ryker have been strained ever since."

I sat back against the headboard. The picture on his bedside table...her hair had been the same shade as mine, but the face was a mystery. It would certainly explain why Ryker was so protective over me and why Rivers had been so weird around me to start with.

Cassie picked up the nail polish and unscrewed the lid. "Yep, this place is filled with secrets and pain, what with Ryker and Rivers and Dray—" She snapped her mouth closed.

"It's okay, I know about Viola. We met at the cemetery."

Her eyes widened. "He told you what happened?"

Oh man, this was the perfect opportunity to find out the truth, but damn my dicky moral compass. I blew out a breath. "No. He didn't."

She made an 'o' with her mouth. "And you could so easily have tricked me into telling you." She shook her head. "Man, you are really something else."

I gave her my best cheesy grin. "Now that I've been so honest, any chance you'll tell me anyway?"

She snorted. "No way. If I had spilled the beans and Dray found out." She made a slashing motion across her throat with her index finger.

That bad huh? My curiosity would have to remain unsatisfied. "What about you and Orin? I'm glad to see you sorted things out."

She shrugged, her eyes on her hands as she painted her neat finger nails. "Orin knows the score. We're not exclusive, even though he chooses to be."

"Do you love him?"

She glanced up sharply. "For now." She went back to painting her nails. "And he loves me. But love doesn't last. Best not to get too hung up."

Between me and my aversion to relationships but my desire for love, and her and her aversion to love but desire for relationships, we made one fucked up pair.

"Pass me the purple one, will you."

She picked it up. "Oooh, look it's almost the same shade as Bane's eyes."

Was that a sly look she slid my way?

But then she was blowing on her nails to dry them. Once again, my imagination was getting the better of me, but she was right, the purple was almost the same shade of violet as Bane's eyes.

The sun beat down on my face, its heat a gentle caress. The world was bathed in vibrant greens, deep earthy browns, and an azure sky hung overhead to cap it all off. Cotton wool clouds peeked at me from between the slender branches of the trees above. The forest opened out into a clearing dominated by a sparkling lake. The grass beneath my bare feet was soft as down between my toes.

I needed to see what was under the water.

There was something beneath the serene surface, tugging me forward. My knees kissed the fragrant earth at the lakes edge, and I leaned forward to stare into the clear depths of the pool. My reflection blinked back at me, bewildered and mussed, as if I'd just got out of bed.

Bed.

Wait, I was sleeping.

Dreaming

What was the swirling black stuff in my reflection? It was getting bigger. I wanted to pull away, but my body was frozen.

Don't be afraid. This is what is meant to be.

The darkness wanted out. It wanted to be free.

Don't fight it, child. This is salvation.

Not salvation, this was destruction. I couldn't, I wouldn't let it take me.

With every ounce of strength I had, I strained against the invisible bonds holding me by the lake.

Stubborn, willful, child.

The darkness surged outward ready to obscure my reflection, and I fell back onto the grass. The sky stared back at me, peaceful and tranquil and at complete odds with the galloping of my heart. *Knock, knock, knock.*

Was that my pulse?

Knock. knock.

"Harker. Harker, you there?"

I sat up in bed, the dream still clinging to my mind like sticky ribbons. "What? Who is it?"

"It's Ryker."

I rubbed sleep from my eyes. "Come in."

Ryker popped his head round the door. "Hey, sleepy head. There's a call for you in the study."

A call? For me? Who'd be calling...Jesse! I was out of bed and through the door before

Ryker could say anymore. The stone steps were cold against my bare feet, but I barely felt the chill. There was a phone call for me. She'd found a way to get in touch.

The study door was open, and I rushed in and picked up the receiver. "Hello, Jesse?"

"Harker?"

My heart sank. "Nolan. Hi."

Not Jesse then. But Nolan may have news about her.

"Harker. It's good to hear your voice." He sounded gruff, his voice hoarser than usual.

"Are you all right? You sound odd. How are things? How's Jesse?"

He cleared his throat. "I've been sick. Got taken down by this bug that's been doing the rounds. Was out of it for over a week."

"I'm sorry to hear that." But how the hell is Jesse?

"I'm only just back on my feet, and I called in to check on Jesse...she's gone, Harker."

Gone? My mind went blank for a moment. "What? What do you mean she's gone?"

"She's no longer in Sunset. I did some checking. She voluntary moved to Midnight a week ago."

The ocean roared in my ears.

"Harker? Harker? Can you hear me?"

Jesse was in Midnight? Had been for a week? What had happened to her? Anything could have happened to her.

"I'm sorry, I was sick. I dropped the ball, I — "

"Have you any idea where she was headed? Any clues."

"I'm sorry, no."

I hung up.

"Serenity, are you all right?" Ryker said from the doorway.

I turned to him, hands clasped together to stop them trembling. "My sister is in Midnight. Please, help me find her."

His frown deepened and he bridged the gap between us and cupped my shoulders. "Hey. It's all right. If she's in the district we *will* find her. Just let me make a few calls. She'd have come through district immigration, and they'll have a record of where they housed her."

"Why didn't she come find me?" I rubbed my temples. Pull it together, Harker. This was salvageable. We'd locate her and everything would be fine. "She should have come straight here."

He winced. "She may have tried but our base location isn't common knowledge, not to mention the wards we have around the place to deter humans." He led me to the seat behind the desk. "Sit and let me find her for you."

He picked up the phone and dialed, and I did my best not to wring my hands. What had possessed her to do such a thing? She should have known better. God, what the hell had possessed her! The shock was replaced by anger—at my sister, at myself, at the whole damned fucked up situation, and the fact that I loved her so damn much that my chest felt as if it was being squeezed in a vise and my heart would burst at any moment.

Ryker's voice was a soothing rumble in the background. A click followed as he hung up the phone.

"Get dressed, we have an address."

Drayton caught us as we were on our way out the door. "Where are you two off to?"

I paused with my hand on the door handle. "My sister is in Midnight. I need to see her."

Drayton's brows shot up. "Damn. Go. If I hear anything on the warrant, I'll let you know."

The warrant? Of course, we had a case and a warrant, and I had a job to do. I'd been so excited about that, but it seemed insignificant now. I smiled and nodded though, feigning enthusiasm.

"Any news on the toxin?" Ryker asked Drayton.

Could we just go already?

Drayton shook his head. "No news yet. I'd chase Tristan if I wasn't afraid of getting my head bitten off. He'll call when he has something. He always does."

"We should go," Ryker said.

Thank you! I flung open the door and stepped out into the night, which was actually the morning, but heck, it was too much of a mind boggle to dwell on. We took the Range Rover with the big wheels, and Ryker drove quickly through the streets. The world was still waking up, lights coming on in the stores we passed.

"The electricity bill for this district must be huge." Where the heck had that come from?

Ryker chuckled. "I guess it balances out with Sunset not needing it as much."

True. Hang on, he hadn't actually told me where we were headed. "Where is Jesse? Which sector?"

His lips tightened. "Sector one."

My stomach dropped. "No..."

He kept his eyes on the road. "It will be fine. We'll find her and everything will be all right."

Sector one was a mess. The scourge had hit it hard and Jesse had been there. She'd been in the midst of chaos and I hadn't known.

My knee began to jiggle with anxiety. "Can we drive faster?"

Ryker stepped on the gas and we pulled up outside a neat little bungalow, or it would have been neat if the windows hadn't been smashed to bits. The garden had been torn up and the bins lay on the pavement, spilling debris. A scream caught in my throat.

"Don't," Ryker said. "You don't know for sure." He unlocked his door. "Stay here. I'll take a look around."

Sod that. If she was in there...hurt...dead...I needed to know, to see. I climbed out and jogged to catch up to him. He tried the door which swung in easily, probably because it was hanging off its hinges.

My throat tight, my lungs frozen I followed him into the dark interior. My gut told me there was no way she'd survived this total decimation but my heart screamed that she was still alive.

We searched the whole house. No blood, no body. That was good news, right? Don't think about the fact that she could have run, been chased, and died elsewhere. She could have been dragged through the streets like the twins' mother.

Where the heck was she?

"The house is clear," Ryker said. "Let's canvas the area. Talk to some neighbors."

I nodded, not trusting myself to speak.

We were headed toward the stairs when the crunch of glass being crushed underfoot filtered up the steps. A strangled sob followed. Ryker froze and turned to look at me. Could it be? I walked slowly to the top of the stairs, not daring to hope. A woman stood in the entrance way, her hand covering her mouth, eyes bright with tears.

Oh, God.

I climbed down a step and she glanced up. Our eyes locked and then she was rushing up the steps, and I was rushing down. We met in a tangle, in a frenzy of tears and hugs.

I squeezed her tight. She yelped and I smoothed back her hair. "Sorry, I just... You're okay."

She pulled back. "I couldn't find you."

"You shouldn't have come. You have to go back."

She jerked out of my grasp. "I am *not* going back."

I stared at her defiant face. That familiar expression that told me there was no point arguing, and for anything else I'd have backed down, but this was life and death. I grabbed her hand and tugged her the rest of the way down the stairs.

"Look!" I pointed at the carnage. "Look at this. This shit happens every month. If you'd been here, you'd be dead. Do you understand?"

She tried to pull her hand from my grasp, but I held firm. "You could have died."

"I was fine. I stayed in a friend's basement. He says he'll save a spot for me next month too. If you can handle it, so can I. I want to be with you. I *need* to be with you." She stopped trying to pull her hand free and moved in for a hug.

My arm came up to embrace her on instinct, but I forced myself to stop. She could have died, and every day she stayed was another day she was in danger. My eyes burned with the knowledge of what I was about to do. I grabbed her by the shoulders and pushed her away from me, allowing my fingers to dig in and bruise. "*I* can handle being here because *I'm* not human. I'm not weak and breakable like you."

She winced. "Serenity, you're hurting me."

"Yes, I am." I injected as much derision into my tone as I could muster. "I'm hurting you because I'm not human. I'm a fucking energy sucking neph. Do you want to know how many times I wanted to feed off you? How many times the hunger almost got the better of me?"

Her eyes were wide as she scanned my face.

"Too many times." I spat the words out in disgust. "I had to pretend every day to be something I wasn't, and I hated it. But now, when I can finally be free, when I can be the monster I am, you show up here to fucking ruin it." I shoved her away. "There is no place here for you. I don't want you here. Do you understand me?"

The horror and hurt on her face and the tremble of her bottom lip almost undid me, but she could have died. I held fast to the anger, the fake derision I'd dredged up and folded my arms. "Get the fuck out of Midnight, Jesse. You're not welcome here."

She spun on her heel and ran out the door.

"Serenity?" Ryker placed a hand on my shoulder. "Are you sure about this?"

His face blurred in my vision. "Can you please..." I jerked my head toward the exit.

He nodded curtly and followed Jesse outside.

I strode back upstairs, locked myself in the back room and cried.

We were seated at the kitchen table, pot of tea on hand and some shortbread to take off the edge—although, I wasn't feeling the buttery goodness today. I nursed my cup of tea, warming my hands against the porcelain. How'd I gone a whole day without caving and going to see Jesse?

"What you did was incredibly selfless," Ryker said.

"No, it wasn't. It was completely selfish. Having her here would mean worrying about her every single second. I need her to be safe or I won't be able to function."

Ryker picked at his noodles. "You could have arranged for her to have sanctuary every month. We could have found her accommodation in a better part of the district, checked up on her regularly. We'd all have chipped in. The Protectorate is your family now, and Jesse is your sister which makes her our responsibility too."

"And what kind of life will she have here? Living in fear of the next breed or scourge attack? Living in darkness without the touch of the sun? No. She's better off in Sunset."

"Well, I've lodged the request with the immigration department. She came here voluntarily so I'm sure they'll allow her to return."

"How soon will we know?"

"A couple of days at the most. Meanwhile, she's staying with her teacher friend in sector three. Did you know she was working at the Griffon primary school in sector two?"

"She has a job?"

He nodded, lips turned down. "She seems to have got her shit in order."

My lips curled in a small smile. "Yeah,

that's Jesse. Always one with the plans. You know she's an amazing cook, right?" I laughed. "Oh and she tells the most awful jokes, like super corny, and then she laughs at her own puns."

Ryker's lips twitched. "You know, you *can* change your mind and tell her the truth. Tell her you love her and want her to stay. We can keep her safe."

The temptation was a warm tug at the back of my mind. To have her close by, to be able to see her all the time, speak to her, have dinner with her. I'd give anything for those things, but she deserved better than Midnight. She deserved Sunset.

"Thanks, but I'm good."

Ryker picked up his empty plate and walked over to the sink. "Go find Drayton. Maybe the warrant came in?"

I nodded and drained my cup.

"Leave it. I'll wash up."

He was trying to distract me, and boy was I grateful. My seat scraped across the stone floor. He held his hand out for the cup, a gentle smile on his face, and something inside me melted, propelling me into his arms. I pressed the side of my face to his chest and hugged him tight.

"Thank you. Thank you for being here for me."

After a second his arms closed around

me and he rested his chin on my head. "Anytime, Serenity. Anytime."

"Ahem."

Ryker tensed and then released me abruptly. I turned to see Drayton standing in the doorway.

I offered him a smile. "I was just about to come find you."

"Ahuh. Why don't you go check on the computer and see if that warrant came back yet? I'll join you in a sec."

Why did he look so strained? "Sure." I brushed past him, inhaling his familiar core tightening scent, and walked part way up the stairs, but damn, curiosity had me stalling and tiptoeing back down, far enough so I could hear their voices clearly.

"You need to tell her. Now," Drayton said.

"I don't need to do anything. It's not like that between us," Ryker said.

"Maybe not for you," Drayton said.

"She doesn't look at me like that," Ryker insisted, but his voice sounded strained.

"Really? You both looked mighty cozy a second ago. Trust me, Ryker, I know a few things about the opposite sex and they always fall for the guy who can be there for them, and you're turning into that guy for her."

"Your jealousy is making you crazy."

"I'm not jealous, I'm just...I don't want her to get hurt."

"Maybe you should have thought of that before you started to cozy up to her in the first place. You know what you are. You know your limitations. If anyone is likely to hurt her, it's you."

"Fuck you, Ryker. Just tell her the truth and nip things in the bud."

"No."

"Why the fuck not?"

"Same reason you haven't told her about Viola, because it fucking hurts, that's why."

There was a long beat of silence.

"I'm sorry," Drayton said.

"Yeah, so am I."

I backed away from the doorway and ran lightly up the stairs to the upper floor. Drayton thought I had the hots for Ryker and he was jealous, which meant that Cassie had been right that Drayton had feelings for me. There was no ignoring the fact that he liked me more than he should, and there was no getting away from the fact that nothing could ever come from it. The last thing I wanted to do was cause friction in the work place. The Protectorate functioned well because everyone got on, and could rely on each other to have each other's backs. I'd need to find a way to fix this, and soon.

Cassie was in the study pinning something to the corkboard.

"Rota," she said. "And you're on it. You're with me tonight."

My stomach fluttered in excitement. My first official patrol. "What area are we patrolling?"

"Up by the human hospital." She stepped away from the board, her face crinkling in concern. "I heard about your sister. You made the right call."

"Yeah, I know I did. Still sucks though."

She sighed. "I'll see you later, Harker. And maybe we can grab a quick drink after shift?"

"Wait, can you log me into the computer? Drayton asked me to check if the warrant has come back from District council."

"Sure." She parked her butt in the swivel seat and tapped away at the keyboard.

The phone rang shrilly.

"Can you get that?" she asked.

I picked up the receiver on the third ring. "Hello, Um, Protectorate here."

Cassie snorted.

"Yeah, I know who you are. This is the MED. We have another missing person's situation, Several in fact. The Griffon school bus was on a field trip to the beach. The bus was found abandoned two miles off course near The Deep. Fifteen children and two teachers are missing."

My scalp prickled. "The Griffon school?"

"Yes, you took on the damned case so get off your arses and find these kids, and while you're at it you can find the other people in the files we sent you too."

"The teachers? What are their names?"

Cassie slammed her hand down on the desk making me jump. "Sorry. Spider."

The rustle of paper drifted down the phone line. "Michael Walden and Jesse Harker."

Oh, God. My hand tightened around the handset. "How long have they been missing?"

"They were due back at the school by lunch time. They never made it."

I glanced at the clock on the wall. It was almost two p.m. "Thank you. We're on it." I slammed the receiver down, my pulse fluttering in my throat in panic.

"Harker, what the hell was that?"

"Twenty missing kids and two teachers. Cassie, my sister is missing."

This was our case, Drayton's and mine, and Bane gave the go ahead to investigate with strict instructions to call for back up if needed.

It no longer looked like our missing persons case was connected to the Sanguinata. According to Bane, the Sanguinata weren't interested in children. They needed mature adult blood to sustain themselves. If they had been kidnapping humans for some nefarious plan like a secret blood bank, then children would be useless to them. It still left us with the case of the illegal recruitment, but even though the warrant had come through, this development trumped a visit to the House of Vitae.

Thank goodness, because if they'd insisted on acting on the warrant first, I'd have told them where to shove it. Kids were in danger. My sister was in danger. That trumped everything.

We parked the van on the road leading down to The Deep.

"Looks like the MED is gathering evidence," Drayton said. He twisted in his seat to scan the back of the van and the faces of our squad for this mission, Gary and a shy guy called Carl. "Spread out and look for clues, anything suspicious."

"You got it, boss," Gary said.

"We jumped out and headed down the track toward the sand. Gary and Carl leapt out behind us and split up to look for clues.

Lights had been set up around the perimeter, and the yellow school bus sat in the center. Two humans—MED officers no doubt—strode over.

"What have you got?" Drayton asked.

The older of the two humans flipped open his notepad. "The bus is clean of any evidence of violence, no blood. There are a bunch of footprints leading around the side of The Deep, just beyond that bank and then they just vanish." He pointed to a rise bathed in moonlight, either side in shadow. The club lay out of sight beyond it.

"Wait, we found our Jane Doe on the opposite side of the bank, remember? Half buried in the sand." My head was whirring and an awful terrifying conclusion bloomed in my mind. Oh, God. Oh, fuck. "Drayton I think they're in the earth,"

Drayton cocked his head. "What are you talking about?"

The MED officers exchanged confused glances.

"The Jane Doe was found partially buried. On the night of the scourge run, I followed the tracks that a ripper left when dragging a woman away from her home. They ended at a mound of earth. It looked freshly turned. And now this. The tracks end at the bank."

"Serenity, I get what you're saying but what could possibly have dragged them underground. There are no creatures like that in Arcadia."

"But you said new creatures were showing up, remember? You said you didn't know how. Maybe this is something new." Yeah I was clutching at straws, but my gut was screaming that I was right.

"Humans cannot survive in the earth," the MED officer said patiently. "We need to breath."

The older guy rolled his eyes. "Nephs need to breath too, you idiot."

"Not all of them."

They thought I was crazy. "I need a spade. Get me a spade!"

"Serenity," Drayton said. "I get it. You're worried about your sister but—"

"Get. Me. A. Spade." I glared at him.

He held up his hands and retreated to the van returning a moment later with a spade and squad in tow. I grabbed the tool and jogged toward the bank. Locating the spot easily using the yellow cones the MED had set up, I began to dig. The other joined me, watching but not helping. Fuck them. It was here, the entrance to whatever. I could feel it like a tingle under my skin.

"This is ridiculous," the MED officers said in unison.

I continued to dig in the spot where the tracks ended. The earthy sand came away easily, almost too easily, as if it had been recently moved. I was right. I had to be.

The squad stood a little way off, whispering among themselves about the new Protectorate who was acting all crazy. Drayton had planted himself behind me, his shadow a comforting presence at my back.

And then his phone rang. "It's Tristan." He took the call. "Yes. You have?... What?... You're sure?...How? Okay, thank you."

I paused in my manic digging and looked over my shoulder at him "What did he say?"

Drayton's chest was rising and falling rapidly as if under the influence of some terrible revelation. "Tristan succeeded in identifying the toxin. It's *not* a toxin. It's venom. Spider venom." He licked his lips. "Similar to the kind produced by the black widow." He glanced at the squad. "Everybody fucking dig."

The squad began clawing at the sand.

Spiders? I stared at the bank. "No, it would take shed loads of venom to have incapacitated her like that. Not to mention there were no wounds, no bites on her."

Drayton shook his head. "I think you're right, we're dealing with something new here."

The hole I'd dug was getting deep. I plunged the shovel in one more time and the world gave way beneath me.

"Harker? Harker? You all right?" Drayton called.

I sat up, groaning as my back pinged with pain. Shit, I'd landed hard. And where the heck was I? It was dark and musty but dry. I lifted my chin to the moonlight filtering in through the hole I'd just fallen through. The hole was at the end of a slanted chute at least two meters above me, and I was in some kind of tunnel. Could I stand? How high was this thing? I pulled myself up, bracing myself against the earth. This far down it was all hard packed earth. Something had built this tunnel.

"Harker?"

I stepped into the chute. "I'm here. I'm all right. Drayton, you need to get down here."

"Gary's gone to fetch some ropes from the van. We're loading up. Just hold tight. Do not go anywhere."

"You don't need to worry about that. We'll need torches too."

A scratching sound behind me had me spinning round. But it was so dark it was impossible to make out anything.

"Drayton. Please, hurry."

The scratching came again, and something else...something that sounded suspiciously like breathing. Oh, fuck. I wasn't alone.

The scuffling grew closer, and the air closed in. My hands began to burn. The daggers were coming, thank God, and then a rope appeared in front of me and a moment later Drayton landed in the tunnel. I threw myself at him. He wrapped his arms around me, lifting me off my feet.

"It's all right. I'm here," he whispered in my ear.

I nodded. "There's something down there. I heard it."

Gary landed in the tunnel and chucked a flashlight to Drayton. Drayton caught it neatly, and turned it on. He shined it to our left. A shadow withdrew around the bend.

"What the fuck was that?" Gary asked.

"I think we're going to need to find out," Drayton said.

Be wary

The daggers were already in my hands.

There was mortal danger down here and we had no choice but to advance into it. Carl joined us, and with Drayton leading the way, we followed the shadow.

The tunnel was wide enough for two of us to walk abreast of each other, so I walked abreast of Drayton with Clay and Gary making up the rear. The flashlight made the tunnels even creepier, intensifying the darkness outside its shaft of light. The ground underfoot was smooth as if someone had taken the time to carefully pat the earth back into place. And then we came to an intersection with three tunnels leading off from it.

My scalp crawled and my stomach clenched. "It's a burrow."

"Yeah, a fucking huge one," Gary said.

"I really don't think I want to meet the owner," Carl said softly.

Drayton ran the light from his flashlight across the three entrances. "Eenie, meenie, miney, mo." He swung the light back to the first exit and then stepped through.

A scuffle drifted down toward us and Drayton paused, swinging the flashlight this way and that. The glint of eyes and then a flash of hairy limbs.

Gary yelped. "Mother of shit."

"Was that a... Oh, man." A spider. It had looked like a huge, inhumanly sized, monstrous spider. My palms were instantly coated in a sweat and if the daggers hadn't been magically stuck to me, I'd have dropped them.

Breath, just breath.

"I am breathing," I snapped.

"What?" Drayton asked. "Are you okay?"

"I'm fine. I was just talking to..." the voice in my head? Er nope. "I'm fine."

But that was a lie, because my knees were ready to knock, and my heart fit to burst because spiders were supposed to be more scared of us than we were of them, right? Not one that size. One that size could eat my face.

Drayton hadn't advanced either. "Maybe we should head back and call for that back up." I'd never heard him sound unsure before, and it sent a chill up my spine, but Jesse and the kids were down here with the huge spider. I couldn't come this far and then back off.

"I think we should just go a little farther. Just to scope it out. That thing hasn't attacked us yet."

Drayton nodded. "Fine just a little farther and then we head back and get a few more boots down here and some more light."

We continued in silence, the only sound our rapid shallow breath and the scent of our fear. Was it my imagination or was the tunnel getting wider?

"Drayton, I think that—"

A yelp slammed into us from behind but was cut off too soon.

"Carl!" Gary swiped at thin air, the flashlight went wild.

"Argh!" Gary reached for us before being whisked back into the darkness.

Drayton grabbed my hand. "Run."

We barreled down the tunnels, taking one turn after the other. I wasn't keeping track and I doubted that Drayton was either, all that mattered was getting away and then we slammed into something sticky and strong.

"A web, dammit!" Drayton said. "Don't move. The more you struggle the more tangled you'll get. My arm was stuck above my head, face buried in the sticky, silken strands of the massive web, and my hands still clutched the daggers. The daggers that could cut through anything.

Hell, yes.

I tested what little movement I had. All I needed was to angle my wrist enough to allow the blades to make contact with the threads, but the bonds were too tight. There was no wiggle room.

You can do this. Just drop the shields.

What? No. Now wasn't the time to let the hunger out. The need to feed would take over everything including logic.

Listen to me, child, the sentinel approaches, there is no time.

The web began to vibrate, and ice filled my veins. The sentinel? We had to get out. Biting the insides of my cheeks I cracked open my shields and waited for the hunger, it surged to the surface, flooding me and lending my limbs a boost of strength. My wrist snapped taut and then this time when I strained against the bonds they stretched and my blade made contact. My wrist was free.

"Harker, what are you doing?"

"Cutting myself free." I worked carefully, strategically, while the web bounced, announcing that the sentinel was close.

Faster.

I was going as fast as I could, and then the web released me, and I fell through to the other side. Drayton cursed and when I turned to him I could barely make him out. The threads that I'd cut had rolled back and wrapped around him. His body was coated and the only visible part of him were his eyes and mouth.

"Go," he said. "Go get help. Now."

"I'm not leaving you." I began to slash at the web, desperate to get him free, the whole thing was bouncing now, yanking Drayton out of my reach. He slammed into the roof of the tunnel and stuck there.

No.

The flashlight, which had fallen to the ground flickered.

"Serenity, you need to leave before whatever is coming gets here."

"The sentinel."

His eyes widened. "The daggers told you that?"

"Yes." A sob caught in my throat. I couldn't reach him. Even if I wanted to cut him down, I just couldn't.

The light flickered over his face, catching the whites of his eyes and making them gleam. And the scrape of talons on flattened earth echoed down the tunnel, clip, clip, clip. Scrape.

No.

I reached for Drayton and his gaze softened.

Then the flashlight went out and the tunnel was filled with an inhuman screech,

"Run!" Drayton ordered.

This time I listened.

The darkness was complete, and yet I ran. The daggers in my hand tugged me forward.

Left.

Right here.

There's an intersection coming up.

My disembodied companion could see in the dark it seemed.

I'd left Drayton behind.

The sentinel had him

Keep moving. Do not stop. They are behind you. They do not want you to escape.

Duh? I'd kinda figured that one out.

Sarcasm will not serve any constructive purpose here.

What? Could he read my mind?

Irrelevant.

It was highly relevant but escape was more so.

Stop, here, turn to your right, move forward.

I followed his direction and something bumped my knee.

It's a chute. Climb it. You will need to dig your way out but it is not deep.

How did he know all this?

I don't, but you do.

What the heck did that mean?

Not now. Later.

I climbed, my knees scraping on the bumpy earth and then I came up against soft soil. Freshly turned soil.

Dig.

Using my hands as spades I did just that. The earth shifted around me and behind me, and I was cocooned in it. My hair my face, my eyes—I was burying myself alive. Panic took hold of my lungs and used them as a squeezy toy,

Focus, child. You're almost there. Can you feel it? Can you feel the air?

Now that he mentioned it, I could. Tamping down on the horror, I pushed on and then my hand thrust into nothing. No. Not nothing. Air. With a final push I broke the surface into the moonlight.

Keep moving. There isn't much time. It knows you have found its home and it will act to protect itself.

"What is it?"

Something ancient and wily. Something I had hoped never to see again.

And what the heck are you

A friend.

I stared at my hands. The daggers were gone, they had been for a while and yet he was still speaking to me, which meant he'd been there all along—when I'd kissed Drayton, when I'd fed off River, when Bane had saved me from Abigor.

I do not invade your privacy. Ever. I will always make myself known when it is time to fight or guide your hand. The daggers respond to danger, but I cannot always be there.

"And where do you go? I mean, where are you?"

Somewhere you do not want to be.

Enough with the cryptic. "How about just leaving me be?

A chuckle. *That I cannot do. Not yet.*

I pulled myself free of the earth. I was in the park, the one that the ripper had dragged the woman to. This is where he'd brought her, to this chute. The rippers were feeding this thing?

What the fuck?

I began to jog to the road. I needed to get to Bane and the others. We needed backup. A mile and a half on the ground, but if I took the roofs I could cut that journey in half. I cracked open my shields a little more, allowing the power I'd taken from Rivers to seep into my limbs. There was enough. There had to be.

Just bring the shields down.

No. There was no need for that. I could do this. I had it under control. And then I launched myself up onto the nearest roof and began to fly.

The Mansion door swung open and I staggered in. My legs were rubber, and they gave way as soon as I hit the foyer.

"Ryker! Bane! Someone!" I couldn't move. I'd used my final reserves of power and the craving spread through my limbs like fire ants over my skin. The shields had fallen. I needed to put them up now. I tugged mentally but they refused to budge.

No. Oh, shit. No. Why had I listened to the voice?

"Serenity?" Ryker's face floated above mine.

"Get away." My lips felt strange, as if they belonged to someone else.

He reached for me, and I tried to roll away but the fire ants on my skin pressed down, holding me immobile.

"Get away from her." Bane's voice reverberated throughout the corridor. "She's craving, can't you feel it?"

Ryker's eyes widened. His mouth twisted and he backed up. He had shields too, he must have dropped them. Good. He was safe. I didn't want to hurt him, because this was a new kind of craving, something primal and raw and dangerous. I'd fed, I'd controlled the hunger and I'd kept the shields up a fraction, so why had it got so bad? How had the hunger forced the shields all the way down?

Because it isn't enough. You must feed the darkness not throw it scraps.

Go away, just leave.

Bane's face replaced Ryker. "Harker, can you hear me?"

The fire in my veins intensified and a scream tore from my throat. My body bucked of its own accord.

"What's happening?" Ryker said. "Why is she glowing?"

Solid arms scooped me off the cool flagstones and pressed me to a different kind of furnace. My body wasn't my own, gripping, and writhing, wanting. Oh, God. The shame.

And then we were on the move.

"Where are you taking her?" Ryker asked.

"To be fed."

"Bane, what—"

"Do *you* want to do it?" Bane snapped.

Ryker was silent. He couldn't, wouldn't open up to me like that. My eyes burned because even though I understood why he wouldn't, this would be so much easier with him. He grounded me in a way I didn't understand.

The world was a blur and Bane's skin was velvet and taut and, yes, it tasted salty. Had I just licked him? Oh, fucking hell? Please, this had to end. Silk sheets kissed my fevered skin. Skin...where were my clothes. Rational thought fled my mind as a body covered mine. His skin brushed mine, his muscles sliding over my sensitized flesh

"Feed, Harker." Bane's voice in my ears.

My shields were down and I had no control so why wasn't the darkness feeding?

Because you are always in control, Serenity. Don't you understand yet?

"Harker, feed."

Yes.

I latched on to him, wrapping my arms around his torso, hooking my legs around his. It was intimate and crazy and delicious, and his power — that honey syrup edged with cinnamon — poured into me. My heart pumped hard, pulse thudding in my ear, my core tightened and tightened as if...oh, god. No.

"It's all right, Serenity. Just let go." Bane's voice was rough, hoarse and breathless.

No, no I couldn't. This wasn't how I fed.

This was wrong.

He smoothed my hair back from my face. His thumbs brushed the curve of my jaw, and then his lips brushed the delicate skin under my ear. His tongue flicked out to taste me, and I lost my grip. The orgasm ripped through me like a mini tornado, tearing a throaty groan that would have me mentally closing my ears for years to come.

Bane's body pressed into me. His huge hardness rubbed against my sensitive parts, and, damn it, I was grinding up against him, wet and slick and wanton.

Drayton's face flashed through my mind. The webbing was wrapped around his body and over his face. The sentinel had him. We had to save him.

"Enough." I bucked, and twisted and Bane rolled off me.

My hand went to my chest where my heart felt as if it was about to crash through my rib cage and make a break for it. I slammed my shields down, but the juncture of my thighs still throbbed hungrily.

"Harker?"

My body grew liquid as lethargy infused me. Last time I'd fed off him, I'd slept for hours. No. Not this time. I jumped off the bed, shaking my arms and hopping from foot to foot. I needed to stay awake. I needed to. Hey, the floor was rising up to say hello.

I opened my eyes on a snort.

Bane's deep violet eyes drank me in from his position on the side of the bed. His chest rose and fell erratically.

"How long have I been out?"

"Twenty minutes," he said.

"We have to go. Right now." I swung my legs off the bed, my knees brushing against his chest. His huge hands closed them. They were bare. I was naked. No. I still had my underwear on but still.

"Calm down. Tell me what happened."

He was so close. Too close, and the memory of his powerful body pressed against mine was too fresh for this proximity. I'd wanted him, writhed under him, and — oh, God — he'd licked me.

"Harker, focus."

I shook my head, dispelling the final vestiges of the feeding. "Drayton and the others are in danger." My voice was a rasp. I cleared my throat. "There are tunnels underground. Spiders." I filled him in as quickly as I could. "And I think the daggers know what we're dealing with, at least the voice that goes with them does."

Bane stroked the tattoos on my wrists. "Can you speak to him now?"

I closed my eyes and reached out. Hey

are you there?

Nothing.

"He's not here. He did say he wasn't always here."

Bane's lips compressed. "Fine. In that case we'll have to work with what we have. We're dealing with spiders, big ones, but still insects. So let's treat them like what they are."

He rose and held out his hand. "Let's go crush some eight legged beasts."

Ryker pulled me into a hug in the foyer. "You scared me half to death."

Orin and Cassie were by the door, adjusting their weapons belts.

Rivers bounded down the stairs. His sword had been replaced by a smaller blade tucked into a sheath at his waist, and his sword spot had been filled by a canister strapped to his back.

"What is that?" Ryker asked.

"Bug repellent." He shrugged. "It won't kill them, but it will slow them down."

Bane grinned. "Good thinking, Rivers."

Orin clapped his hands together. "Let's do this thing."

"Wait," Bane said. "Cassie, Ryker alert the MED and rally reinforcements. Cover the two chutes and kill any threat that emerges."

Ryker's body tensed. "Like Hell. We're

coming with you."

Bane growled and his lip curled to showcase his fangs. "Don't test me, Ryker."

Ryker bristled, his gaze sweeping over me, his brow crinkling in concern. "Damn it, Bane."

Bane's eyes narrowed. "She is with me. She will be safe."

Ryker closed his eyes briefly and nodded.

Cassie placed a hand on his arm. "Come on, let's round up the troops and get going. If anything goes horrifically wrong, I should feel it, we'll get down there asap, I promise."

Ryker nodded reluctantly.

Rivers joined us by the front door. "Do you need to feed?" His expression was impassive, but the rapid pulse at his throat told a different story.

"I'm good, thank you."

He nodded curtly.

Bane yanked open the door and we piled out and headed for the van. When we got there, Rivers and Orin climbed in, but Bane took a few steps away. I turned to him enquiringly.

That smile again, with the fangs. "I'll see you there."

His wings shot out, huge obsidian things and he launched himself up into the air.

"Serenity?" Rivers held out his hand, and I clasped it, allowing him to haul me into the van. The door slammed and we were off.

"It never gets old," Rivers said. "First time I saw him fly, my heart was in my mouth."

Orin snorted. "The guy's a demon in the sky."

We could see him through the windscreen careening through the stars, moonlight on his wings.

"He can go faster," Rivers said. "He's just keeping pace with us."

I gripped the dashboard, my knuckles white. He was so high up, so fierce and dangerous.

Rivers hand slipped over mine. "He'll be all right." He swallowed and then quickly pulled back his hand.

The van swerved as we turned onto the track that led to the beach. It was the closest chute and the one where, hopefully, the MED would still be set up.

Sure enough, the place was crawling with officers. The hole we'd dug was cordoned off. It didn't look like anyone had gone down after us then. My chest heated in indignation but I staunched it. How could I blame the humans for their self-preservation instincts? Putting our lives in danger was the

Protectorates' job. I climbed out of he van as Bane landed lightly on the sand a few feet away.

We approached the chute.

"Any movement?" Bane asked the nearest human.

"No," The man stumbled out of the way as Bane stepped over the hastily erected barrier.

"Hey, didn't you go in earlier?" someone called out.

I ignored them and followed Bane down into the tunnels.

Rivers and Orin flicked on their torches, but Bane didn't seem to need the light. He barreled ahead.

"Objective is to find the humans and get them out," Bane said. "Humans first. Neph second."

We rounded a bend, and then another. A mental map was forming in my mind, but after several more turns I lost the thread. But Bane moved as if he had an actual map to hand.

Finally, he came to a standstill. "Something has changed." He took a step to the side and reached for the wall. He pulled his hand away quickly. "Silk."

Rivers shone the light directly on the walls to reveal silken threads woven to create a crude kind of wallpaper effect. There was even a pattern.

The tunnel widened and opened out into a vast chamber that glowed eerie green and clinging to the walls and the ceiling were at least a hundred monster sized spiders. My palms were instantly slick, and in the next moment they were clutching my daggers.

She is here.

He was back.

Who is *she*?

The ground shuddered and something rose up to greet us. It was a spider out of nightmares. Its body suspended a meter above the ground, its legs...oh, God. It's hairy legs. But then the eyes opened and it looked right at me.

We were so screwed.

Every creature has an Achilles heel.

"You are here for the humans." The voice was a wet gurgle that turned my stomach.

"Yes," Bane said. "Where are they?"

She chuckled, and it was a horrific gurgling sound that made the hairs on the back of my neck stand to attention. "Some are inside me." Her distended stomach pulsed. "Digestion is a little slow these days."

Oh, God. I pressed a hand to my mouth, not sure whether I wanted to puke or scream.

"The rest are...hanging around."

Hanging? I looked up at the weird white

hanging things. Were those the humans? Oh, shit. Jesse was one of those parcels.

"The humans on this land are protected," Bane said, his tone even and unperturbed. "You cannot hunt here."

She laughed, her body vibrating with the effort. "It has been eons since someone dared to tell Arachne what she can and cannot do."

Oh, man she was speaking in third person, and if the whole spider thing wasn't enough, then this would have just pushed it over the ledge into creepy town.

"Arachne, was drawn here," she continued. "Arachne was summoned, and Arachne must feed to regain strength. Human souls are nectar and their flesh is tender."

Orin cursed softly under his breath.

She'd been drawn here. By what?

"How did you get in?" Bane asked.

"There are cracks which Arachne and her children can slip through. The cracks grow larger and more hungry come."

"So there *are* ways out of Arcadia," Orin said.

Arachne laughed again. "No way out. Only in. So, now we are here. Now this is our home. Arachne must feed." Her tone was matter of fact. "You are not human. Your flesh is tough, and your souls are tainted. Arachne does not like. But the spiderlings are always hungry."

The spiders on the walls quivered as if in anticipation.

"Arachne's children are obedient. They bring her food. They do not steal, they do not take. They see you in our home and they do not attack. They tell Arachne and Arachne counsel them to wait. More will come. More will come and then they will feast." Her body pulsed. "More will come?"

Oh shit. More *would* come. If we didn't make it out Cassia and Ryker would come down here with reinforcements, but they would be no match for the hoard clinging to the walls.

I reached out to the voice. He knew what this thing was. Maybe he could help us identify a weakness. Are you there? Hello, dagger voice.

Dagger voice?

Well, what should I call you?

Call me Ambrosius.

What are we dealing with here? You said you knew.

Her name is Arachne, and she was once human. There are many tales of how she became what she is, many legends, but the truth is that her vanity in her craft led to a curse that transformed her into a spider.

What was her craft?

She could weave the most amazing fabrics.

And now she's here. What does she want?"

To feed, to live. To belong. Arachne is a complex creature. A human soul trapped in a monster's body. At first she would have fought her new instincts but eons have passed. I doubt her humanity has survived.

An idea bloomed on my mind.

"I noticed the silk wallpaper effect in the tunnel beyond." I jerked my head back the way we'd come. "It's really gorgeous. Um, did you do that?"

Her many eyes googled at me. "You like Arachne's weaving?"

Oh God, she was fixated on me now. It's a monster, just like the scourge or the bloodsuckers, not a crawly. Don't think about how it moves. "Sure. It's really intricate and, um, pretty."

A sigh rose up from that black mouth. "Arachne does love to weave. Soon Arachne's home will be draped in intricate silk patterns. Strong, resilient and beautiful. My silk is unbreakable, did you know that?"

Vanity, her Achilles heel was vanity.

Good, yes. Now use it.

"It hardly seems fair that such gorgeous work should be hidden all the way down here, with no mortal eyes to appreciate it. I mean you have a serious talent." I took a step closer to her, keeping my movement casual and unthreatening.

"What are you doing, Harker?" Bane hissed.

I ignored him, and tilted my chin to look up at the ceiling. "If you got rid of some of your, um, children, like asked them to move out of this chamber you could do wonders with this place. With the green glow reflecting of your wonderful patterns, this chamber would be a sight to behold. But then," I tapped my chin. "Only you would see it." I shook my head. "It's such a waste, you know?"

I was so close, one lunge and slice and I'd have her.

"You speak Arachne's heart. You bring memories of a time when Arachne's creations were sought far and wide. A time before..."

Her body shifted as she scuttled to the side and I bit back a scream, part fear, part disgust, and part frustration. Bane caught my eye. He'd cottoned on to what I was trying to do.

"She's right," he said to Arachne. "There is a need of your skill above ground. Why hide away your talent underground?"

Arachne let out a snort. "Ha, you think they would receive Arachne? That they would allow her to live, to feed above ground? No. They would kill. Arachne is no fool." Although, she didn't sound too sure.

"How long have you been underground?" Rivers asked. His tone was polite and enquiring.

"Forever it seems."

"The world has changed. Monsters walk among us. Creatures much more frightening than you."

"Monster, yes. Arachne is a monster." She said it as if reminding herself.

Maybe that hadn't been the best direction. I shot Rivers an annoyed look. He winced. But now Arachne's attention was on him. I took another step toward her.

Bane's body was a mass of tension as he kept his eyes on Arachne, not daring to glance my way just in case he alerted her to my plan.

I lunged and slashed. The spiderlings screeched and Arachne moved so fast she was almost a blur, her leg slammed into me sending me flying into the wall.

"You play with Arachne. You mock her!"

I sat up, head spinning from the blow.

"Others will come, but for now, Arachne will give her spiderlings a small feast."

The spiders clinging to the walls dropped.

The next few moments were a frenzy of slashing and stabbing, rolling, ducking and leaping. A spiderling landed on me and got the pointy edge of my dagger and then Bane was tugging me to my feet and we were fighting back to back. Rivers and Orin cut their way through to us and we formed a circle facing outward. We had each other's backs, and fuck, a hundred spiderlings was nothing. Rivers let loose with the repellent and the spiderlings scuttled away, out of range.

"We need to get out of here," Orin said. "We can't take them all out."

"We need to find the humans," Bane said. "If we leave then there is no way she's allowing us back in."

Jesse. I had to find Jesse. The only way to do that was to bring down Arachne. She was right before us, just outside the gas cloud. Her many eyes gleamed with a green tinge. If I could just get past the spiderlings...

Arachne's scream was a living twisted thing. "Use your venom, you fools."

The spiderlings ran back and forth and then right at us, right into the repellent. A hiss filled the chamber and air wafted against my face. It rushed into my lungs, stinging and biting. My body began to tingle.

Venom. Child, do not inhale.

But it was too late. The shit was in my blood stream. So, this is how the venom had found its way into Jane Doe's system. It was delivered as a fucking spray. I toppled to the ground, and a moment later Bane hit the ground next to me. His eyes were open, teeth gritted, clearly furious with this turn of events.

My pulse was growing sluggish. I couldn't fight. I couldn't...

You can't, not alone. Drop the shields, child, let the darkness in.

Fuck you. Last time I did that it almost killed me.

Did it? Did it really? Or did it simply take its fill once you permitted it to?

Every part of my mind protested. The darkness was dangerous, alien, hungry and uncontrollable.

No, not uncontrollable.

He was right. It hadn't fed on Bane, not

until I'd given it leave to do so, even though my shields had been useless and I'd been insane with hunger.

Drop the shields and let it help you.

The years of holding back, the years of keeping the hunger locked up pressed down on me, mingling with the venom in my veins. The spiderlings closed in, eager for their meal.

I dropped the shields and released the darkness. It tore through the venom, obliterating it from my blood, and I was free to move. Bane's power thrummed in my veins, thick like honey infusing my bones with a new kind of strength. I'd fed the darkness well, and left enough to be held back in reserve. I drew on that reserve now, rolling to my feet and leaping over the spiderlings.

Arachne screeched. And my daggers sank into her hairy flesh, cutting through her like she was a knob of butter. I slashed and stabbed to the accompaniment of her screeches. No not screams, laughter. She was laughing — cackling like she was fit to burst.

I jumped back, landing lightly on my feet.

"Fool, you can't kill me."

Arachne is cursed. A curse complicates thing. I'm not even sure she can die. For what is the purpose of a curse such as this if she could simply end her life?

Oh, shit. I glanced over my shoulder where behind me the spiderlings circled, torn between feeding on the venom incapacitated nephs or coming to their mistress' aid.

Power thrummed in my veins and my mind whirred. I couldn't kill her but something she'd said echoed in my mind. *My silk is unbreakable you know.*

Unbreakable.

I couldn't kill her, but I could trap her.

"Your pathetic," I spat. "Relying on your minions to do your dirty work?"

She bristled.

"If your silk is so strong why haven't you used it to trap me yet? You just let me stab you? You know what I think? I think you've lost your touch. That your silk is no longer quality. That the stuff in the tunnels is just like any other spider silk."

"You do, do you?" she sneered.

The silk came shooting out at me so suddenly, I almost didn't jump out the way in time. Almost.

It hit the wall behind me and I leapt, aiming for the wall opposite. Using the power inside, I kept moving evading her silk shots, as they hit and clung to the walls, back and forth, over and under.

Yes, it was working, her silk was everywhere and she... she was in the center of it all.

Good girl. Good girl!

Yes!

I fell to my knees and stared at the dome of silk that encased Arachne.

"What have you done?" she battered into the wall of interwoven threads over and over again but it wouldn't give.

The spiderlings attacked her prison, crawling all over to try to find a weakness but Arachne had told the truth. Her silk was unbreakable. And now she was trapped.

Behind me, Bane groaned and sat up. His neph body must have fought off the venom. Rivers and Orin broke from their paralysis a moment later.

I gripped my daggers tighter. "Have I ever told you how much I hate spiders?"

Bane's lips curled in a sadistic smile. "Time to do a little pest control."

Bits of dead spiders were strewn around the green glowing chamber by the time the cavalry arrived. Ryker, Cassie and half our Protectorates came spilling into the chamber. Several MED officials streamed in after them.

"Shit, we missed all the action." Cassie looked put out.

Ryker came to a standstill, his face contorting in disgust at the sight. "Maybe if you'd had your *feeling* a few minutes sooner, we could have been down here to help." His eyes widened as they fell on the caged form of Arachne. "What the fuck is that?"

Arachne was silent and still. "You think you're safe?" she snorted. "You are fools. Something is coming. Something darker than your most terrifying nightmares, and when it arrives I will be here to greet it." She gurgled. "When it arrives, I will be free."

I stepped closer to the wall of silk. "Who is coming? Tell me?"

Her laughter echoed throughout the chamber.

"Ignore her, she's just baiting you," Orin said. He lifted his chin. "We need to focus on getting the humans down."

Everyone looked up at the bodies dangling from the ceiling.

My mouth went dry. "Are they alive?"

"They should be," Rivers said. "Hopefully."

The MED jumped into action, radioing for supplies and paramedics and all kinds of shit. It took a few hours to get all the cocoons down. We started with the smaller ones, loading the unconscious children onto stretchers and getting them the heck out of the tunnels. There were so many more humans than we'd realized, and each time they cut through the cocoon binding a person my pulse leapt. And each time it was a stranger. My eyes searched for Jesse and Drayton. I'd failed them both. I should have made Jesse stay with me until it was time to go back to Sunset. I should never have left Drayton to the sentinel and run. What if Arachne had eaten them? No, she wouldn't have eaten Drayton. He was a neph, but Jesse was human...what if she'd eaten Jesse?

Ryker pressed a hand to the small of my back. "They're here. We'll find them. Drayton and Jesse."

I nodded dumbly, my hands itching to rip the cocoons to shreds but the MED medical guy was adamant that we hang back and let him work. It was excruciatingly slow. And then a familiar spill of blonde hair had me rushing forward.

"Jesse?"

"Stay back, please," the MED guy said. He checked for a pulse. Did it have to take him so long? Finally, he nodded. "She's alive." Two other officials hauled her up onto a stretcher. The MED guy glanced over his shoulder. "Friend of yours?"

I swallowed. "My sister."

He frowned, probably wondering how a neph could have a human sister, but then he smiled reassuringly. "She's going to be fine. Her pulse is strong."

I sagged in relief and Ryker wrapped an

arm around me.

"We have Drayton," Orin called out.

I rushed forward and fell to my knees beside the incubus's unconscious form. "His pulse, check his pulse."

The second medical guy shot me an irritated look and then did as I asked. He pressed his lips together and shook his head.

"What? What is it?"

He looked shifty, afraid. "I... I can't find a pulse."

My stomach dropped and my eyes burned. "No."

Orin shoved him aside. "Idiot, you're dealing with an incubus. Pulse is at the back of the fucking neck."

He slipped his hand under Drayton's head. I held my breath.

Orin's shoulders relaxed. "It's weak but we have a pulse."

Bane hoisted Drayton over his shoulder. "I'll get him back to the mansion."

"He needs medical attention," the MED insisted.

"Yes, he does," Bane said. "But the neph kind."

Ryker slipped his hand into mine. "He'll be fine. Come on. Let's wrap this up.

Drayton's screams echoed around my skull, and my hand shook as I sipped the brandy Cassie had poured for me. We were in the lounge, as far away from the agony as we could get. Cassie nursed a glass of wine, her eyes going to the door every few seconds.

The cocooned humans had been evacuated, the tunnels swept for spiderlings and Arachne's chamber bricked up. It had taken a couple of days, but it was done. The cracks she'd mentioned hadn't been found, and Arachne was no longer speaking. She'd gone into some kind of spider coma. It was over. The missing person files had been closed, everyone we had on file accounted for, and there were some extra people who the district was still trying to find homes for. Jesse's companion, Michael, the other teacher, hadn't made it. His heart had stopped on the way to the hospital. The kids were in intensive care. We still had no clue how the bus had ended up at the beach, or at least we wouldn't have until Jesse awoke. She was stable for now, but still unconscious. There was nothing more I could do for her until she woke up. But Drayton was another story.

I gulped the last of my brandy and poured another. "What are we going to do?"

Cassie shrugged. "I don't know. He can't feed, not like this. He'd kill the human."

There were faded scars on his body where the sentinel had attacked. Wounds his power had repaired, and while in his cocoon his incubus had continued to work on him, saving his life but draining his power. So, now he needed a fix, and he needed it bad.

I took a huge sip of my drink. "Have you seen him?"

She sucked her head. "No, and I don't want to. Orin says it's bad. Drayton has left the building. We're dealing with the incubus now, and the incubus wants to feed."

I ran a hand over my face. "What about a neph? Could he feed off a neph?"

Cassie snorted. "Sure, he could. And in the process, he would probably kill her. There would be no holding back for him. He'd fuck until his lover was dead, and then he'd probably fuck her some more."

"Stop." I held up a hand. "There has to be a way to take the edge off."

He needed a boost, and it had to come through sexual contact. I'd siphoned off him using a kiss. Could I siphon sexual energy *into* him using a kiss? And where would I get that kind of energy. I wasn't an incubus, I didn't feed off sexual energy.

You choose not to.

My hand shook, and I almost dropped the glass.

"Harker, you okay?" Cassie asked.

I nodded. I focused on Ambrosius. What do you mean?

When you fed from Bane, it was sexual

energy combined with his power that you drew from. You are a cambion, part incubus. The difference is that you have a choice of the energy you take. There are many to choose from: a neph's power, a human's life force, sexual energy, rage, to name just a few.

I had a choice?

I put my glass on the table and stood. "I think I have an idea."

Bane stood with his back to me, looking out at the night sky. It was chilly this high in the roost, but the air felt pleasant on my skin. The muscles under his t-shirt rippled with awareness.

"I don't know how to help him," Bane said.

"But I think I do."

He turned to look at me, his dark brows snapping down.

I licked my lips. "I can help him, but I'm going to need you to do something to help me help him."

"Name it."

I took a step closer, enough to feel the heat from his body. "I need you to kiss me."

His nostrils flared and a low growl rumbled in his chest. "Harker..."

"Please, trust me I—"

His mouth cut me off, and my feet left

the ground as he gathered me up easily. I was a doll in his arms, a plaything, and he devoured me with kisses that burned my soul. My shields melted and the darkness purred, drinking him in. Every last drop of his sizzling energy tugged and stoked an icy heat to life at the apex of my thighs. I moaned into his mouth, my hands sliding up his thick neck, into his silken hair, over his shoulders and back again. He was the pitcher of chilled water I needed to quench a thirst I'd been denying for way too long. His power surged into me along with an edge that I recognized as sexual energy. It had been present last time too, even though that hadn't been his intention, or had it?

I should break the kiss now. The darkness' hunger was sated, but there was a different hunger—almost as insatiable as my cambion craving—and it was all mine. The shock of the revelation had me jerking back and tearing my mouth from his.

His breathing was ragged against me. His eyes narrowed, and his expression shuttered. He lowered me to my feet and stepped away. "Was that what you needed?"

I nodded, unable to form words around the crazy lump of yearning in my throat.

"You intend to feed that to Drayton, don't you?"

"Yes." My voice was a whisper.

"He isn't there right now," Bane said. He folded his arms across his gargantuan chest. "You know, the White Wings used to call the Black Wings demons. They said that the hunger inside the nephs, the powers we could wield, were all part of the demon essence donated to us by the Black Wing blood. Right now, Drayton is gone and only the demon remains. Right now, there's only the incubus and the incubus is ravenous."

"But if I can feed it some sexual energy then Drayton can take control, right?"

Bane shrugged a massive shoulder. "I don't know. Drayton is asleep. Buried deep in his psyche. The incubus may just take and take, and it could kill you. But maybe..." He studied me speculatively. "If you have a connection with him, you can draw him back. It may take some acting on your part."

"What kind of acting."

"The incubus can't know you're willing. You must show you're afraid. It will excite it. It isn't often the demon gets to take its fill without the effort of glamour. And maybe...maybe your terror will nudge Drayton awake."

I wiped my sweaty palms on my jeans. "Okay."

He cocked his head. "It could go horribly wrong."

This was Drayton we were talking

about. My heart ached. "I'm doing this."

Bane glanced at my hands. "We'll have to bind your hands behind your back."

The daggers. Of course. If I felt like I was in danger, then they would materialize. "Fine."

He stepped around me and opened the door. Was he deliberately avoiding touching me?

"I'll take you to him," he said.

The basement was a dungeon. A cold, stone chamber filled with cages and shackles and racks laden with implements of torture. What the heck did they do down here, and to who? Drayton's screams of rage had ceased as we began our descent, almost as if he'd sensed our arrival and was satisfied that the ruckus had done the job of drawing us to him.

"The scourge we bring back from Sunset spend a little time here," Bane explained. "It's not usual for them to venture past the border, but over the years it has been occurring more and more frequently."

"Do you think it has something to do with the cracks Arachne mentioned and the other creatures that seem to be making their way into Midnight?"

"It seems too much of a coincidence not to be connected."

Drayton wasn't visible yet, but something inside tugged me forward, warning me and compelling me at the same time. He was close. Bane led me past several cells. This chamber probably stretched under the whole of the north wing, which was pretty huge. How many people could you cram into this space? Yeah, I was focusing on random stuff to ignore the shiver in my chest. My palms were clammy too.

Drayton came into view, not locked in a cell but shackled to the wall, his chest was bare and his trousers hung low on his hips, his eyes blazed in triumph as he caught sight of me, and he licked his lips. His features were sharper and his eyes were so dark they were almost black. The man I'd grown to care for wasn't there, instead I was looking at his demon. A demon who wanted to hurt me, the horror was real and I let it rise.

"Drayton." I took a step forward. "What have you done to him?" I shot Bane an appalled look. Or at least I hoped I did.

Bane grabbed me and cuffed my hands behind my back. I struggled and kicked out, and he released me, chuckling softly.

"You brought me a treat, Bane," the incubus said.

"Yes, I guess I did," Bane said.

The pulse at the base of my throat was suddenly thudding way too hard, this felt way too real.

Bane grabbed me by the back of the neck and dragged me toward him. His violet eyes gleamed and I crushed the urged to smash a fist into his face, not that I could even if I wanted to, cuffs and all. This was just a ploy. Wasn't it?

He cupped my head with his huge hands and ran his thumb roughly over my mouth. "She is sweet. I hope you don't mind, but I had a quick taste."

The incubus laughed. It was a dirty sound that made my skin crawl. Where was the charismatic entity I'd seen working The Deep? The thing hanging on the wall was all sharp angles and greyish skin. Yes, it had Drayton's features but all the softness, all the beauty had been stripped away.

This was the demon that controlled Drayton. Did I have one? What did she look like? Rivers' awed face came to mind along with his words when I'd fed from him. He'd said I shone. I blinked away the memory and gasped as Bane ran his nose up the column of my neck.

"Bring her. Bring her to me now." The incubus' tone had grown thick with desire.

"No, please." I strained trying to get away from Bane. "Please, let me go!"

The incubus laughed. "Oh, this will be sooo good."

Where was Drayton? Could he hear my screams? They filled the dungeon, echoing hollowly. Bane carried me to the incubus and held me up by the back of my neck. This close up, the inhumanity in the things eyes was like an ultraviolet light exposing every dirty stain. Real visceral fear flooded me, and I twisted from side to side convinced this was no ploy, this was real and Bane intended to sacrifice me to save his friend's life. The daggers filled my hands but trapped behind me they were useless pieces of metal.

"Kiss her," Bane urged. "Take what you need. Take it all."

He pushed my face toward the demon. And the thin cruel lips grew nearer and nearer. A strangled cry escaped from my mouth and then something flashed in the incubus's eye. The dark brown hue lightened a fraction and the pupils dilated and contracted.

"Please, please, Drayton, don't hurt me. Don't—" my words were cut off by the pressure of his lips and then his tongue was in my mouth.

My shields were batted aside and the incubus began to feed. I wanted to heal him, but I needed him to fight, to rise from his slumber and take the reins. I needed him to know it was me he would hurt if he didn't stop, and so I closed my eyes and focused on this intimate connection.

It shone bright—amber power laced with violet. It was Bane's power and the sexual energy we'd conjured together. Drayton was taking it, absorbing it. Drayton, can you hear me. Please. You need to stop. You need to stop or you'll kill me. Please...I pushed my thoughts down the connection. He had to hear me. The power was coming to its end, he was drawing too fast and soon it would be my life force he'd be feeding off.

Drayton, if you don't stop you'll kill me. I'll be dead, just like Viola.

His lips slid from mine and Bane yanked me back. I sagged against his chest.

"Drayton? Drayton are you there?" Bane asked urgently.

The incubus raised his head, and stared at us with green flecked, brown eyes. "I'm here. I'm here."

It had taken almost a week for humans who'd been abducted by Arachne to recover. Many of them didn't recall much leading up to the attack. The Deep, the park and a spot behind a bowling alley on the south side of the district were the danger zones. The MED located and cemented off the chute by the bowling alley. Jesse was interviewed and explained that they'd stopped at the beach to collect shells to take back to the school. That was all she remembered.

I stood in the doorway to her hospital room, watching her tie her laces. It was almost time and my chest ached with goodbye.

She looked up and locked gazes with me. Her mouth tightened. "What are you doing here? Making sure I leave?"

I swallowed the lump in my throat. "Making sure you don't get yourself into any more shit, yeah."

She stood and smoothed down her shirt. "Well, fuck you, Serenity. I don't want you here. I have a ride out of Midnight."

"Yeah, I know. One I arranged for you."

Her mouth trembled and she turned away, giving me the second I needed to bite the insides of my cheeks and prevent a tremble of my own. This was the best way. Cut ties to keep her safe. Cut ties so she would never come back.

Her shoulders rose and fell in a shudder and then she turned to face me, her expression cold and distant. "You can rest assured that I will not be attempting to contact you in the future. As far as I'm concerned, I was always an only child."

Her words were shards of glass burrowing into my chest. But I smiled sadistically. "Trust me. I've wished the same thing every fucking day."

A rap at the door signaled the arrival of her ride.

Orin smiled kindly at her. "Are you ready?"

She nodded curtly.

"I've collected your stuff from your house. It's all loaded up in the van."

She smiled stiffly. "Thank you."

I pushed away from the door jamb. "Yeah, well drive safe." I turned and walked away. No goodbye hug, no kiss, no I love you. The ladies' toilets were just down the corridor and I clipped quickly toward them, pushed through, locked myself in the nearest stall and began to hyperventilate. I could do this. I wouldn't cry. I wouldn't break. This was the right call. She'd almost died, twice, but the tears were leaking out anyway and ruining my resolve.

A soft knock interrupted my tight-spot pacing.

"It's taken." I wiped at my face.

"Open the door, Serenity,"

"Ryker?"

I unlatched the door and Ryker stepped in and locked it again.

"This is the ladies toilets." I sniffed.

He picked me up, pushed the toilet lid down and then sat down on the loo with me on his lap.

"I know." His emerald gaze was filled with empathy and the final vestiges of my control crumbled. I buried my face in the crook of his neck and sobbed my heart out.

The best formula for a broken heart was to get out there and kick some arse, which was why I was hovering in the hallway waiting for Drayton and the continuation of a case that had begun over a week ago. The case of the illegal recruitment. With the house games a mere month away, it was imperative that we resolved this issue to maintain balance.

Drayton strode into the foyer, shrugging on his jacket. "You ready to execute a warrant, Harker?"

He'd been all stiff and formal with me ever since...well, since our moment in the dungeon. We'd barely spent more than two minutes alone in the same room, and to be honest I'd thought he'd go without me, hence the hovering, but it looked like Drayton was a neph of his word.

"Yes, sure. Let's do this."

We headed outside and climbed into the range rover.

"So, how you liking Midnight so far?" he asked. He wasn't expecting an answer. He was making small talk. He was putting up walls, but my mind was already, sincerely, pondering his question.

Let's see...This was Midnight, the district where the scourge ran once a month and the residents cleaned up after as if they'd just had a rave. It was the home of ghosts who lived forever in a cemetery at the top of a hill. It was residence to the Breed, the Sanguinata and the Lupin. Midnight was one huge hot spot, and if Arachne was telling the truth, there was a whole load of crap headed our way. Midnight was a cesspit of danger and the darkness inside me had never been so uncomplicated.

I sat back in my seat. "I think it feels like home."

His eyes narrowed, and his lips twitched and for a second I caught a glimpse of the Drayton I'd come to lo—know.

He started the engine. "Yeah, in that case, Harker, you're royally fucked."

To be continued...

Serenity's story continues in Champion of Midnight.

Check out the excerpt below

The drive to the House of Vitae was mostly a silent one, not for want of trying on my part, mind you, but Drayton was determined to keep conversation limited. If I'd known helping him push back his demon would result in this distance I would have ... still done it, damn it. The atmosphere was strained. The memory of what had happened in the dungeons hung between us. I'd seen him stripped bare, out of control. I'd seen the darkest part of him, and although he was grateful for my help, he'd said as much, there was obviously a part of him that was ashamed. Maybe it was time to open up and talk about it? Just push the issue, and clear the air instead of tiptoeing around the subject. I slid a quick glance his way. His jaw was tense, and his eyes were on the road in total focus, a little too much focus, if you asked me. Yeah, maybe talking about stuff could wait.

It was strange having my shields partially down, but Drayton had made it clear that going to visit the Sanguinata reeking of human was a bad idea. Besides, it was best to keep the number of people who knew about my shielding ability to the minimum. Ambrosius's words echoed in my ears, his assertion that I controlled the hunger whether the shields were up or down. He'd been silent since the Arachne's attack underground. Was it strange that I missed his voice in my head?

A huge set of iron gates came into view with the words *Domus Vitae* emblazoned across a crest on an arch above. The crest was a shield depicting a serpent and a sword. Neat script reading *perpetua vita aeterna et sapientia* ran along a plaque under the crest.

"Life everlasting and wisdom eternal." How the heck did I know that?

Drayton shot me a curious glance. "You learned Latin?"

I shook my head. "No. I didn't."

"Then how —"

The gates swung soundlessly inward with the help of two silent, stoic-faced guards. They stood back stiff and distant in their purple livery as we drove through the gates.

"We're expected," Drake explained. "I called ahead."

"You have the warrant, right?"

He nodded tightly. "I do, but they don't know that. This is a social call." He slid a warning glance my way.

Bane had made it clear that we were to do this one by the book. "Drayton, Bane said—"

"Look, let me just try it my way first, okay?"

I blew out a breath. It was impossible to make a valid argument with so little information on the Sanguinata, or this dude, Dorian. There was no choice but to follow Drayton's lead. I was a newbie to the protectorate, and although Bane had released me for patrol, this was still meant as an observational learning exercise.

Drayton steered the Rover through the entrance and down a neat, cement pathway bordered by clean, crisply kept gardens. The roses looked black and gray in the moonlight, but they grew here in abundance. The fact that any plant life grew in Midnight was still a mind boggle, but the magic of Arcadia was strongest in this district, whether due to the concentration of nephs, or the ministrations of the Order of Merlin, who knew. It just was.

The driveway seemed to stretch forever. And were we on an incline? "How much farther is the house?"

Drayton's lips lifted in a wry smile. "The *house* is just over this rise."

What was with the emphasis on the word house? We reached the top of the rise, and my question was answered. House of Vitae was no *house*; it was a freaking castle — a castle with a huge-arse moat around it.

"Shitting hell!"

"Right?" Drayton snorted. "The Sanguinata have some serious money and clout in the city. We do *not* want to piss them off."

Good to know.

We hit the bottom of the rise, and Drayton sped up a bit down the long stretch of road leading up to the bridge spanning the moat. Water gleamed in the silvery rays of the moon. A dark shape cut through it, slipped under the bridge and came out on the other side.

I craned my neck to try and get a better look at it, but it dove underwater. "What the heck was that?"

"Dorian's little pet."

"I would not call that little."

"Yeah, Mitch has grown a little since I was last here."

"Mitch?"

"That's what Dorian calls it."

"What is it?"

"I'm not entirely sure."

Great.

We slid under the archway into a stone courtyard and Drayton parked the car. Balustrades depicting beautiful women and men in poses of a sexual nature dotted the pretty quad, and ivy crawled up the stone walls as if desperate to reach for the moon. A stone archway and a brick wall cut off the courtyard from the main castle.

We exited the vehicle and waited. Long minutes passed, and then the echo of boots filled the courtyard.

"That'll be Dorian's butler, Jeffery," Drayton said.

How many times had Drayton visited the Sanguinata and why? A slender, somber man appeared under the arch. He stopped and pressed his heels together. "Please, do follow me."

He led us through the arch and a set of thick, wooden double doors into a brightly lit stone entranceway. Unlike the mansion, the castle was spotless and modern inside. Someone had gone to a whole lot of trouble to get this place into order. The walls had been plastered and hung with pretty landscapes and portraits of severe, beautiful people. The floors were carpeted in thick pile, muffling our footsteps as we slipped through corridors and up stairs. So many little details to take in, but my attention was on the exits — the windows that were too high up, and the doors that seemed to be locked. As we took twists and turns, my mind made a mental map in case we should need to make a hasty escape. Drayton seemed familiar with the castle, relaxed even, but I knew enough about Drayton to know how easily he could slip in and out of the chilled persona he liked to don. And with my shields semi-down, the tension buzzing beneath his mask was static against my skin.

We stepped onto a foyer on the third floor. Double doors again, this time cream with ornate brass handles barred the way. Jeffery walked briskly toward them and flung them open.

The hum of voices and the tinkle of music drifted out to greet us followed closely by the scent of roasted meat and something else, something coppery and tangy.

Blood.

"Master, your guests have arrived." The butler bowed and then ushered us through into the room. The chamber was long, and we entered at one end. On either side were two

long banquet tables occupied by nephs —
Sanguinata no doubt. Gold, cream and
crimson were the themes here, no windows it
seemed, unless they were hidden behind the
thick velvet drapes that spanned the length of
the wall to our right. Heavily made up
humans dressed in flimsy garments worked
the tables, serving and ... Wait, was that a
Sanguinata filling her wine glass from that
human's wrist?

"Stop staring," Drayton whisper hissed.

Tearing my gaze from the display, I
focused on the cream tiled walkway which
cut between the tables. It led to a man
lounging on, what looked like, a mini throne.
It was even set on a dais. He was blond and
powerfully built which he obviously liked to
show off as he wasn't wearing a shirt. His
eight-pack was on display, and his bare feet
were propped up on a cushy footstool. A
small table sporting a bowl of fruit was
placed within reach. A pale, ornately-dressed
woman sat on a chair to his right, and a
human female sat on the floor by his throne.
She was dressed almost indecently in a see
through nightgown. Her feet were also bare,
and gooseflesh peppered her skin. Her hair
was clean and shiny though — the only part of
her that looked healthy. Other than that, she
looked like she was about to topple onto her
face. Wait, what was that red pipe peeking

out from under her hair?

"Drayton, how good to see you," Dorian said. "It has been too long."

"Indeed." Drayton inclined his head. "How have you been?"

"Oh, you know, surviving." He lifted something to his lips, the red pipe ... Not a pipe, a fucking straw.

He sucked on it and waved us forward. Taking my cue from Drayton, I walked closer to the imposing Sanguinata, coming to a halt about three meters away.

The human at Dorian's feet groaned, part in protest, part ecstasy. Dorian ran a hand over her head. Her eyes rolled upward, and then her lids drooped. She slumped against his thighs. His lips turned down in disgust, and he jostled his leg, sending her toppling to the floor.

My chest tightened and I took a step forward. Drayton gripped my arm and squeezed in warning.

"I despair," Dorian drawled. "If we don't win the games this year, I fear we shall all starve."

The gathered Sanguinata chuckled, but the sound was more polite than genuine. As if laughter was the expected reaction. I thought they needed the blood to survive due to a deficiency, not to use as a food source. I tried to catch Drayton's eye, but he was resolutely fixated on Dorian.

Dorian smiled, but the action was cold and devoid of any real emotion. "Jeremy, please take this one away and bring me a fresh one."

He said it like he was asking for a refill on a cocktail. The butler reappeared as if by magic which, who knew, it may just have been. He gathered the human into his arms without effort. She probably didn't weigh more than a child. Blood trailed from the tube, spattering the floor as he carried her from the room.

My stomach turned.

What the fuck?

The rest of the Sanguinata continued with their meals, sipping crimson fluid from crystal cut glass. Blood … They were drinking blood, probably taken from the humans serving them. Why had I thought that humans donated blood and that was that? I'd never expected them to be treated like blood bags, to be fed off directly.

"Don't worry, little neph," Dorian said. "We do not bite,"

I blinked at him. He was talking to me. "You don't?"

He shrugged. "Of course not. That would be against the district laws."

Someone to my left snickered.

Dorian was lying.

Beside me, Drayton tensed. Why wasn't he saying anything?

"So, what is the real reason for your visit, Drayton?" Dorian leaned forward, plucked a grape off the table and popped it into his mouth. He chewed slowly. "Tell me what is it I can help you with?"

God, I wanted to smash the smarmy look off his beautiful face.

Drayton sighed and held up his hands. "You got me, Dorian. Can't get anything past you. But, it's actually something I was hoping to help *you* with. Give you a heads-up."

"Oh, really?" Dorian sat up a little straighter. "Information, eh? We love information don't we?" He transferred his attention to his court, and a hearty murmur of agreement skittered across the gathered. "Go on."

Drayton winced. "It seems like one of your Sanguinata has been attempting to recruit humans."

Something dark flitted across Dorian's face, but it was gone too quickly, replaced by an appropriate expression of concern. "No." He placed a hand on his heart. "That cannot be true. One of mine would never break the law in such a blatant way, especially when we know what's at stake if we do."

He was lying. Again. It dripped from his voice and settled around him like a bad smell. With my shield's partially down, it was easy to pick up on the untruth. Drayton tensed. Had he sensed it too?

"Well, it's happening," Drayton said. His tone remained easy and light. "We spotted him at The Deep just over a week ago."

"A week?" Dorian's brows shot up. "And you leave it till now to come and see me."

"We had another case to deal with that couldn't wait."

"Ah, yes. The underground tunnels and the monstrous spiders."

Man, news got around quick in Midnight.

"So, tell me. What did this lawbreaking Sanguinata look like? You know most of my men. Is it someone here?" He waved an arm to encompass the room.

Drayton turned to me. "Serenity?"

"You didn't personally see the lawbreaker?" Dorian said. He focused his attention on me. "Your colleague did. The *new* member of your team." He smiled, flashing fang. But while Bane's fangs gave me delicious shivers, his just turned my stomach.

"Yeah, I saw him." I lifted my chin. "I can identify him too."

I swept my gaze over the Sanguinata to my left and to my right, searching each face for the one that was etched in my mind. My brain was funny that way, capturing details like a photograph when I needed it to and, sometimes, even when I didn't.

Damn it, the culprit wasn't present. "He's not here."

Dorian stuck out his bottom lip in mock sorrow. "In the absence of a positive identification, I'm afraid all I can do is reinforce the rules at our next meet. Give the house a talking to."

"And when is the next meet?" Drayton asked evenly.

Dorian's lips twitched in amusement. He ducked his head and studied his nails. "The night before the games."

This was all a joke to him. My face heated in indignation. The fucker had no intention of doing anything to stop the illegal recruitment. Drayton had been right about being able to get him to talk without use of a warrant, but not using the warrant had also given him a sense of security. He was toying with us, thinking there was nothing more we could do. Drayton had asked me to take a backseat on this one, but there was no way I was letting that smarmy fucker get away with breaking the law. Dorian deserved a rude awakening.

I ripped the warrant from Drayton's back pocket and fanned myself with it.

"Sorry, not good enough. I suggest you call a meet immediately. Now. Right here, so I can find the perpetrator and *you* can punish him."

Dorian's eyes narrowed and his lip curled. "What is the meaning of this?"

I unfolded the paper. "Oh, this?" I widened my eyes as if surprised to see the warrant in my hand. "This is a warrant giving us authority to question and search the premises in an attempt to locate the lawbreaker."

"Serenity..." Drayton's tone was laced with warning.

"No, Drayton. We tried it your way, but this *isn't* a social call. This is official business." I crossed my arms. "I suggest you cooperate, Dorian. You wouldn't want a copy of this warrant to find its way to the House of Mort, would you?" I tapped my chin. "Wouldn't that mean forfeiting the games this year?"

Dorian's already pale expression paled even further, and the gathered broke out into excited whispers.

Dorian slumped back in his seat and waved a hand in my direction. "There is no need for a meet. I may have an inkling who the perpetrator is. He *will* be reprimanded."

His word wasn't going to cut it with me. "Maybe we should—"

"Enough!" Drayton snapped, his eyes

blazing down on me. He slowly turned his head to look at Dorian. "Thank you. Your assistance in this matter is very much appreciated. This will stay between us. I give you my word."

Dorian pinched the bridge of his nose, doing a great impression of someone stricken by remorse. "This is most embarrassing, highly irregular, but you have no idea how difficult the past two years have been for our kind. There will always be weak links in the chain, but please trust they will be purged."

Drayton smiled tightly. "And that is all we ask. Best of luck with the games." He gripped my hand, a sign that we should leave, but the doors behind us opened and a whirlwind of kicking and screaming was dragged into the room

Dorian sat up straight, his eyes lighting up at the sight of the golden-haired female who was flinging every cuss word she could muster into the air.

"No. Let me go. I want to go home. Let me go!" She thrashed and bucked in Jeffery's arms.

I caught a glimpse of her face — the curve of her jaw and the arch of her brow. Jesse?

No, it wasn't my sister, just someone who looked similar.

Jeremy, the butler, dropped her on the

ground by Dorian, and she was on her feet in a second, her arm winding back to strike the lord.

"Stop!" Dorian's voice was a whiplash command.

The woman's hand halted an inch away from his face. "I fucking hate you. I hate you all. Let me go. I don't want to do this. This isn't what I signed up for. It isn't what any of us signed up for. You can't just keep us here."

"Enough."

Her hand dropped to her side. Dorian's thin lips curled in cruel smile, and a moan rippled across the room, almost sexual in nature. Something was about to happen. The anticipation was a buzz in the air. Dorian turned the woman to face us, gently swiping her hair away from her neck. His tongue flicked out to moisten his lips, and his lips peeled back. There was something marring her creamy skin.

"Bite marks." My eyes widened.

Dorian's lips dropped over his fangs, hiding them from view. "Jeffery, you fool, you forgot the needle and drip."

Jeffery inclined his head and hurried from the room.

The woman's body trembled with impotent fury, and tears leaked from the corner of her eyes. Her body was locked in stasis by Dorian's command, but her gaze dragged to me. Rage and imploration mingled to stab at my heart. Fuck this shit.

"Let her go, Dorian." The words dropped from my lips like ice chips.

Dorian's jaw tensed. "Excuse me? You dare to order me?"

There it was, that primal edge that had been missing from this encounter all along, buried under a persona of civility — the lethal glint in his dark eyes, the pinprick of crimson that spoke of unbridled rage and insanity.

"This human belongs to my house. She belongs to me." His cultured tone had slipped into something guttural.

"Serenity," Drayton said. "He's right. She agreed to this. She signed a contract."

I rounded on him. "Agreed to being bitten? To being used as a walking fucking blood bag? You do see the bite marks don't you?" I waved a hand toward the servers. "You do see what the fuck is happening here, don't you? Donating blood is one thing, but this … This is fucking insane."

Drayton's jaw flexed. "I'm sure Dorian has addressed the oversight with regards to the biting."

The fuck was his problem? Why was he covering for this piece of shit?

Dorian inclined his head. "Of course."

The woman's eyes widened.

My pulse hammered in my throat with

the need to hurt someone. "How about you let her speak for herself?"

Dorian stepped away from the woman and padded toward me, a panther on the prowl

Drayton took a step forward to shield me. "We're leaving. Now."

Dorian ignored him and kept his gaze fixed on me. "We bid for what we want here. We win and we get to reap. It's the way of Midnight. Everything is a gamble. I suggest you educate yourself on the ways of Midnight before you get hurt."

Drayton's control snapped. "Do not threaten her, Dorian."

Dorian blinked in surprise. "Or what, Drayton? You'll fuck me to death?"

The gathered broke into laughter — genuine this time — and Drayton bristled. His hands curled into fists. Shit. As much as I despised Dorian, as much as I wanted to punch his face in, we were in the lion's den. Two nephs surrounded by at least fifty or sixty Sanguinata.

It was my turn to grab Drayton's arm. "Let's jet.

We turned toward the door.

"Please!"

I spun to face the woman who had, by sheer force of will, broken Dorian's compulsion. She fell to the ground, exhausted, her hand reaching for me. "Please, don't leave me here with them."

She was someone's daughter, someone's sister. Somebody loved her just as I loved Jesse. I'd thought the winged were bad, but this ... This was something else. Rage bubbled up inside me, and my mouth developed a mind of its own.

I approached Dorian, not caring that he was a head and a half taller than me, that his fangs could tear me to shreds, or that we were in his territory at his mercy. Yeah, my mouth didn't give a shit about that. "You like to gamble, huh? Like to bid and play to win?"

Dorian cocked his head, intrigued. "You want to play, little neph?"

I licked my lips. What the heck was I doing? But the human's eyes had lit up with hope, and there was no going back now.

"Yeah, I want to play."

He crossed his arms. "I'm listening."

"Let me take part in your house games. I win, and every human gets the option to leave if they want."

"Serenity, no," Drayton cried.

A tray or something metallic clattered to the floor to my left. I kept my gaze on Dorian, my muscles vibrating with adrenaline. "Unless you're scared your big, bad Sanguinata players will lose to a girl." I batted my eyelashes. "I mean, they've already lost to the Lupin two years in a row. Maybe you're just not that good."

His lips twisted in amusement, and some of my bravado evaporated. What did he have to be cocky about?

"Do you even know that the games are, little neph?" Dorian asked.

Shit. No one had filled me in on the details, but there was no way I was telling smug-arse that. "Of course, I know what they are."

"Damn it, Serenity," Drayton snapped.

"Hush!" Dorian replied. "Let her speak. She has fire. I like that in a woman."

Ew. I crossed my arms under my breasts. "Do we have a deal?"

Dorian's lips peeled back exposing lethal fangs. It wasn't a snarl, it was more of a … a come on? "You have deal, neph. But I have a condition of my own."

My mouth was suddenly dry as a subconscious part of mind picked up on a threat I'd failed to consciously recognize. I shrugged, feigning nonchalance. "Go on."

He leaned in, so his sweet, coppery breath wafted into my face. "If you lose, you give yourself to me."

"Serenity, no." Drayton yanked me toward him. "Stop this. Stop it now."

But I couldn't, not with all those eyes on me—the serving girls and boys with their hearts filled with the possibility of freedom.

I gently extricated my arm from Drayton's grasp and turned back to Dorian. "*If* I lose, you can do what you like with me. If I win, you let go every human who wishes to leave, *and* you change the house recruitment contracts to allow future recruited humans to leave if they wish."

Dorian smiled smugly and my hands itched to slap him.

Time to take a step away from temptation. "We have a deal?"

"Oh, yes, neph. We have a deal."

Other books by Debbie Cassidy

The Gatekeeper Chronicles
Coauthored with Jasmine Walt
<u>Marked by Sin</u>
<u>Hunted by Sin</u>
<u>Claimed by Sin</u>

The Witch Blood Chronicles
(Spin off to the Gatekeeper Chronicles)
Binding Magick
Defying Magic
Embracing Magick
Unleashing Magick

The Fearless Destiny Series
<u>Beyond Everlight</u>
Into Evernight
Under Twilight

The Sleeping Gods Series
<u>Forest of Demons</u>
<u>Desert of Destiny</u>

Novellas
<u>Blood Blade</u>
Grotesque – A Vampire Diary Kindle World book

ABOUT THE AUTHOR

Debbie Cassidy lives in England, Bedfordshire, with her three kids and very supportive husband. Coffee and chocolate biscuits are her writing fuels of choice, and she is still working on getting that perfect tower of solitude built in her back garden. Obsessed with building new worlds and reading about them, she spends her spare time daydreaming and conversing with the characters in her head – in a totally non psychotic way of course.

She writes High Fantasy and Urban fantasy. Connect with Debbie via her website at debbiecassidyauthor.com or on her twitter account @authordcassidy.

Made in the USA
Monee, IL
13 November 2023

46475851R00224